AN OUTSIDER

"Some people don't think well of a Chinese man consorting with a non-Chinese lady," David said.

I straightened, hearing him refer to me as a lady. My hands and fingers worked and fretted as I gripped my reticule. I knew all about it, I wanted to say. All about that skin that didn't quite fit. "Maybe they were talking about me. About how I look." I'd heard the name-calling. Heard the references to the blood that flowed in my veins. "Maybe they weren't talking about you at all. It might have been about me."

"If they talked about your looks, it'd be because you're so pretty." His cheeks went dark, and he stared at his feet. "Sorry, I didn't mean to blurt that out. It was supposed to be a compliment."

And I lost words. He stood there, this kind young man who had just saved me, his hands thrust into his jacket pockets, thick dark hair slicked back, his dark eyes lifting to mine and then dropping away in shy retreat . . . I didn't know what to think. He was sweet and nice-looking, no doubt about it; he lit up some feeling deep in my heart.

Kula Baker keeps her wits about her. Kula Baker does not go soft over a young man.

OTHER BOOKS YOU MAY ENJOY

Aurelia	Anne Osterlund
A Company of Swans	Eva Ibbotson
A Countess Below Stairs	Eva Ibbotson
Impossible	Nancy Werlin
Just Listen	Sarah Dessen
Let It Snow	John Green, Maureen Johnson, and Lauren Myracle
Lock and Key	Sarah Dessen
The Morning Gift	Eva Ibbotson
The Reluctant Heiress	Eva Ibbotson
A Song for Summer	Eva Ibbotson

Forgiven

Forgiven

JANET FOX

speak
An Imprint of Penguin Group (USA) Inc.

SPEAK
Published by the Penguin Group
Penguin Group (USA) Inc., 345 Hudson Street, New York, New York 10014, U.S.A.
Penguin Group (Canada), 90 Eglinton Avenue East, Suite 700, Toronto, Ontario, Canada M4P 2Y3
(a division of Pearson Penguin Canada Inc.)
Penguin Books Ltd, 80 Strand, London WC2R 0RL, England
Penguin Ireland, 25 St Stephen's Green, Dublin 2, Ireland (a division of Penguin Books Ltd)
Penguin Group (Australia), 250 Camberwell Road, Camberwell, Victoria 3124, Australia
(a division of Pearson Australia Group Pty Ltd)
Penguin Books India Pvt Ltd, 11 Community Centre,
Panchsheel Park, New Delhi - 110 017, India
Penguin Group (NZ), 67 Apollo Drive, Rosedale, Auckland 0632, New Zealand
(a division of Pearson New Zealand Ltd)
Penguin Books (South Africa) (Pty) Ltd, 24 Sturdee Avenue,
Rosebank, Johannesburg 2196, South Africa

Registered Offices: Penguin Books Ltd, 80 Strand, London WC2R 0RL, England

Published by Speak, an imprint of Penguin Group (USA) Inc., 2011

1 3 5 7 9 10 8 6 4 2

LIBRARY OF CONGRESS CATALOGING-IN-PUBLICATION DATA IS AVAILABLE

Speak ISBN 978-0-14-241414-9
Printed in the United States of America

Designed by Jeanine Henderson
Set in Venetian 301 BT

For Jeff and Kevin, with all my love,
and for Leda, with deepest thanks

Forgiven

PROLOGUE

JANUS, THE ROMAN GOD OF GATES AND BEGINNINGS wore two faces.

The Spanish named San Francisco for a saint. The Celestials met their Demons on its streets. Called Golden Mountain by those in the Middle Kingdom, it perched precarious on a cracking plate. Children's sad eyes pleaded in the stench and filth of its tight alleys, where hawk-nosed men slithered and the unwary were shanghaied. San Francisco's gilded halls and palatial homes held wealth beyond dreams. For some, it was a prison. For some, it was release.

I went to San Francisco to uncover secrets locked tight in its man-made canyons. But the earth shuddered and heaved and unleashed a consuming storm, and I saw its walls leveled. I saw what dissolves in a shivering fire and how that fire purifies. I witnessed how gates tumble and life begins new from ash. I found what is important, and what is too easily lost.

I discovered in that Janus place the secrets locked inside my own divided heart.

Chapter ONE

November 27 1905

> *"Whether I shall turn out to be*
> *the hero of my own life, or whether*
> *that station will be held by anybody else,*
> *these pages must show."*
>
> —*David Copperfield,* Charles Dickens, 1850

WITH ONE SHAKY HAND I RAISED THAT BRANCH. AN INCH only. I quaked like an aspen leaf in a tricky breeze. Not from the cold, though there was that. But from the fear.

"Come on out, girl." The voice of this intruder with the evil snaky eyes rang through the clearing, bell-like in the frost morning.

I eased back deeper into the tangle of chokecherry. Snake-eyes had his back to me, and I fixed my own eyes on the ripped edges at the bottom of his pants leg, watching those frayed threads as the knitted branches that hid me sliced up his form. If I could crawl back silent, if I could just belly back far enough here, if I could get on my feet again, could get enough ground between us so he couldn't shoot me, I could outrun him. Because when I had to, I could outrun a deer.

"I ain't gonna hurt you, now."

Liar. The bruise on my upper arm spoke to that lie. The bruise where he'd grabbed me, surprised me, and I'd twisted around and whanged him good with that fry pan, giving myself just enough time to scrabble into the thicket where I hid now, my stomach on the frozen ground.

I wished I'd nailed him harder and less glancing and laid him flat. I'd be clear to the safety of the fort at Mammoth Hot Springs by now if I could've kept on moving.

Snake-eyes grunted as he rubbed at what must've been an egg-size lump forming where my whale of a swing with the pan had connected with his shoulder. He moved to the left, shoving the barrel of his rifle into the brush barely five feet from where I lay trying to make myself smaller, invisible. "You come out now, it'll go easier for you. I'm gonna find you, one way or the other."

Come back, Pa. I whispered the plea in my brain, begged. I sent that plea out over the trees and snow-dusted hilltops. I couldn't hide here forever.

Snake-eyes moved away from me, and I took that as an opening. I could ease back a little bit more, just catlike . . .

Snap.

Snake-eyes whirled, came at me so fast I didn't have time to get farther than my knees. He reached into the thicket and had me by the hair and he yanked.

Kula Baker doesn't scream.

"I got you now, you sorry little . . ."

My feet jabbed on the hard ground and slid on the snow patches, as my hands went up for my scalp, where he pulled on my braid so hard I thought he might snap my neck. He jerked me back into the clearing while my feet fought for purchase and found none, and then he threw me toward the fire ring at the center, where the fire smoked and sputtered.

I landed hard on my knees, the winter soil like bare rock. I thanked the good Lord and my pa for those thick denim overalls I'd borrowed, as I rocked forward onto my hands. The pan, my only weapon, lay too far away.

"Now I will ask you nicelike and you will answer." Snake-eyes cradled his rifle with the barrel pointing in my general direction. "I want something I 'spect to find in this camp. Something of Nat Baker's."

Nat Baker: Pa. "Then you ask Mr. Baker himself, why don't you?" I braced my palms on my thighs, trying to coil back, trying to be ready, trying to ignore the smarting pain where more bruises were forming and where I'd surely lost some hair from my scalp.

"I'm asking you." He leaned forward, his lips curled in a sneer. "If you run, girl, I'll plug you." He straightened again. "There's a box. About as big as a badger. Has a brass clasp and a lock. Now, you tell me if you've seen this box."

Box? What box?

Kula Baker can keep a stony face.

"Spill it, girlie. You seen it, or ain't you?"

If I told Snake-eyes the truth, he'd plug me. If I lied and he believed my lie, I might stand a chance of escape.

I lied. "I've seen it. If I tell you where, you'll let me go?"

He snorted. "Once I have it, I'll let you go."

"Fine, then. It's about so big, right?" I made a shape about as big as a badger with my hands. "Baker hides it in Cookie's tent. Underneath the flour sacks."

"Stand up." He waved his gun at me.

I stood, wobbly, as if the ground beneath me quaked, and then with all my strength pulled my muscles together, ready.

Snake-eyes looked me up and down. "Thought you was just a girl. You more like a woman."

He stepped closer. I stepped back.

I clenched my hands into fists, gave him the slit-eye look, but, oh. Pa, hear me. You must come back. My plea went up into the crystal sky, curling like smoke and vanishing.

As far as I knew Pa and the men would be off for hours. Who knew where they were—I never truly knew where Pa and his gang went. Never needed to. Saving myself now was all up to me. I could smell Snake-eyes's sour breath from here, the stench of his filthy clothes. My stomach knotted.

But I pointed with a steady arm. "It's over there. Hadn't you better go get it if you want it so?"

"You surprised me once, girlie. I ain't turning my back on you again. You lead me the way to that box."

I stepped farther away, glancing sidewise to keep my footing; the last thing I wanted was to fall now. I knew what happened to a prey animal once it fell. I moved toward Cookie's tent and calculated my options.

They were not good. I decided I would just as soon die with a bullet in my back as enter Cookie's tent with Snake-eyes. Inside that tent I'd be as vulnerable as a fox in a leghold; and I hated closed-in spaces. I figured then I was done for. My skin prickled with sweat even though my blood ran cold. I sent up a last prayer to the sapphire sky; I had no hope for it.

To hear it answered was something of a shock.

Snake-eyes heard it, too, the drumming of hooves as Pa and the men returned to camp. He cursed and spat and reached for me fast, but I was faster.

I spun away and ran as hard as I could in the direction of the hoofbeats. I expected that bullet in my back at any second, but it didn't come, and I figured old Snake-eyes was more bent on saving his own skin than on shooting me.

I ran out of the clearing, through the ring of trees, and met the men on the hillside as they came near to the camp.

Pa, riding at the front, saw me coming, and he slowed. I threw my arm toward the camp. "Stranger, Pa! In the camp! He . . ."

I had no need to finish. Pa read the rest in my face. He alone could read me like a book. His jaw set, and he reached down and took my arm and swung me up behind him in one swift move.

Snake-eyes was on his way, spurring his horse in the opposite direction, already crossing the Yellowstone, the water rising around him like blasts from a geyser.

Gus leveled his rifle. But Pa said, "No."

"You sure, Nat? It's a clear shot."

"Kula?" Pa asked.

Snake-eyes scurried up the slope, kicking that gelding's belly for all he was worth. "He didn't hurt me," I said. I knew my pa had never killed a man. Never. Had never let any of his men kill anyone. All those years living as outlaws, hiding out in the woods, robbing trains, stagecoaches, my father as the head of his gang had made sure they'd done no killing. I didn't want this to happen now on my account. "Don't, Gus."

"Let him go," Pa said to Gus. And to me, "What happened?"

"He was looking for something." I didn't say how scared I'd been; I didn't need to. Pa could surely feel my thumping heart.

And Kula Baker doesn't speak of fear.

The rest of the men dispersed ahead of us into the camp. Pa

spurred his horse. When we reached the picket rope, Pa helped me slide off before he dismounted and faced me. "What'd he say he was looking for?"

"He wanted a box, about this big. I had no idea what he was talking about."

"He didn't hurt you?"

I touched my scalp, still burning. Anyone else, I'd lie, say, "No." But I couldn't lie to Pa. "He grabbed me by the hair. Bruised my arm some. And my knees."

Pa touched my head, all gentle, but his jaw was set so I could see his teeth.

"But I gave him one heck of a whack on the shoulder."

Cookie, bent over by the fire, retrieved his fry pan from the dust and wiped it clean with his bandana. Pa brought this on me, had practically invited Snake-eyes here seeking a box the gang had likely stolen. I was tired of this life, sneaking, thieving, hiding. I wanted Pa out of it. To leave and take me with him. But I had to approach it sidewise. I dropped my voice. "What box was he looking for, Pa?"

"Can't truly say." He had his back to me as he lifted the saddle and let the mare off to graze. He chewed his lip as his hands finished working through the rest of the tack. "But this settles it. I should've seen this coming, you being of age and all. Strangers take one look at you . . . Kula. It's time for you to be off."

I scurried behind as Pa walked away from the camp to the line of trees. "So it's time for what you've been promising me? You'll quit. We'll go off together, you and me."

Pa lifted his chin toward the snow-covered mountain peaks. Here in the valley snow cast a thin blanket, too, but russet patches of bare ground showed where the chinook winds of the past week had blown through and warmed things a little. The sky was the same color as Pa's eyes.

I waited. What I wanted, more than anything, was a yes. Leave, Pa, yes. Come with me, Pa. Help me get up in the world. I held my breath, hoping.

"I can't go yet. There's one more job I've got to do. I can't leave here until after the new year."

And hope crashed. "What job, Pa? It's time you quit. You promised me."

"Don't try to tell me what to do, girl."

Only one person in the world was as stubborn as me, and that was my pa. But my recent fright set my tongue loose. "You said when I turned seventeen, we'd go. I want to be out in the world. I want to move up in the world."

"You will be out. I'm sending you out. This is no fit place for a grown girl."

No fit place for a grown girl—I wasn't sure what it meant to be a grown girl, with no one to teach me the ropes. Times like these were when I missed my ma the most. A girl needed her mother, and I'd never known mine. Now if Pa sent me away, I'd really be alone in the wide world. "You can come with me. Leave this place and let's both go."

"Not yet. Not for me. You'll have to make do."

"But not without you!"

"I can't go yet. I won't say it again."

Pa's final word. And another broken promise. My cheeks burned, and I stabbed the toe of my boot at a lump of dirty snow. "But without you, how am I supposed to make do?"

He pursed his lips and raised his hand to lift his hat and scratch up his hair. Snatches of gray ran through it, like the rivers of old snow that dressed the distant slopes. He looked older than his years. "I've been thinking about that. I've been thinking about that for a while, and this business makes me see that I was right for thinking ahead. I took the liberty of writing a letter to Mrs. Gale a month ago. You remember her."

"I remember the cleaning and the washing and the mending." I also remembered Mrs. Gale as kindly, but I wasn't about to say so. She had treated me well when I was employed by Maggie even before we knew about our connection, Maggie's and mine. I'd admired Mrs. Gale for her pluck as she came and went through the park in summers, where she took modest rooms and worked hard as a photographer for the Haynes Studios, but I wasn't about to say any of this to my pa. My words came out all grumbly. "I remember the work, all right."

He raised his hand to silence me. "I sent her back her rings." His mouth twisted a bit. "Kept those rings all this time, instead of selling them. Anyhow, I returned them to her a few months back as a token."

"A token? A token of my eagerness to spend my life scrubbing other folk's things?"

"So she'd not think ill of me. She's already fond of you, girl. She sent word back. She remembered you. And she's got a nice place in Bozeman. She's ready to take you in. You can live with her and earn your keep."

A nice place in Bozeman—what I wouldn't give for such—but Pa wouldn't be there. And I'd be slaving for a rich woman. Again. Hurt rose in me like bubbles in a spring. "I'm tired of earning my keep!" My voice rang, and a couple of the men looked our way.

Pa's eyes cut at me, but that spring was hot.

"I've waited and waited for when you'd quit this business and leave here with me. We'd go together. Don't send me away. You have to come with me."

I bit my lip till my eyes smarted.

"My mind is set. You're going. I'm sending word to her today and sending you after. You'll leave tomorrow, Kula. Get yourself ready." Pa left me with my hands gripping the picket rope like it was a lifeline.

I should've known—I wanted to hurl the words at his back. I should've known I couldn't trust you.

I marched away from the camp and up the hill, my knees complaining from their bruising and my heart breaking from Pa's words.

I should've let Gus pull the trigger. Got rid of those snake eyes, those yellow teeth. This was his doing, Snake-eyes.

I strode right up to the crest, to where the valley pulled away south with the bright silver thread of river that wove through it, patches of snow in the hollows, pale ovals in the piney blue-black, and the mountains all snow covered at their sharp tips. Steam rose up from spots where the hot springs vented into the cold bright air. My lungs contracted, and a little sound escaped me that was too close to a sob.

Kula Baker doesn't cry. Pa'd just given me what I'd wanted, hadn't he? I'd leave this rough place. I'd be in Bozeman. A city, brimful with possibility. A place for me to rise up in the world, raise my station.

No. Pa was packing me off to another wretched situation, where my station would be that of slave. Cleaning and washing for Mrs.

Gale. Suffering the rudeness of men who'd think nothing of open gawking at a girl with native looks.

I had this dream. In the whispering restless dark I saw myself dressed fine, because my pa and I had made a proper home, because Pa had taken on proper employment. I could read books all day long if I wished, in my own parlor, in my own silks and velvets. I could catch the eye of a gentleman. A gentleman who would treat me right so I'd never have to cook or scrub or sew again. A gentleman who'd look on me with soft eyes.

I had been a maid before, seen how gentlemen treated a lady. I never would understand Maggie—she'd been rich once. And as good as she'd been to me, I took her for a fool. Turning her nose up at an offer of marriage. I'd have left with that rich gentleman if he'd asked me, but he didn't. And a man like him would not ask me, a ladies' maid—at least, not until my pa and I together had a fresh start. That's what we both needed. A fresh start at a new life.

A new century lay open before us, where all things could be made clean and shiny, even a man's soul. Why, I'd heard that men could get up in the air in flying machines, men flying like birds. If that were true, why then, anything was possible. It might even be possible for me, the part native daughter of an outlaw, to become a lady.

Wasn't it? Couldn't I lift out of here until I was wrapped in the blue bowl of the sky, free? Couldn't I fly like a swallow out over these thick-timbered woods, these braided rivers and steaming rocks and sullen springs and hulking peaks?

Oh, I'd leave these woods, yes, but without Pa and without that fresh start. I'd still be a servant. Even with Mrs. Gale, nice as she was, I'd still be her servant.

I tightened my hands, balled up my fingers, raw and callused. Whatever start I made would be fashioned by me.

"Hiya!"

Gus galloped away north, snow and mud spitting up behind his mount's heels. Carrying Pa's message to Mrs. Gale, no doubt.

I turned back toward the camp to make my preparations with an unsettled mind.

Chapter TWO

November 28, 1905

*"She had thrown the dice,
but his hand was over her cast."*

—*The Golden Bowl,* Henry James, 1904

MIN WAS THE ONLY CHINESE I'D EVER MET.

I didn't live in the camp most of the time. Pa'd reared me and schooled me in my letters and numbers, and his men were like a passel of uncles teaching me this or that about hunting, or scouting, or sensing change in the weather.

He'd seen to it I'd never met a true threat. At least not until recently.

Once I'd reached an age where my two good hands could be of service, Pa'd found me work here and there in the park. Someone was always looking to have their clothes washed and mended, or their tea served, and I'd scrub the sour look off my face and pull back my hair in my blue ribbon, and they'd pay the poor sweet Indian-looking girl to take care of their things. Even house me pretty nice, some of them, so I didn't have to stay in Pa's camp.

Min showed up in Mammoth Hot Springs a few weeks earlier, and I noticed her right off. She was like me, foreign-looking. There weren't many of us in Mammoth itself.

She floated in and out of Yellowstone Park, from Mammoth to Gardiner and back, picking up chores, washing, and mending. We'd exchanged only a few words, but straight off I thought of her as kin. Both of us wore our skins like they didn't quite fit.

Now, in the railway station in Gardiner with travelers and tourists, Min came to my mind as I felt the appraising stares, the bold ogling looks, the recognition that I didn't fit, and I shrugged in my discomfort.

An animal that shows fear is easy pickings.

Kula Baker does not show fear.

The train from Gardiner to Livingston was near empty, and I sat alone by the window with my gloved hand pressed flat against it. The valley rose hard and knifelike to either side of the train: it rose steep, offering the way forward or back, and I was going forward past the edge of known territory.

When that valley broadened out under a gray sky, under the snow-covered hills and flanking mountains, the Yellowstone slowed as it tumbled out of the mountains, easing out into the plains and into the broad unknown beneath the bare cottonwoods and perching bald eagles. I tried to slow my own breath and let myself flow out with the river, even while my heart was galloping down the vertical face of a cliff.

I'd learned a thing or two from my employers, and most from Maggie, who had tried over the last year to school me in worldly things. Now she was off at that college of hers, and I hadn't seen her since summer. But it didn't matter what she'd taught me; I'd never ventured this far out of Mammoth, out of the park. Terror blazed through my innards. And then I tucked in tight.

I touched the cameo that had been my present from Maggie, and beneath it and hidden by the placket of my shirtwaist I felt the small key Pa had given me just before I left. "Keep this key close," Pa'd said as he slipped the chain around my neck in the early morning light. "You may have need of it."

At the ticket window in Livingston, I asked after the Bozeman train.

"Three o'clock," the man replied, his head bowed over his paperwork. "One way or round-trip?"

"One way."

He glanced up at me through the iron bars, and I could feel his eyes take in my features. "Second class'll be a dollar fifty."

I glared. But I curbed my tongue, wishing I had the money to demand first class. I slid the coins across the wood counter and took my ticket and sat on the oak bench near to the door with its arched sign: LADIES' WAITING ROOM.

I would've gone into the Ladies' to wait, but did I dare, with my second-class ticket? With me being so obviously not a true lady? I squared my shoulders and stared at the wall.

Men prowled the station, catlike.

Cougars came into the camp on a rare occasion, and I knew well what to do when facing down a cougar. Stand tall, do not run, show no fear—that's best. Cats do not like to be challenged, but they love a chase. I straightened my shoulders and made sure my thick hair was still pinned well up. Everything about me, still tucked in tight.

One man took a turn around the long room and came and sat next to me on the bench and cleared his throat. He was outfitted in an old, out-of-fashion frock coat. His shoes were scuffed. I twisted my head away and leaned my arm against the rest.

"Know yer way around Bozeman, then?"

I glanced; a mistake. For one instant, with his hungry expression, he looked like Snake-eyes. In that instant the fear must've been plain as day on my face. I drew up, but not before a sly smile played on his lips.

"You traveling alone? Course you are."

"I have friends in Bozeman."

"Whereabouts?"

My heart hammered. I had no idea whereabouts. Pa said Mrs. Gale would fetch me at the station in Bozeman.

"Pretty gal like you, traveling alone. Darn shame." His voice dropped. "You maybe a Crow? Or Sioux?"

"No."

"Sure," he said. "Sure thing." He slid down the bench right up next to me. "I know gals like you. Can't fool me."

My hands tightened around the drawstring of my reticule. "I've got a knife handy, right here. You don't move away, I'll stick you." I kept my voice low and even, hoping he wouldn't hear the tremor hiding behind it.

He clicked his tongue, but slid back to the far corner of the bench. After a minute he moved off, and I let the air out of my lungs.

This was not my dream, where I was treated so. My gentleman would treat me decent.

On the train as it climbed up and over the Bozeman pass through snow-covered hills and under gray skies threatening new snow, a knot grew in my stomach, tighter than a burr in sheep's wool. I touched the key again, felt it beneath my shirt.

The train eased into the station in a cloud of steam. I made my way down the steps and found my trunk. The porter who pulled it off the train for me took in my meager offering of pennies and frowned. I frowned right back, knowing from experience, from my years of service, just what he was thinking. Those pennies would have to do. I had no more to give him.

From behind me came, "Miss Kula?"

The voice was so unexpected that I turned sharp as glass. I looked down into the anxious face of a boy who stood twisting his cap. "I'm Caleb, Miss Kula. I do for Mrs. Gale from time to time, and she sent me to fetch you."

I relaxed. He seemed more nervous than I was. "I see. How did you know . . ."

"It was you?" He smiled. He was pleasant enough, maybe three or four years younger than me. "She told me. She said you were pretty. Dark-haired. Native-looking." At this last he blushed.

As well he should have.

I narrowed my eyes. "My trunk." I pointed, leaned toward him. "Don't go getting any ideas," I said low.

"No, miss, I sure wouldn't. Never. No." He stared at me, abashed, and I realized with a shock that it was the first time anyone had ever called me "miss." The very first time, in all my years. I forgave him right then.

I stood straight and mustered up a smile. "Then I'm sure we'll be friends." I stuck my hand out. "Friends?"

He pulled back from my hand as if it would bite. He nodded. Then he took my trunk and dragged it out across the platform and through the station to a small carriage waiting by the curb.

As I made to get into the carriage he stuck out his hand to help me up. "Friends," he said, soft and shy, as our hands met.

Caleb drove down Bozeman's main street. I'd never seen so many shops in one place. This was nothing like Gardiner, let alone Mammoth.

"That's the greengrocer," Caleb said. "There's the pharmacy."

Such a variety of people, all dressed fine, even though wrapped against the chill wind. Such a hubbub and slop, garbage and calling out.

"Lookie!" shouted Caleb, and he laughed. He pointed at the horseless carriage belching and rattling down the street in front of us. When it pulled over with a whine and a clattering halt, Caleb shouted, "Get a horse!" as I twisted right around in my seat to eyeball the thing.

Such noise and confusion reigned that if I hadn't been in control of myself I'd have slapped my hands over my ears and shut my eyes. The ride to Mrs. Gale's house may have taken ten minutes, but it felt like ten hours.

And then—there she was. In the middle of the chaos. Min.

She glided down the street, head bowed, hands clutched at her middle. I lifted my own hand to call out to her but drew back just in time. For she'd walked right up to someone I knew, even if he was dressed decent. Even if he did sport a waxed mustache and a shiny star on his lapel. She walked up to Snake-eyes, and it was clear from the way he laid his hand on her: she belonged to him. Bitter saliva filled my mouth.

Snake-eyes. Min was his. And he was the law.

Chapter THREE

November 28, 1905

"All I have done so far is to survive as nothing more than a humble worker like pigs and cows. Is my youth being wasted? No. I have dreams. I have hopes. Life means nothing if you don't try to better yourself."

—*Diary of Henry Hashitane,*
Japanese rail worker in Montana, 1905

I TUGGED AT CALEB'S SLEEVE, POINTED. "IS THAT THE SHERIFF?" I could hardly choke the words out.

"Him? Don't know him. But that looks like a marshal's badge. Must be from someplace else."

And Min. There she was. Almost like I'd conjured Min by thinking of her. And she was connected with him. My skin was a prickle all over, and that closed-in space feeling came over me and I smelled a trap, set and ready.

Kula Baker knows predators.

Pa'd said he'd come for me here when he was ready. I had to bide my time working for Mrs. Gale. Now I'd be biding with a wary eye and a worried heart until Marshal Snake-eyes returned to his someplace else. I put my hand up to hide my face as we drove by.

We turned onto a broad avenue heading south, and I let out a long breath and shoved the thought of Snake-eyes from my mind.

"There it is," said Caleb. "Mrs. Gale's."

I knew Mrs. Gale was a photographer who sold her photos, as well as being a widow of independent means. That was a startling fact all by itself—that she worked. But now that I approached her town home I saw Mrs. Gale through fresh eyes, and wide ones at that.

Her house was the largest I'd ever seen up close, a brick three story with a full front porch like the one on the National Hotel in Mammoth, with tall windows draped in lace. A neat little picket fence surrounded the front yard with its sprawling bare-branched elm.

Mrs. Gale herself came to the door when Caleb rang. She was just as I recalled her: bright-eyed, plump, thick fingers of gray woven through the brown coils of her rolled-up hair. I curtsied, a rare thing for me. I was humbled by all this splendor.

"Kula." Mrs. Gale smiled. "No need for formalities here. Come in." She drew me into a front hall larger than most houses.

Caleb followed me in with my trunk; I slipped my fingers into the bow of my bonnet while my eyes swept this grand space.

Mrs. Gale lectured on about mealtimes and expectations and duties and other things I should be attending to. But my senses were otherwise occupied. I stopped in front of the tall clock in the hallway and listened to its deep, slow tock.

"Because I live alone, I have no cook, so you'll help in the kitchen as well."

"Yes, ma'am," I murmured.

"Let's see you to your room." She turned and led me up the stairs.

The window that faced the landing was stained glass, a picture of a girl admiring flowers in a vase. I stopped on the landing and traced my fingers over the smooth glass, over the lead that held the glass together, over the body of the girl with her pretty white gown, the gray light coming through the glass and staining my fingers red and deep purply blue and yellow. Fruitlike, ripe and luscious.

I wanted to be that girl. I could be that girl. If I found myself the right husband.

"Kula?"

I went on up the second flight.

"There's no need for you to sleep on the servant's floor with just the two of us in the house. I didn't take on boarders this winter. Both our rooms are here on this floor. That one's mine, and here's yours."

I had my own room. My own. I stepped into the room with Mrs. Gale.

"Are you all right, my dear?"

I raised my fingers to my face and rubbed my cheeks dry.

"I'll leave you here. When you're ready, come downstairs and join me for tea." Mrs. Gale went back downstairs, leaving me in my room.

My own room—with a bed, my own bed, a real four-poster with a lacy canopy. With linen sheets. With a private water closet, my own private water closet with a pull chain toilet that I flushed three times in a row just to watch the water wind down in the shiny white bowl.

I sighed. I knew who would be cleaning that shiny white bowl. Still . . . I had my own wardrobe, with hangers for my clothes. My own writing desk and chair.

The seat on my chair was embroidered with a stitch so fine it made my fingers ache.

Caleb had left my trunk in the middle of my room. I bent and unlatched it. I had a few nice things: the pale lemon shawl Maggie had given me, her blue velvet gown. Pa doled out most everything from the runs to his men, or sold it. He didn't want to turn my head with pretty baubles. Except for the few books he'd given me, everything else I had I'd earned myself.

I was ready to change all that. Ready for a man to raise me up.

When I joined Mrs. Gale, she'd set out the teapot and a plate of sugar cookies in the front parlor.

"This is a fine house," I said into my teacup.

"Kula, I like you. I know you've had a hard life. You'll work hard here, too, but when your father asked me, I took you in because I like your company."

"Yes, ma'am." I was pretty certain Mrs. Gale's notion of hard work was nothing like the ill treatment I'd received from time to time in the past. Still and all, I was a servant. I knew what would be expected of me.

Kula Baker won't be taken for a fool.

I lay in bed that night and recalled how I'd parted from Pa what seemed a hundred years ago but was in fact only this morning and that key he'd handed to me, saying, "Keep this key close."

"What's it open?" I'd asked.

Pa had glanced at Gus, who stood nearby, waiting in the slant dawn light with the pair of horses to ride with me into Mammoth to catch my coach. "You'll know if the time comes. Choices. But just remember, not all choices are easy, girl."

"Pa, I don't understand. Please come with me. Let's go together. Don't send me off alone." I whispered it so low I was sure he didn't hear me. Sure he didn't hear me because he stepped back and let Gus hold the mare's head for me. All he did was lift his hand goodbye before he turned away.

Now I lay in the pitch-dark strange room in Mrs. Gale's house and ached all over in spite of the soft feather mattress. I wasn't truly sure why Mrs. Gale had taken me in and was acting so nice to me. I wasn't sure at all what I'd do if I ran into Snake-eyes or even Min on the street. I wasn't sure about a thing in my life, not even Pa.

I loved my pa. How I loved my pa. But for me love alone wasn't enough.

FOUR

November 1905—March 1906

"Thus conscience does make cowards of us all."

—*Hamlet*, William Shakespeare, 1602

WINTER BLANKETED BOZEMAN, COLD AND DRY. SNOW FELL from the sky at regular intervals, smoothing the rocky, bare-limbed edges of the city.

I worked for Mrs. Gale, but it was easy work. I still wasn't sure of her intentions—what kind of lady didn't work her servants hard?—but her kindly demeanor let me down gentle. For one thing, she truly admired my skill with the needle. My embroidery was good, that I knew, but it meant something to me to hear Mrs. Gale say as much.

And I was also quick with numbers—my pa had taught me—and Mrs. Gale let me help her with her affairs. I cleaned, but she was such a tidy person by nature and things were so well scrubbed to begin with that it was like putting the polish on a church.

I learned from her how to cook in ways other than over a campfire and with ingredients like anchovies (which I did not like) and capers (which I did). And I learned to eat at a table laid with more implements set out only for the two of us than outfitted Pa's entire camp. Sometimes, gazing at the finery around me, I wondered at it all.

Growing up with outlaws made me a hard case, especially for a woman, and I still couldn't figure why Mrs. Gale took me on and treated me so kind. There were many rocky, bare-limbed edges of my own to be smoothed, and Mrs. Gale was a fine-grit sandpaper.

After my first few weeks in Bozeman, Caleb and I did the regular shopping together. I never let up keeping my eyes open for that devil Marshal or for Min, like worrying about running into a bear that lurked unseen in the woods, but town shopping became my delight. I determined not to let worries rule my life. As Caleb loaded the grocery items, I wandered the dry goods aisle of the general store, fingering satin and lace ribbons and sniffing jars of cold cream. Then Caleb and I would spend a handful of pennies on small glasses of Coca-Cola at the soda fountain just so I could stare after the ladies and examine their fashionable costumes. One day, perhaps that would be me . . .

A few times I caught the eyes of men. Men who seemed quite proper and of means. I took to mimicking the actions of the ladies—tried to put a lick of polish on my figure even to the point of acting shy and demure, which was so against my nature. And I listened, and polished up my speech by imitation, too, so I could meet my opportunities with a gracious tongue.

On one of those occasions a young man smiled and tipped his hat. He approached me and would have engaged me in a conversation if Caleb had not appeared at my elbow, tugging at me like an annoying little brother. I hid my disappointment, but gave the young man a willing smile.

There were opportunities in Bozeman for me.

Kula Baker knows what she wants.

When some weeks had passed and I'd seen neither Snake-eyes nor Min, I began to relax. I decided they'd returned to wherever they'd come from. It pained me to think of Min with him, but there was nothing I could do about that.

The holidays came and went, but I heard nothing from Pa. Maggie and I had exchanged letters, and she was friendly and I swallowed my jealousy of her good fortune. As a Christmas gift, I sent Maggie a stack of five new hankies that I'd embroidered, and she sent me a pair of pearl earbobs that I put on at once and didn't take off except to sleep.

Bit by bit the hard knots I carried around from seventeen years of ups and downs began to unravel. I began to realize that maybe I didn't need my pa to help lift me into a comfortable life. I could make my own way to a life of contentment, to a respectable life. I could find a man who would treat me well. Be he young or old, it didn't matter. I was certain that somewhere in this small city were a man and a future, waiting for me.

I'd been in Bozeman almost five months, and still I did not hear from Pa.

Pa had done his best. That I knew. He'd had to raise me up in the company of a rough bunch without a mother, but I was always clean and well fed and nurtured by books and ideas. Even once he'd started me working he'd seen to it I had what I needed. He'd tried, he'd cared. So why was I not surprised when he all but disappeared from my life?

I had thought that he'd given up on me; I never thought I'd give up on him.

Routine wears a groove so that you forget what matters. I was in such a groove one snowy March day when Caleb and I picked our way through ice to the greengrocer's door. A fine snow drifted down from a gray sky. I was caught by surprise.

"Kula?" The voice came from behind me, hoarse and ragged, muffled by the snow.

"Pa!"

There he was, big as life, and I didn't think; I threw my arms around him.

But he drew away, and then I truly saw his face. Lined, thin, gray stubble knotting his chin. His hair too long. His eyes darting and fearful. This was not the Pa I'd left behind. I dropped my arms and took a step back.

"What's wrong?"

"It's bad, Kula. That stranger in camp . . ." Snake-eyes. "His name's Wilkie. Josiah Wilkie."

All my muscles were tensed now. Snake-eyes had a name. "Josiah Wilkie. He's a marshal, Pa—I saw him here in town. What about him?"

"You've got the key—now you've got to go to San Francisco, and quick, Kula. I didn't know what Wilkie was up to. How could I have known?"

Passersby on the sidewalk, casting scathing looks at how we blocked their passage, churned around us like river eddies. Caleb chewed his thumb, his eyes as big as two moons.

I tugged at Pa's sleeve to pull him against the window where through the glass the winter vegetables—onions, parsnips, carrots—stretched out in stiff rows. Pa's eyes were not on me but traveling up the street, down the street. My body tingled; my nerves were on fire, muscles ready. My voice was a soft hiss. "Pa, I don't understand. What are you talking about?"

"You stay away from him. Stay away from Wilkie. You promise me: you stay as far away from him as you can."

"Pa—"

"You still have the key, don't you?" My hand traveled to my throat. "Good. That key is for the box. Find the box in San Francisco. It's all I've got."

"The box! The one that Wilkie wanted? What about it?"

"It's in San Francisco, girl." He gripped my arm so tight I felt the bruise form. "Go to San Francisco."

I shook my head, bewildered. "Go to San Francisco?"

"You have to go, right away. Kula, there's no time. You have to promise me you'll go there and find the box. You—"

I set my lips, pushing back. He was not making sense. "Pa. I'm not going to San Francisco. I'm making a new life, right here, in Bozeman, Montana."

"You must. It's the only way. Listen to me now, remember. You'll need to find Ty Wong."

"What in heaven and earth are you talking about?" I tugged my arm out of his grip, the blood pounding through me. Was I feeling anger, or fear? I had a life here, a life I was not about to leave.

But he blundered on. "Ty Wong. He'll tell you where . . ." We heard a shout from behind us, in the street.

Pa let go of my arm and staggered into the street, leaving me rigid against the window. "Hoy!" A man shouted, a horse reared. Pa raised his arm and leaned away as the buggy driver reined back; and then I heard the whistles coming from the end of the street, wagons screeching through the throng, men yelling, horses screaming, all clatter and confusion and Pa in the middle, snow drifting down, his head lowered as if he waited for the axe to drop.

And me, still standing rigid, trying to distance myself from him, trying to make myself invisible. They were after Pa, and all I wanted was to melt into invisibility.

"There he is!"

"Get him!"

"Don't let him get away!"

My feet were fixed as if I stood in a sucking swamp. Pa did not move as the men, most wearing a blazing star, surrounded him, rifles at the ready, Colts drawn and cocked.

All of Bozeman was transfixed. On the sidewalk between Pa and me two men had stopped to watch; I had to stand on tiptoe to see past them to Pa. I heard the one say to the other: "That's the man murdered Abraham Black. Shot him in cold blood. I heard it was his young son found Abe dead in a pool of blood in his own barn. Terrible thing. And all for a couple horses."

I shrank against the building. My pa? Pa wasn't a horse thief, much less a killer.

"He's a well-known one, that one, so I hear. That's Nat Baker. Nat Baker's been robbing coaches in the park for years. They finally got him now."

The other man nodded. "He'll hang for sure."

Pa. My pa will hang. For murder.

From the crowd around Pa a man pushed forward, wearing a silver star all shiny and spiked right there on his chest. I knew him right off, those snaky eyes of his, that man Pa'd said was Josiah Wilkie.

Wilkie pointed at Pa. "That's him, boys. Cuff him good. He's a slippery devil."

The men closed ranks around Pa, and my heart thudded slow, slow beats that pounded in my ears as I tried to take it all in. I should stop it. I should step up and say, "No, that's my pa; he'd never kill anyone."

Wilkie stepped back and spun those snaky eyes around as if he expected to find someone in the crowd, and I froze solid.

I tipped my brimmed hat low over my eyes so Wilkie couldn't see my face. I stood with my back against the glass as rigid as those lined-up vegetables, the snow like a curtain between Wilkie and me. If I stood there silent and still, no one would notice me. No one would notice a native-looking girl in a plain woolen skirt and jacket. Here in Bozeman, no one took much notice of native girls—they faded into the shadows like smoke. Here on Main Street I was only a shadow, unconnected with the killer.

The shock of thought ran through me: the killer of a man found dead by his young son, a man killed for a couple of horses.

The crowd around Pa moved and shifted, and his eyes met mine, just for an instant. And then I dropped mine away again, my hands plastered flat against my skirt, my gloves pulled tight. I sensed the movement of the men as they shoved by me in a chorus of triumph pushing Pa before them, his feet catching on the cobbles. His stumble, their rough yank and grab. My palms sweaty inside my gloves, my hands shaking as Pa—my pa, not a murderer, not the killer—was swept away from me and into the closed carriage with its bars, slam, slam, and the "hiya!" as they took him away. And I denied him, stepped deeper into the crowd, melting like late snow, melting in my shame and agony. I denied my pa.

Caleb was at my elbow. "That's your pa?" He spoke softly, but awe colored his words.

"No. Forget it. Let's go." I yanked him past the greengrocer and down the street, opposite to the direction of the police wagon.

The sharp teeth of denial, like coyotes on a downed elk, tore me to shreds.

Kula Baker does not forgive. Especially not herself.

Chapter FIVE

March 24, 1906

"His mind ran over past years, and pieced together the recollections of a long-past scandal. "'Of course! Of course!' he said to himself, not without excitement. 'She is not like her mother, but she has all the typical points of her mother's race.'"

—*Lady Rose's Daughter*, a novel by Mrs. Humphrey Ward, 1903

I SLAMMED INTO THE FRONT HALL, SHAKING ALL OVER. Mrs. Gale, sitting by the fire, lifted her head.

"Kula?"

I fled upstairs, my skirts hiked high, taking the steps two at a time.

In my room, I put my hands on the window and shoved, heaving up the stubborn sash. I leaned my head into the frigid air now thick with blowing snow. I gulped in the cold and my body constricted against it, but I didn't care. Pa should've left the woods before this. He could've left his outlawing long ago, and changed his tune and been a free man. Instead, my pa had doomed himself by getting caught—maybe even murdered a man, though my heart wouldn't admit it—and my whole life was inside out.

The snow hit my cheeks like sharp pins, sticking onto my skin and sending little frozen threads into my heart.

I pulled back inside and closed the window and all my skin

burned and I shook all over like a rabbit in a snare. My room was freezing cold now, and I tugged my yellow shawl tight around my shoulders as I sat on my chair and rocked and shook.

I reached for the key that hung out of sight round my neck, and I thought about what Pa had said. About San Francisco and that box and what might be in it. It had to be valuable, or else Wilkie wouldn't have wanted it so bad. Whatever it held, Pa needed it. Choices, Pa'd said.

Go to San Francisco, and find someone named Ty Wong. I had to go to San Francisco. But how could I make my own way to California—the end of the earth as far as I was concerned. And to find a complete stranger in a huge city to retrieve a box that I hadn't even known truly existed until now?

How in heaven was I supposed to manage all that? And what of my life, of my plans? How could I find someone to help me make a safe life for myself in San Francisco, just when Bozeman was starting to become home?

My teeth were chattering so hard I sounded like a sapsucker on a hollow tree. I went downstairs to seek some warmth.

Mrs. Gale stood at the bottom of the stairs, waiting for me. On seeing her, prickles rose on my neck and gave me pause. I stopped on the landing with my back to the stained glass.

"What?" I asked.

"Someone came by looking for you."

I hadn't been upstairs more than fifteen minutes. I tugged the yellow shawl up to my chin. "Who?"

"He wore a badge and an unpleasant expression. He said he'd followed your father to Bozeman and had somehow connected your father with me." Mrs. Gale knew what my pa was. She knew why someone with a badge would be looking for him.

"Did he know about me? That man?"

She shook her head. "Not from me. I didn't invite him in."

My legs were so shaky it was like standing near one of the geysers when it erupted.

"Kula, what's happened?" Her voice was soft, gentle.

"Pa. He found my pa. That man arrested Pa on the street. Caleb and I saw." My suspicious nature slipped as I sank down on the step. "I didn't try to stop it."

Mrs. Gale came to sit on the stair below me, her dress billowing around her.

"He said Pa killed a man . . . He would never . . ." I blinked, keeping my misery locked up tight. "Pa might be a thief, but he's not a murderer. But I didn't say anything. I didn't try to stop them . . ."

Mrs. Gale placed her hand on mine.

I didn't know what was safe to tell her, what to hold back. I still didn't altogether trust her. I didn't really trust anyone. And now I wasn't even sure I could trust my own pa.

What if he *had* killed that man? How could I ever forgive him?

"Can I help?" Mrs. Gale asked.

I shook my head. "No. Except to release me. I have to leave." I had to go to San Francisco.

"Of course."

I dropped my voice to a whisper. "Maybe Caleb could take me to the train."

She looked puzzled. "I can arrange that. But Kula . . ." She hesitated. "Running away won't help."

I yanked my hand out from under hers. Anger pushed the words right out of me before I could stop myself. "I'm not running away. Pa needs me to go to San Francisco."

She sat back, her eyebrows up. "Really."

I nodded. I picked at the edge of the shawl. "Pa said. Go to San Francisco."

She pursed her lips. "I was born there."

This was news. "What's it like?"

"A busy seaport. There are many diversions, and not a few dangers. Especially for a girl traveling alone. Why must you go to San Francisco?"

I put my head down, resting my forehead on my folded arms. I spoke into my arms. "To find something of my pa's." Because Pa told me I must. Maybe it would help him. But I didn't say this; I didn't want to tell her more.

She asked, "For how long will you be there?"

"For as long as it takes me to find someone and this thing Pa needs."

"My sister-in-law lives there," she said. "I can ask if she would take you in."

I rubbed my eyes hard before I lifted my head. "Take me in?"

"You're a capable young woman, and if I made the right entreaties . . . she might work you harder than I have, but she's not cruel. You'd have a place to live."

I wrapped my arms around my waist. I saw no choice. I'd be serving but this was nothing new. I'd be dependent upon a stranger, a rich matron who'd take one look at me and make assumptions. "How can I leave my pa?" I murmured, speaking my thoughts out loud. "How can I leave him now? He needs me here." My eyes smarted and my throat stung.

"I can help with that, if you'll let me. I'll see what I can discover. And I can keep you informed as to what's happened to him."

I met her eyes. "You'd do that?" I shook my head. "Why? Why would you care about me and my pa?"

Her eyes darted away. "In my years I've learned a thing or two." I frowned. She went on. "I have no children."

I gazed at her soft cheek in profile, thinking on this, thinking on her livelihood, her independence, her loneliness. I had to trust her. I had no choice.

And I had to have that box. I had to go to San Francisco, even if I had no idea where to begin once I got there. San Francisco, a city beyond my wildest dreams of a city, and me alone there. Where to find that Ty Wong, and how to balance my search with a servant's necessary work. Would I find what I needed? This stranger, a missing box . . . and maybe even, with luck, someone to treat me right?

I doubted it. I squared my shoulders even as I pulled that shawl double tight around me, like a swaddling.

I had to trust that all things would be made plain in time. I had no other choice.

I might as well have been leaping off the cliff into the gorge of the Yellowstone, the great raging river and jagged rocks waiting for me at the bottom.

Mrs. Gale wrote a letter for me to carry to her sister-in-law. I packed in haste. Thus without further warning or mental preparation or shoring up of any kind, the very next evening I was on a train steaming west to San Francisco.

Chapter SIX

March 25–28, 1906

"California . . . His description of the beautiful flowers blooming in winter, of the great herds of Spanish cattle in lovely fields, of glorious scenery, and of the ideal climate and blue skies, made me just crazy to move out there, for I thought such a country must be a paradise."

—Mrs. F. A. Van Winkle, interview,
The San Francisco Chronicle, September 9, 1900

RACING.

My train: racing across the west, a great lumbering mechanical beast charging bullheaded toward the ocean and the edge of the continent and away from the snow-covered mountains, with me on board wishing I could turn myself right around and run straight back to the high rocky fortress of my youth.

My heart: racing with fear and an anxious dread at what lay ahead for me when this beast finally arrived in San Francisco. City of saints and demons—or so Mrs. Gale had said in one of her few choice descriptions.

My brain swirled with awful imaginings. The worst and most terrible was of my pa, hanging. Then there was Wilkie, his snake eyes devouring me. The box, which was hidden who knew where and which held secrets and choices of who knew what kind. That huge city waiting to swallow me alive.

While I packed my things—a quick task, in the face of my small collection of belongings—Mrs. Gale had painted me a portrait of San Francisco. She told me of Chinatown: "a precarious world unto itself. You'd be best to stay away. The Chinese call themselves 'Celestials' and we non-Chinese are 'Demons.'" She also warned me against venturing into a vile place called "the Barbary Coast," "where that name, Demons, is most fitting."

Kula Baker pays careful heed to warnings.

Once on the train I tried to concentrate on the pleasant images I'd see in California. Mrs. Gale reminded me that I'd see the ocean, and I'd have that view best from the top of Mount Tam, "a more glorious place you can't imagine." I'd read about the ocean often enough, that blue and endless expanse. I'd read about what lay across it, about the Far East, with its rich embroideries that put my simple threads to shame. But as fast as I could think these soft pictures transformed: the ocean hid leviathans and serpents in its vast depths; the Oriental silks sported fire-spewing dragons.

I clung to my hamper of food and drink, taking but a little due to my unsettled stomach. The train lurched side to side. I tried to sleep on the fold-out berth, hanging my wool skirt and jacket beside me, drawing the broadcloth curtain tight shut, but the night was long and haunted as the miles slipped past.

On the second day, I made my way to the dining car. I sipped an iced beverage at the table with its fine linen cloth and silk-shaded electric lamp, but this was a luxury I did not allow myself twice.

Not just for the expense. From the moment I stepped into the car, there were eyes on me. I was watched there, and I knew why. A native-looking girl in plain unfashionable dress in the dining car, sitting alone. I didn't belong. But there was something else . . . I had the eerie sense someone followed me into the car. I lifted my gaze from my sweating glass, half expecting it to meet Snake-eyes Josiah Wilkie.

I squelched a shiver, gulped that drink, and hastened back to my seat in the second-class coach.

Before leaving Mrs. Gale, I'd looked at the maps of California and San Francisco in her atlas. Pa had taught me at an early age how to read a map. The great long bay that lay east of San Francisco was bigger than my Yellowstone Lake. And the Pacific Ocean to the city's west, and Mount Tam to her north—I'd traced them with my finger over and over, making that map lay out in my head so I could watch it all unfold as we got close.

We hurtled and lurched through snow and narrow mountain passes and down onto plains all brown and frozen up, through spires of trees and out into flats that stretched into broad rolling hills, until after three bone-jarring days we entered the city and I pressed to the window to see the fields and homesteads at its borders and the waters of the bay for the first time. I tried to make myself ready for arrival as best I could, splashing my face with the lukewarm water of the tiny lavatory.

The train pulled into outskirts and tight packed brownstones and finally into the roundhouse, where we lurched and shifted in the darkness for some minutes.

That darkness, it was wicked. I pressed myself right up against my window, starting when the electrics overhead blinked once or twice and faces pulsed in and out of my sight.

At last we pulled alongside the platform, where the light flooded from skylights, the train squealing and belching to a stop.

I stepped stiff-legged from my coach, and a smell so foreign assaulted my nostrils that I drew up. Damp and mildewy. It reminded me of fishing at the lakeside in midsummer, but not so pleasant. And the air was chilly but not biting as it had been when I'd left Bozeman. It sank on me . . . heavy. Penetrating. It sank right into my bones and settled there.

My trunk and hatbox were hauled out of the baggage car and dumped without ceremony upside down, the hatbox ribbon chafed and dirty. I took the handle of the trunk and righted it and, there being no other clear means of transport, dragged it along behind me down the endless stretch of platform toward the station. Around me all was chaos: steam welled from beneath trains, people shoved this way and that, shouts and catcalls flooded the air, and engines roared to life in this great hall of trains and tracks; such confusion reigned that my instinct was to climb back onto the train and hide until I saw my high and silent mountains again.

Kula Baker does not shrink. Even in the face of chaos.

I dragged my trunk bumping and scraping into the relative peace of the station's waiting hall—although it was a hubbub there, too, people crowding me and glaring at my trunk and me, and I stopped dead center in the hall in despair. There were great doors on all sides.

Which way should I turn? I had no notion where I was. I tugged the folded note of Mrs. Gale's instructions through the drawstrings of my reticule.

Miss Phillipa Everts, near the intersection of Clay and Jones streets. Find a coach to take you northwest from the station. Or take the trolley if you find a sympathetic soul to guide you.

Mrs. Gale hadn't been back to San Francisco since she and her husband left some twenty years earlier; what if everything had changed? And despite the patient instructions Mrs. Gale had given me, I'd only half listened to her through my mental turmoil. I wasn't truly sure what a trolley was, much less how to take one.

The back of my neck prickled, and I turned right around, feeling I was being watched. Nothing. Shifting crowds and shadows, that was all. Little spasms ran up and down my back, and I gripped my trunk handle tight, searching the crowds, coming up with nothing. Just that uneasy tremor.

Then a cloud withdrew and the sun slanted in arched windows in the high walls above, and I lifted my eyes heavenward and took a breath. I could navigate. Years in the woods hadn't taught me how to fold a napkin or use the right fork, but I knew northwest by the light of the sun.

I dragged my trunk, which seemed to have grown heavier by the minute, out of the biggest doors in the place, doors that faced westerly. Where I stopped again, once more befuddled and overwhelmed.

Chapter SEVEN

March 28, 1906

> *"San Francisco is a mad city,*
> *inhabited for the most part by insane people*
> *whose women are of remarkable beauty."*
>
> —Rudyard Kipling, 1889

THE STREETS OF SAN FRANCISCO WERE A BEDLAM, A WILLY-nilly confusion.

For one thing there were horseless carriages. Automobiles. I'd seen only the one in Bozeman. Here they were everywhere, crisscrossing the roads, making terrible noises, belching and coughing, braying like sick mules. People paraded by me on foot, of course, men, women, boys—lots and lots of boys. How, I marveled, did those boys ever get schooling, all running wild through the streets as they were?

The most fashionable women wore the largest hats I'd ever seen, far larger and more adorned than those I'd admired in Bozeman. I reached up and touched my plain little out-of-season out-of-fashion straw boater, embarrassed.

And mixed up in all this madness, horses pulled everything from small one-seaters to laden wagons, and these, too, were weaving in and out among the people and the automobiles, the horses leaving behind their own fragrant residues.

But most astonishing to me were the trains that were not proper trains but single cars running on tracks embedded in the paving. These must be the trolleys Mrs. Gale spoke of. People jumped on and off them at random—these trolleys never stopped, or so it appeared. Two or three boys, laughing themselves silly, hung off the rear bumper of one passing close by where I stood.

In every direction buildings and smoke and noise and confusion and signs and color and people rose up around me, and a raw stench of mixed soot and horse sweat and fish and damp wool.

I gawked like a perfect fool.

"Miss! Help you, miss?" He was tall and gangly, the boy who stood now at my elbow. "This way, miss! Have a cart right here, waitin' right for you!"

"I . . ."

He already had my trunk by the handle, wrestling it from my grip.

I let go. He heaved the trunk into the back of the cart, and behind it tossed my hatbox and picnic hamper, and then he clambered up on the bench quick as you please, leaving me to fend for myself. I yanked up my skirt and clambered up next to him.

He slapped the reins and the cart took off at a pace, and I grabbed the seat with one hand and my hat with the other.

"Don't you want to know where I'm going?" I shouted, for the noise around me seemed deafening.

"Oh, I 'spect you're headed for Nob Hill, ain't you now." He turned toward me and flashed a toothless smile. "Sure."

"I'm going to Clay and Jones streets. Clay and Jones. Not Nob." I held on tight as we wove between two turning carriages. "What's Nob?"

"You? Clay and Jones?" He looked me up and down. "I'll be. Dressing countrylike and all that. You're a Nob snob after all."

"Clay! Jones!" I shouted. "Not Nob." I bristled at the "countrylike," and tucked my old boots under my skirt. I figured three days on a train might be enough to take the starch out of any gentlewoman.

The boy smiled again, but this time kept his eyes forward. "All's the same to me."

At least I could tell from the sun in the clear bright sky we were headed west.

The cart moved at a clip, the boy managing to maneuver the horse between all the honking, bell-clanging, screeching, mechanical contraptions and the people. He turned the cart deftly more to the south, a quieter street, and moved at an even more rapid clip.

At one point I caught a glimpse of water again—the bay, for the hills rose behind—but it went by in a flash between the tight packed buildings, and I held on to the wagon seat for dear life.

"I'm going to the home of Miss Phillipa Everts," I shouted. "Do you know her? Where she lives? On Clay?"

"Can't say. But, oh, sure. We can find her. You bet." He spit off to the side. The cart lurched around another corner, and we entered a terrible place.

Hurdy-gurdy music poured from buildings whose thin walls

seemed on the verge of collapse. Wretched women leaned over windowsills, their faces so painted they were distorted. Men lurched and staggered, drunk in broad daylight. I turned my eyes away from the sight of those low bodices and leering smiles.

The boy stopped the cart. "There you are!" He flashed a huge gaping grin.

I shook my head. "What? No. That's impossible."

He pointed.

A dance hall raked sidewise; a scanty-clad woman, her back propped on a sign, sat smoking a fat cigar. I turned back to the boy, narrowing my eyes. "Where are we?"

"You look! It's right there, right at that corner." He waved his hand. The sign read Clay Street, all right, but this was not the Clay I expected. Then, since I made no move, he jumped down and came round to my side of the cart and took my arm, yanking me down to the street. "There you go."

I smoothed my skirt with my palms and tried to pin back my hair. "No. This isn't right. It can't be." Curls tumbled out beneath my hat, and the loose hair occupied my hands and fell over my eyes.

"Sure is." He flashed me his toothless grin, hopped back onto his cart, slapped the reins, and was off before I could blink.

My trunk! "No!" My shout landed dead in this noisome place.

All my things—everything I owned in the world, my belongings were all in that trunk, my trunk that was still, with my hatbox and hamper, in the back of his cart.

"Stop!" I yelled. "Thief!" I ran and flailed, heart pounding, stomach lurching. "Stop him!"

I tried to run after him, but he moved that cart so fast through the staggering populace I was sure someone would be crushed, and before even a block I was trying to press through a crowd myself, helpless, watching as the cart carrying all my worldly goods turned a corner and disappeared.

Chapter EIGHT

March 28, 1906

"The Barbary Coast is the haunt of the low and vile of every kind . . . Licentiousness, debauchery, pollution, loathsome disease, insanity from dissipation, misery, poverty . . . and death, are there."

—*Lights and Shades of San Francisco*, Benjamin Estelle Lloyd, 1876

I SLOWED AND SWALLOWED THE LUMP THAT FILLED MY throat. Smells assaulted my nostrils, and I pressed one gloved hand against my nose and mouth. The crack of glass mixed with the raucous music. I didn't know which way to turn.

A man came up from behind me and gave a firm squeeze to my backside.

I whirled, aghast, and he lurched backward, which didn't stop him leering and moving back in on me. "Just wanted to know how much you're charging. Pretty thing, you are."

"Be off!" I shoved him away, my voice shaking. A titter floated down from one of the windows looming over the street.

He muttered something unrepeatable, and then said, "You come back here at dusk. Maybe then you won't be so uppity. Native girl like you shouldn't be uppity anyhow." He glowered at me as he stumbled away.

I clutched my reticule tight to my body and pushed down the

middle of the stinking street, moving as fast as I could, running, in fact, back in the general direction from which I'd been driven.

Within a few blocks I was able to slow down, as the passersby were less threatening and better dressed and the number of bawdy houses and saloons thinned and disappeared. And as I slowed, the shock of what had happened set my body to shaking all over.

I hadn't been in San Francisco an hour, and already I was robbed and abandoned. Touched in disgusting familiarity. A victim. And what an idiot I was. Shouldn't I have known better? Mrs. Gale had warned me about the Barbary Coast. Named after the place of pirates, somewhere in Africa. Barbarous, that's what it was. Filled with pirates.

No police stood around this neighborhood. And except for his gap teeth, how could I even describe the boy robber? I'd been hoodwinked but good. Was this what it was like, when my pa and his gang stopped a coach or a train, was this how a passenger felt when liberated of her possessions? The heat of shame crept up my neck.

I straightened my back, set my jaw, moved my trembling legs. My anger was mostly directed at myself. Stupid me, taken in by a robber, stupid, stupid, stupid.

I pressed on, following the growing crowd of pedestrians and coaches onto a larger avenue. I might as well have been in the buffeting current of the Yellowstone River, pressed this way and that and helpless against that current, alone and lost and stripped of most everything I owned.

I'd worn my meager collection of jewelry on the train, thank goodness—the cameo, my one pearl necklace, the earbobs, the chain with its key. Those were still with me, as was my money, what little I had. But all my clothes—gone. The blue velvet gown and yellow shawl I treasured. My handful of books—gone, including my favorite Dickens. My embroidered gift for Miss Everts—my attempt to win her sympathy and show her my skill by crafting elegant flowered tea towels—gone.

What remained, save my jewels, were the dark plaid traveling skirt and jacket I wore now, and those garments were in sore need of a cleaning after three days on a train.

I gave up on my hair, letting it tumble down my back, and I plastered my boater on top of my head, and let my legs work through the shakes.

Clay and Jones. I stopped walking and looked up. I was still on Clay. I wasn't about to go back the way I had come. I made to turn up another broad street—Grant Avenue. Above me stood a building adorned with curving tiered roofs capped by red tiles. Chinese lettering covered the signs; a painting of a red dragon curled over one doorway. I remembered the other things Mrs. Gale had said. Chinatown.

She'd warned me against Chinatown, too. But I had to press through if I was to reach my target, and nothing, I thought, *nothing* could be worse than the Barbary Coast. I'd seen a few other Chinese, including Min, on the streets of Bozeman. Mostly men who'd come to work on the railroads and stayed after the railroads were finished. They'd stuck to their odd clothing and kept to themselves, their lives lived quiet and secretlike. I remembered sipping Coca-Cola with Caleb while I'd watched such a one make his way down Main Street, his coat buttoned slantwise, his small flat hat perched back on a high broad shaved crown, his long braid strung down his back, his hair as raven black as my own.

I didn't see how this Chinatown could be threatening. Nothing like what I'd just been through. Surely not.

I pressed on. The narrow street was packed with black-suited men, and there were vendors everywhere—and stands with everything from live chickens and ducks in cages to dead chickens and things I didn't care to even wonder about, to vegetables I didn't recognize. People shouted and called out in their mother tongue, and I was buffeted by rank smells that made my lip curl. Chinese people around me gave me no heed at all.

I got turned around for a minute and froze, trying to avoid the crush of a moving cart.

I stood inches taller than most. A tickle of fear rose up from the small of my back. I stood out like an aspen in a pine grove. Eyes locked on me from all directions. Not friendly eyes. What had I done now?

I fixed my shoulders, making force of will my strength.

I turned right around quick and ran smack into an old woman. She tripped backward, dropping the sack she carried on her head, and that sack hit the ground with such an impact that it split and spilled its contents: rice. She began to chide me at once.

"I'm sorry." I lifted my hands in the air, trying to calm her, getting the full meaning of her words despite not being able to understand a one. "Please. I'm sorry." There wasn't a thing I could do; the rice was scattered, ruined. She waved her hands in the air, scolding, as a crowd gathered around me, nodding and adding their own accusations.

I knew I should compensate her. But my purse held so little.

"I'm sorry!" But words served only to inflame the crowd and the old woman.

"Here, missy!" A man waved to me, his broad face bearing a smile—but I didn't trust something about that smile. It was false. "You come with me now. We take care of." Even in the midst of this tirade, I knew I shouldn't go with him. But what was I to do? I took a step toward him.

"Come, missy!" His smile dropped, and he became more demanding, reaching his arm through the crowd to grab my wrist.

And then from behind me came a gentle low voice speaking Chinese. So soft and gentle I turned at once. I came face-to-face with a young Chinese man, as tall as me. He leaned around me and spoke in hushed tones to the old woman, who turned her chatter on him until he'd soothed her like my pa soothing a panicky horse and then he put a few coins in her hand. She lowered her voice to a mutter, cast me an evil glance, but went off. The crowd dispersed, and the young man took my elbow and steered me away.

I searched the street for the other man—the broad-faced one—but he vanished with the crowd.

I turned to my rescuer. "Thank you." I mimed with my hands; I didn't expect him to understand me.

I pulled right up in surprise when he returned, with no shade of an accent, "You look more than a little out of place." And his face lit up with a smile so like the sunrise that I melted before it. "In fact, you stand out like a sore thumb. Come on. Where're you supposed to be?"

Chapter NINE

March 28, 1906

"As long as California is white man's country, it will remain one of the grandest and best states in the union, but the moment the Golden State is subjected to an unlimited Asiatic coolie invasion there will be no more California."

Organized Labor, Official Organ of the State and Local Building Trades Councils of California, San Francisco April 21, 28, and May 5, 1906 [combined edition]

I DIDN'T KNOW WHETHER I COULD TRUST HIM. AS USUAL, I didn't know whether I could trust anyone. But I was alone in San Francisco and had little choice. And he had a quiet, calm manner that eased my mind a little.

He introduced himself as David Wong. He didn't seem to mind my standoffishness when I said only, "Miss Baker."

"How'd you find your way into Chinatown?"

"That wasn't my intent."

His eyebrows lifted. "You don't live in San Francisco." It wasn't a question.

I shook my head. "I just arrived by train. I'm visiting."

"Maybe we should get you out of here and on your way."

I had to follow him—it was either that or stand here, frozen to this very spot. Better this David Wong than the false-smile man who'd tried to snag my arm. Still, my stomach was in knots.

We made our way along this street and then down another, and all at once we were in a different neighborhood of small shops and houses, the signs now in English, no longer in Chinatown. I took a breath of thanks. He looked up and down the street. "Now, then. Where're you headed?"

"The corner of Clay and Jones."

He looked startled. Then he drew up. "All right. Well, you're on Clay now, so all you have to do is walk up about four blocks and you're there."

A group of young bucks, all shined up in bowlers and striped vests, passed us on the sidewalk. One of them narrowed his eyes at David and then gave me a dark glance. They muttered among themselves as they passed and were half a block away when one said, overloud, "Mixed up where they don't belong."

"Let's cross the street," David said.

Once we were on the other side he checked his pocket watch, didn't meet my eyes. "Listen. I'd walk you up there, but you're better off not being seen with me. Some people don't think well of a Chinese man consorting with a non-Chinese lady."

I straightened, hearing him refer to me as a lady. My hands and fingers worked and fretted as I gripped my reticule. I knew all about it, I wanted to say. All about that skin that didn't quite fit. "Maybe they were talking about me. About how I look." I'd heard the name-calling. Heard the references to the blood that flowed in my veins. "Maybe they weren't talking about you at all. It might have been about me."

"If they talked about your looks, it'd be because you're so pretty." His cheeks went dark, and he stared at his feet. "Sorry, I didn't mean to blurt that out. It was supposed to be a compliment."

And I lost words. He stood there, this kind young man who had just saved me, his hands thrust into his jacket pockets, thick dark hair slicked back, his dark eyes lifting to mine and then dropping away in shy retreat . . . I didn't know what to think. He was sweet and nice-looking, no doubt about it; he lit up some feeling deep in my heart.

Kula Baker keeps her wits about her. Kula Baker does not go soft over a young man.

Especially when that young man is just as much of an outsider as she is.

Well. I smoothed my skirt as I averted my eyes from his, while I was as upside down and inside out as if I'd tumbled over the Gibbon Falls.

Tumbled, that was for sure. Up Clay, down Clay; the wind was knocked clean out of me. I was not feeling scatterbrained about just David Wong. It was also this strange city.

I put my hand on my stomach and tried to breathe. It was too confining here. I wanted to break into a run and run until my feet reached a meadow, run until my own familiar snowcapped mountains appeared to rim the sky, the big Montana and Wyoming sky that opened above me in that piercing blue I knew. Here all I could see were snips and snaps of sky, and hills that rose and fell and were all covered with buildings, and I heard the clamor of the city all around. Here there were men who would hurt me, people who would snatch me off the streets, here there were loss and confusion. What was I doing in this place?

This David Wong was my only firm anchor in a shifting sea, and I had to let go and trust him. I took a deep breath. "I was just robbed of all my things."

"Robbed? In Chinatown?" David's face worked, and I nearly thought he would sprint back down the street to recover my goods.

I reached my arm to the air between us, afraid to touch him, even though I surprised myself by wanting to. "No. No, in the Barbary Coast. This boy who picked me up at the station, he took me there and drove off with my trunk."

"Shall we go to the police?"

Police. Men with badges who pretended to be lawful came straight into my mind. All my life I'd avoided the law because of the risk to my father; now I avoided the law because of that Snake-eyes Wilkie.

I shook my head. "I couldn't even tell them what he looked like."

"Is there something else I can do?" His question was so genuine and generous.

I smiled and dropped my chin. "You've done enough. Thank you."

"I've hardly done anything." He'd started my heart pounding, but, oh, this was not something that could ever be. For either of us.

Up the street, the group of boys was now loitering about a shop front, eyeing us. I knew the look of trouble brewing. "I should go on now. I don't want to make trouble for you."

David pointed. "Walk about four blocks, straight up there. You can't miss the corner of Jones and Clay."

I nodded. "Thanks again."

Neither of us moved.

He coughed. "Are you visiting someone there?"

"Yes." Now I stared straight into his kind eyes. His shy sweetness was a balm.

"Can I see you, perhaps? That is, can I come to wherever you're staying and pay a call?"

Pay a call. On me. The first time a gentleman would pay me a call. My heart began to beat faster. Even as the voice in my head said, Kula Baker needs to rise above her station. Needs someone to help to raise her up. This couldn't be the gentleman for that.

Well. It was just a call. And there was no ignoring my thundering heart and flushed cheeks. "I'd like that. I'll be at the home of Phillipa Everts." I hope, I added to myself. She might not take me in.

"Miss Everts!"

"You know her?"

He hesitated, then shrugged. "San Francisco is small, in a funny way. Everyone knows everyone."

My glance strayed back across the street. Those young men reminded me of a pack of coyotes, circling. I wished I could make them vanish so I could stand longer here on this steep hillside with this David Wong. When our eyes met again, my heart took a fair leap and my legs grew wobbly.

But those coyotes menaced. "I should be off. I hope to see you again." And I did hope. Hope fluttered in my chest and forced roses into my cheeks.

He tipped his hat, and I marched on up the hill. After a long block I looked back. David was standing on the street corner. The young men hadn't moved, either. I had the feeling my coyotes were being held at bay by a very determined bear.

I walked on another block, pondering my chance encounter. I wondered if I would see that bear again, that David Wong.

Wong! I clapped my hand to my forehead, right there. With the jarring experience of the robbery and my girlish goggling, I'd forgotten everything, every reason I was even in San Francisco. Even if Wong was a common name, perhaps David was of the very same family and knew Ty Wong. Here had been my chance to find my pa's box, to follow my pa's plea. I turned right around, but David Wong had vanished.

I cursed myself for losing an opportunity to solve my riddle. This day was turning out to hold a long string of curses.

I continued on up the street and breathed more deeply, and not just from all my stirred-up feelings. San Francisco was built on some honest-to-heaven hills. Had I been at home I would have taken my shoes off, for it wasn't the winding of breath that bothered me but my sore feet and the thin soles of my toe-pinching boots on this unforgiving paving. It seemed to take a hundred years and a million unhappy footfalls before I reached the corner of Clay and Jones.

I pulled the note from my reticule again, looked at the address, and up at the street numbers, and then my mouth dropped open so wide I was afraid it would hit my squinched-up toes.

The house hulking above me was a big house in a neighborhood of big houses. Turrets and towers, porches and balconies . . . these only began to describe what looked like a confection of furbelows and curlicues and fancies. It was a giant of a house. This house went up and up, such that I had to tilt my head and squint my eyes to see the whole of it.

Behind the gate was an immaculate garden, dormant now, showing carefully pruned rosebushes laid out in formal beds. I climbed the front steps, shrinking with each footfall. Mrs. Gale hadn't told me the half of it; her sister-in-law, this Phillipa Everts, was over-the-moon rich. By the time I reached for the doorbell, my heart was pounding. I stood and tried to still it. I tried to remember why I was here.

Pa. Love might not be enough, but it was all I had to go on.

Kula Baker musters up.

Summoning my courage, I pressed the bell.

Chapter TEN

March 28, 1906

"The grandeur of the house astonished,
but could not console her. The rooms were too
large for her to move in with ease . . .
and she crept about in constant terror . . ."

—*Mansfield Park*, Jane Austen, 1814

IT SEEMED HOURS BEFORE THE LOCK SNAPPED AND the door opened and a tall, stern-faced man stared down at me. "Yes?"

"I'm here to see Miss Everts, please." I pulled myself up and narrowed my eyes, not to be daunted by a servant. I knew the ropes. How servants were treated. He didn't yet know I was here to serve.

But, as if he read my mind and my past, he'd have none of me. "And who are you?"

"Kula Baker. Miss Kula Baker," I said, with an emphasis on the "Miss."

He looked me up and down, glancing over my shoulder as if to search for my coach—or my accomplice. "For what purpose are you calling?"

"I'm the . . ." Oh. I hadn't thought this one through. What was I to Mrs. Gale? Her servant. I sought the least-humbling truth. "I'm in the employ of her sister-in-law, Mrs. Gale. I'm carrying a letter of introduction."

He raised his eyebrows. He was as starched and pinched as a too-small collar. "Mrs. Gale?"

"Yes." Exasperation filled me. "Mrs. Hannah Gale. Of Bozeman, Montana?" Something was amiss, surely. "This is the home of Miss Phillipa Everts?"

He eyed me up and down. "Wait here." And he shut the door in my face, leaving me on the front porch with my mouth agape.

What if Phillipa Everts's relationship with Mrs. Gale was strained? What if she wouldn't allow me in? I'd have no choice: I'd have to board the next train back for Bozeman.

If I left right this second, I'd be home in three days. I'd be away from this thieving, miserable city and back under my big skies. Just the thought of standing in the cool shadows of tall pines slowed my breathing, stilled my trembling hands. Maybe I could find some other way to help Pa.

But I knew that if I left San Francisco, I would not be able to help my pa. He had sent me here for a reason. I had little money and no idea where to go if I was refused at the house of Phillipa Everts. If I didn't stay here, God knows, there would be no help for Pa.

My pa would hang.

And I would be at the mercy of Josiah Wilkie.

I tightened my grip on my reticule, fussing with the drawstrings like a squirmy child in church. I couldn't help my tumbled-down hair except to push it back from my face.

After a minute the door opened again, and without a word my gangly friend stood aside to let me enter.

"Thank you." I tried to keep my voice from wobbling. I untied the ribbons of my small and (now I knew) unfashionable hat, removing it as I followed him into a drawing room the size of Mrs. Gale's entire first floor, and I halted in my tracks, my mouth dropping open like a baby bird's.

My Montana skies might be bigger than those of California, but houses surely were bigger here in San Francisco. And the decoration of those San Francisco houses was almost beyond the pale.

Ornaments covered every surface. The room in front of me was a trove of tiny treasures: small inlaid boxes, standing frames of photographs, glass-domed still-life scenes—birds on branches, dried flowers—and vases filled with living flowers. Thick tapestry carpets were thrown one on top of the next such that they made a cushion under my aching feet. The furniture was big and dark and upholstered in green-colored velvet. The walls, from floor to ceiling, were papered with art. Oil, watercolor, landscape, still-life. Portraits of grinning dogs. Portraits of frowning old ladies. Portraits of rotting fruit and drooping flowers.

This was quite a house. I froze and let my gaze drift from corner to corner.

"What do we have here? Are you a nincompoop? Come here, girl. Don't stand in the doorway with your mouth hanging open."

She sat in a chair by the fire, looking for all the world like a monarch. Her gray hair was piled high upon her head in waves and folds that must have taken hours of someone else's time; her voluminous dress was of such a fine gray silk that it scattered light; lace lay across her shoulders and knotted over her bosom.

Phillipa Everts peered at me, her lips pursed in a manner that suggested distaste. Or, as I observed her more closely, what might suggest confusion.

She was quite the opposite of my dear Mrs. Gale.

I squared my shoulders. "Miss Everts. I'm pleased to meet you. My name is Kula Baker. Mrs. Gale—"

"Hannah," she interrupted. "You are employed by Hannah Gale?"

"Yes."

"She sent you?"

"Yes."

She smiled. It was a triumphant smile. "Well, well, well. My dear Hannah. Finally come to beg."

"Ah, well, I . . ."

"Oh, come, now." Miss Everts rose. "She's finally broken, alone, poor—probably penniless—and now that Edward is dead, she's desperate to reconcile." Miss Everts went to the window. Swished to the window. "What does she want? My money? My love? My forgiveness?" She turned to me, her back as stiff as a lodgepole. "Well?"

The breath was knocked clean out of me.

"For pity's sake, girl. What message did she send me?"

"None."

"None?" Miss Everts drew back.

"That is, she sent her respects. I have a letter of introduction from her. She wishes you well. And said that if you could see it in your heart to take me into your employ—"

"I don't need an employee. What of an apology? That's what I want! In fact, a grovel would be more like it, but I'd settle for a simple and gracious apology."

"I'm sorry . . ."

"That's a start." She smiled.

I was so confused I must have looked like a fish out of water, my mouth opening and closing. "I don't think you understand my meaning, ma'am."

"We'll discuss it no further. You must return to her with a message from me."

I stepped forward. "But . . . I have to speak!"

"And so you have."

Was she mad? "But I haven't. I'm not here for Mrs. Gale. I've come for my father."

"You've lost me, girl. I do not have your father."

"Please!" All the emotion that I'd been bottling inside bubbled up like a hot spring. It had been a feckless day, a day of ruin and catastrophe, and I was boiling over with it. My mouth ran, and there was no use my trying to stop it. "My father has sent me here. He'll die. I have nowhere else to turn. I've been robbed of all my things, every last blessed thing, including all my clothes and my only gown, and it was blue velvet, too, and I was lost in Chinatown, and saved by a young man to whom I owe everything, except I don't know how to find him, and the only thing I know now is I have to find a man named Ty Wong—"

"Ty!" Her hand flew to her mouth, and Miss Everts whirled away from me. She stood like that for some minutes, while I fought to recover my own self. When she turned back again, she seemed a different person. Now her voice was sharp, firm, her eyes fixed on me like polished gray gemstones. "Are you sure about that name?"

I shifted my feet. "Yes—Ty Wong."

She crossed the room, returning to her chair. She sat and placed her chin on her fist and stared at the floor for some minutes. When she spoke again, it was to the floor, not to me. "Well, girl, you have sent me into a tizzy, and no mistake."

"I'm sorry, ma'am." I picked up my nerve, which lay in pieces on the floor. "I'm here because if I don't find Ty Wong, my pa will hang. That's all I care about in San Francisco. He may hang anyway. But I can't leave this terrible place until I discover what my pa needs me to find, because it may be the only thing that will save him." I straightened. "All I ask is a room, for which I'll work hard. For the rest, I'll make my own way."

Her eyebrows went up. "Well!"

That was it, then. She meant to throw me out. Kula Baker knows when she's not welcome. That was that, I'd failed.

I turned my back on Phillipa Everts and marched across that vast space and was almost out the door when I heard her voice again.

"Girl! You!"

I turned.

"What did you say your name was?"

"Kula Baker."

She looked puzzled. "Baker. Well, we'll see about that." She came to me, and took my chin between her two fingers, turning my face from side to side. "You have a touch of the exotic."

I felt my cheeks grow dark.

"You are quite a handsome young woman." She let my chin drop. "Who are your people?"

"My people?" My cheeks grew hot, now, fairly burning. "My name is Baker. Kula. My given name was also my great-grandmother's."

"Hmph." Her lips pursed. "What's this about your being robbed?"

I cleared my throat. I tried to clear my confusion. "I was robbed by a boy who picked me up at the railway station."

She raised her eyebrows. I met her stare.

"He said he would deliver me here. But he dropped me in a dreadful place. And then I had a problem in Chinatown. Had it not been for another young man who came to my aid there on the street, I might be in Chinatown still."

"Took everything, did this robber? Was there anything of real value?"

I lowered my eyes. "My clothes. My books."

She sighed. "The books—you might console yourself with having aided his education. But the clothes . . ." She waved her hand dismissively. "Inconsequential."

I drew up. "Not to me."

"We can replace the clothing, Miss Baker. The soul is another matter."

"The soul!"

"Yes, the soul. Your soul, I will assume for the moment, is intact. The young thief's soul, not likely. He is sadly duped by the idea that material gain is all that matters. That possessions are of utmost importance. He would be wrong. Possessions, my dear girl, are meaningless."

This woman twisted my mind round like a vane in a high wind. She had possessions aplenty, that was beyond doubt. So what was this talk of soul and meaningless possessions?

"Now there's another issue. Your father. He's about to hang, is that what you said? Men don't hang for no reason."

"He's been wrongly accused." He has his soul intact, I wanted to tell her. He knew possessions weren't the most important thing in life. He did what he did to survive. Not all thieves were the same. And I knew he could change. "He did not commit that crime, the one of which he is accused."

"I see. Not *that* crime, then. And there's something, you say, that will exonerate him from this hanging offense?"

"I think there may be something here in San Francisco—that is, he told me to come here. He wanted me to recover something of his. He said it was all he had. Whether it helps free him, I have to hope."

"And your father is connected with . . ." Her voice trailed off. Her face worked, and I was trying to sort her out. She seemed crazy one minute, clever the next. She lived in a house grander than I'd ever imagined in my wildest dreams, yet she spoke of possessions as soul stealing. And she knew Ty Wong, at least the name. Of this I was sure.

"He said I had to find Ty Wong," I said, making my voice firm.

She tapped her index finger on her lips, as if coming to a decision. "I like you, Miss Baker. Hannah may have opened a door after all, with or without her apology. I've no wish to see you thrown to the wolves, or watch you wander the streets of San Francisco unaided. You are welcome to stay and work for me while you sort this out."

"Thank you, ma'am." The wind was knocked clean out of me, I was so relieved.

She walked into the hallway, me trailing her. "Jameson!" Her voice echoed through the house.

He appeared like smoke in the doorway at the end of the hall.

"Show Miss Baker to the blue bedroom. She'll be my personal maid for a time. And fetch Mei Lien." She turned to me. "You'll need a change of clothing."

"I have money." I began to open my reticule. "Not much, but I can pay for some new things." Not many new things, but I kept my tongue still.

But she waved her hand. "I will send the girl out for clothing. You can purchase things more to your liking later. Remember, girl, possessions. That's all they are. Look to your soul."

I opened my mouth to respond, but she was already gone, back into the drawing room. Jameson hovered, specterlike. He spread his hand, directing me to the stair.

Jameson's eyes were pale and distant; he revealed nothing. In point of fact, he made my skin crawl. I led the way up the stairs, quite alone except for Jameson's eyes on my back.

Chapter ELEVEN

March 28, 1906

> *"The number of servants has increased since 1870 by only half the rate of increase in population . . . The decrease in supply is parallel, too, with the rising demand for servants among wealthy families."*
>
> —"Servant Girls," Editorial, *The New York Times,* November 5, 1906

MEI LIEN WAS A TINY SLIP OF A CHINESE GIRL. She was silent and furtive, and reminded me, in her silent acquiescence, of Min. She smiled shyly at me when she showed up at the door to my room with tea. Until she laid out the tray, I hadn't realized how starved I was; it was now midafternoon and I hadn't eaten since early morning when, just before the train arrived at the station, I'd finished the few scraps that remained in my now long-gone hamper.

The silver tray bore little sandwiches and cakes and a steaming china teapot. The sandwiches were cut in perfect squares and set on lace doilies. This tea reminded me of the most elegant meals served in Mammoth's National Hotel—the ones I cleaned up after, when employment there suited both the management and me.

I'd nipped a few of those cakes as leftovers, but these were far better, sweet and delicate. And I could eat them slow and easy, leisurely. In a small but comfortable room housing me as if I was a guest.

But I wasn't a guest. This I could not forget. I was a servant to Miss Phillipa Everts, however well treated.

Across from where I sat hung a painting. It was a portrait of a young man. Even through my weary eyes he looked so familiar I felt I surely must know him.

Once I'd filled my belly I slipped into an exhausted sleep, right there in the chair.

Two hours later Mei Lien woke me with a soft knock. She carried several large boxes. She placed them on the bed, opening them and pulling aside the paper and spreading their contents for me to see.

The boxes bore a label of shiny, embossed gold—it must have been a choice shop. I ran my fingers over the smooth surface of that label, back and forth. My stomach twisted a little; I didn't know how I'd be fit to pay Miss Everts back. Whatever she thought of possessions, pretty clothing was treasure to me. And make no mistake, I fairly lusted after some of the things I'd seen in Maggie's closet; and my one and only beautiful dress, the blue velvet, was now gone. So my eyes grew wide at the contents of the boxes laid before me now.

I withdrew a simple dark red skirt of fine, soft wool. Three tightly pin-tucked white cotton shirtwaists; silk undergarments. A smart jacket with black and red braiding and a nipped-in waist—the latest fashion from all I'd seen—and the weight seemed right for this damp but not frigid climate. In one box nested a pair of short leather boots that Mei Lien gestured for me to try on at once. Her English was poor, but we understood each other.

The boots fit perfectly. I smiled my thanks to her, and she blushed pink. She pointed at my traveling clothes, miming a scrubbing.

"Yes. I'll change and then they can be cleaned."

She turned to leave, and I stopped her. I pointed to the painting on the wall of my room. "Mei Lin, do you know anything about that?"

Like everything else in this enormous, high-ceilinged room, from the wallpaper to the bed hangings, the primary color of the painting was blue.

Mei Lien shook her head.

I had other questions, and maybe this girl could help. "Do you know someone here, perhaps connected with Miss Everts, named Wong?" And I wondered at myself: was I asking after Ty Wong? Or David?

Even the thought of David Wong caused my stomach to do a surprising little flip.

Mei Lien's eyes widened, but this time she shook her head vigorously and her cheeks grew so scarlet I was afraid she'd faint. I asked no more. I knew how it felt to be put on the spot. And I knew when someone was hiding something. I'd hidden the truth plenty of times myself.

Mei Lien showed me the bathroom that was just next door to my bedroom. She left and I drew my first bath in days. The water came steaming hot straight from the tap. The tub was as big as a horse trough, and the soap smelled of lavender. This bathroom made the bathroom I'd thought so fine at Mrs. Gale's look tiny.

In that bath I had time to think, to examine the threads of my experiences as if I was examining a fine embroidery. My pa wanted me to find Ty Wong. Each time I mentioned Ty's name—to Miss Everts, to Mei Lien—I sensed recognition, but no one would answer me directly. They were keeping some secret; about that, my instincts were good. But could they know Ty Wong? Surely the world could not be that small. Surely the coincidences could not be that extreme. Surely not.

The more I reflected the more those threads began to weave into a pattern. I needed to move quickly, and puzzle out how these connections were made before they wove a net, a snare. I feared a trap that would keep me from helping Pa.

I wondered if that David Wong was connected to Ty, and felt my cheeks color again. I felt a shocking attraction to David Wong. I cupped the bathwater and splashed my face but good. This was no time for such things. I had plans. Plans that did not include attachments to unsuitable men. Suitable men, maybe, if the opportunity presented.

Kula Baker does not fall frivolously in love with unsuitable men.

Even when the thought of that dark-haired David made my stomach do little flips.

My thick hair was damp although I'd given it a good toweling, so I braided it, letting the braid hang down my back to finish drying. I dressed in my new clothes, sniffing at the starch in the brand-new fabric and fingering the tiny stitches on the shirt placket. I noted with satisfaction that those stitches were no better than ones I could make on my own.

Then I set myself to stare at the portrait in my room.

The young man leaned against a pillar—it looked like one of the columns on the porch of the Lake Hotel, those same kind of lengthwise ridges—and he stared out from the canvas with eyes as blue as the rest of my room. Eyes not unlike my pa's. In his left hand was a rolled-up paper; on his right hand he wore a ring. Behind him were hills, covered in green and brown and flecked with the red of some kind of wildflower—bee balm, or poppies, maybe. The hills rolled away and away into the deeper blue of the sky.

I recognized that ring. I stepped close to the portrait, picking myself up on my tiptoes.

It took me only a moment to place it. The painter had executed it with great detail; it was almost as if he was sending a message. Mrs. Gale wore that ring. I knew it without a doubt. It was one of the very same rings that had landed in Pa's hands for a time before he returned it to its rightful owner.

When I'd last seen it up close at Mrs. Gale's, it had seemed too heavy for a lady's fingers, and here was proof that the ring had once belonged to a man. Could this boy have been Mrs. Gale's husband?

I tilted my head to look closer. The golden dragon raised off the surface of that painted ring in such dimension that it looked ready to pounce.

I turned my attention to the rolled-up paper in his other hand. At the top of the paper was a seal or emblem, that same dragon only larger, its head turned to the left as on the ring and a long tongue of flame emerging from its open mouth and spikes running down its back to the tip of its coiled tail. Below the dragon the paper was a rolled-up tube with words written across it, but the young man held that paper pointing heavenward so that it was too far above my eyes to read.

And then another thought crossed my mind. Mrs. Gale and

Miss Everts were sisters-in-law. But how? Why did they not share last names? If this man was indeed Mrs. Gale's husband, then he must also be Phillipa Everts's brother. I had never thought to ask Mrs. Gale, but now curiosity pricked at me. Miss Everts felt she'd been slighted; why, she fairly despised sweet Hannah Gale. All odd little pieces scattered about a game board, and that made no sense.

One thing for sure: Miss Everts put me in this room on purpose.

I heard a soft knock—Mei Lien.

"I show you Miss Everts's room."

Time for me to start slaving away for the peculiar Phillipa Everts. I followed Mei Lien down to Miss Everts's suite on the second floor. Hers was an elegant bedroom with fine furniture of dark wood and a canopied bed and a private bathroom and water closet. Mei Lien opened the wardrobe. Silk and velvet, and delicate embroidered shawls, and polished leather shoes.

My job was to straighten and tidy the room and take out the clothes that needed cleaning. "Chinese laundry," Mei Lien said with a smile. "They pick up."

In about an hour I had the rooms as neat as a pin. I opened the drapes to let in the light and the long hinged windows to let in the air, noting with a sigh the grime on those windows that it was now my duty to wash.

A noise on the street caught my ear.

A smart carriage pulled up in front, and two men emerged, one gray-haired and the other much younger, slender, blond. As I leaned over the sill to watch them approach the house, and my damp braid fell over my shoulder, the younger man stopped short. He raised his face and our eyes met.

He was handsome, so handsome he took my breath away. And

as he stared at me he let a smile cross his face, one that grew like a sweet ripple of spring breeze across water.

But my eyes had been drawn to something else just past the young man, something on the coach behind his head, something on the door of that coach. An emblem. A seal. Something so familiar it made me suck in air.

A golden dragon with a long tongue of flame.

Chapter TWELVE

March 28, 1906

"In China the five clawed dragon is the emblem of royalty. Usually it is pictured as rising from the sea and clutching at the sun . . ."

—"The Chinese Dragon," *Detroit Free Press*, August 12, 1900

THE YOUNG MAN GAZED UP AT ME WHILE I LEANED OUT the window and my braid swung long and free below the sill. He called up, "Rapunzel! Rapunzel! Let down your hair!" And he grinned.

The older man, striding up the walkway, lifted his chin and scowled at me and then turned his face and his ire on the younger man. I withdrew fast, feeling stupid and not a little breathless at seeing that gorgeous face, at hearing that charming prince calling to me as if I was the heroine of a fairy tale.

And the seal—the dragon. It seemed there was a growing riot of links and connections and surprises. I shook myself, rubbed my arms hard. This was San Francisco, after all. In a city known for its Chinese population, dragons were probably common. Even on the coach of a prince of the city.

Now voices drifted up from the front hall; I pulled back the curtain to peer at the coach again. The dragon on that carriage was identical to the dragon in my Blue Boy's painting. There was no mistake.

I crossed the room, pausing in the upper hallway to listen. The men's voices were mixed up with Miss Everts's clear tones.

I slipped along the passage to the stair and started down, trying to creep light-footed, as I had so many times in the woods. The voices issued not from the large front drawing room but from a small parlor closer to the rear of the house. As I turned onto the second flight down from the landing, I realized that I could not only see into that parlor from where I stood, I could see all of them standing there.

The men had their backs to me. The gray-haired man was throwing his hands around like a country preacher; it was his booming voice I'd heard from upstairs.

". . . delivery for next week. This shipment is of especial importance."

"Is that why you've brought the boy?" Miss Everts's tone was light, but I could sense the hostility in it from where I stood.

"I'm putting my trust in young Will. I want to start turning these matters over to him. He needs to learn responsibility." He put his hand on "young Will's" shoulder. "Now, Phillipa. This arrangement has suited us both. I can guarantee that my son will be well trained."

I crept down two more treads. Now I could see directly into the room and into Miss Everts's stony face.

"Hmph. Trained in East Coast behavior, I take it," she said. Her eyes flicked to the younger man. "How old are you, young man? I suppose you have a thorough understanding of the trade."

"I'm nineteen. And I believe I understand perfectly," he replied.

His voice was firm, but he glanced at his father; and in that glance I read deference, even uneasiness.

So. The young prince wants to please his father.

I crept down one more step. It was my undoing. My movement caught Miss Everts's eye. And when her eye lit on me, the two men turned.

"What's this, Phillipa?" The gray-haired man had a lined face, but he might have been about Pa's age or so. "You have a spy in the house?"

"There are no spies in this house, William. The girl was simply descending the stairs. Come down, girl."

I obeyed her, straightening my back and walking with as much dignity as I could muster. A spy. I disliked this man already.

I came into the parlor, clasping my rough hands behind my back, those rough hands that would give me away as a working girl. At least my clothes were decent, thanks to the new things Miss Everts had bought for me. I hoped the men would ignore my damp braid, which even now moistened my shirtwaist right down my spine.

"Kula, this is Mr. William Henderson. Mr. Henderson is a force to be reckoned with here in San Francisco. He owns the two largest hotels as well as our principal bank. I tell you this so that you may greet him properly."

Miss Everts stood behind the two men, all of them facing me. For this reason I could see her face while they could not; her meaning was plain to me. She didn't like William Henderson. She didn't care one fig for all his forcefulness or his hotels or his bank. A game was in play here, and she wanted me in on her side of it.

And I was at Phillipa Everts's mercy. Regardless of how I felt about her or these goings-on, I did play her game. I curtsied. "So pleased to meet you, sir." I turned to the younger Will. "And you, sir."

When I turned to greet that young man, when my eyes truly rested on him, I caught myself. I'd seen him clearly out the window, but his good looks were magnified up close. His thick fair hair curled in all the right places; his eyes were large and deep brown—like a fawn's eyes. I caught myself stargazing into them.

He bit his lip, trying to appear sober, but as his father turned away, the young prince gave me a sly smile.

Kula Baker does know how to breathe. Breathe, Kula Baker.

While I examined the fine Persian carpet under my feet, Miss Everts went on. "Miss Baker is my new protégé. She's an artist's model. I think her exotic beauty will charm San Francisco. Don't you agree?"

An artist's model? I tried to hide my shock by fixing my stare on one particular Oriental swirl.

"Indeed!" William Henderson eyed me like he might eye a prized steer. "Bring her along on Thursday the twelfth, then, Phillipa. Let's introduce her to San Francisco society properly." He stared at me, lines forming on his brow. "What did you say her name was—Baker?"

"I'm Will," the younger man said.

If I fixed my gaze on Will's eyes, I'd fall into them. So I nodded my hello and went back to my carpet. Artist's model? I was a servant, though I longed to be a lady. But, an artist's model?

Miss Everts came around from behind the two men and took my arm with a firm pinch. "Time to take your leave, gentlemen. Thank you for the invitation. The twelfth, then. Kula and I will be there. But at the moment, we have things to attend to."

"I look forward to seeing you again, Miss Baker," young Will said to me, and bowed, which forced me to meet his eyes straight on. He winked, this time, as if we were now the best of friends. Goodness. Such a being walked the earth, and smiled and winked at Kula Baker.

Jameson appeared from nowhere. His voice came out soft. "Gentlemen?" He extended his long arm toward the door, giving them no alternative but to head for it, as indeed they did, hats raised in polite good-bye.

When the door slipped shut and Jameson turned the lock, Miss Everts sighed. "We have a new complication." She and Jameson exchanged a look, and he vanished into the back of the house.

The entire episode left me in a puzzlement. I turned to Miss Everts. I could only address one question at a time, and the first was also the most alarming, at least to me. "An artist's model?"

She waved her hand. "Yes, well. It was all I could come up with on the spur of the moment. I didn't expect to see you make an appearance. Besides, you would make a good model, if that was your inclination. You have a unique presence."

"A model for what?"

"For pity's sake. Posing for paintings and the like."

I blanched, then blushed. "I could never—"

"No?" she interrupted. "Do you have any idea what kind of money an artist's model makes?"

I took a step back. The thought hadn't occurred to me. I'd never examined a role for myself beyond service that didn't involve a husband. I'd been a working girl, of course, but not that kind. I was aghast. "Money?"

"That's right. There's money to be made in many ways, girl, and if money is your object, why, there is your solution." She sounded tired. "I shall be eating in my room this evening. You can take your meal in the drawing room. I wish to be left alone, so there's no need to turn my bed down. You may take care of things in the morning. You should send word to Hannah that you have arrived safely. Send a telegram with Jameson."

But I wanted to know more. I wanted to understand the dragon seal, for one thing. And I couldn't ignore my pressing need to find Ty Wong. "But, Miss Everts . . . I have to ask—"

"No more. I have a frightful headache." She turned and went up the stairs, her gray gown swishing as she climbed in slow pace to her own rooms. Well. That gray silk dress probably cost as much as a month's wages at the Old Faithful Inn. Yet she disdained money—the very thing that kept her in comfort.

My mind was in a muddle, now. I went into the front parlor and paced, one hand to my forehead and the other to my waist, as I tried to put pieces together. I wanted to understand how these pieces connected.

There was that dragon seal for one. I had a good eye for pattern, and I was sure that dragon shooting his flaming tongue was the same on Mrs. Gale's ring, on the rolled-up parchment my Blue Boy held tight in his fist, and on the Henderson coach.

I sat down and drafted a telegram to Mrs. Gale, to let her know I had arrived, and then gazed through the parlor windows across the hills of the city as dusk gathered at the windows and lights winked on here and there.

An artist's model—I wasn't completely ignorant. An artist's

model was no better than an actress or a dancer, performing for money. For all her talk of my soul, Miss Everts was quite content to see me part with my dignity.

Yet because of my new "profession," I'd just been invited to a social event in San Francisco. I'd never been invited to any social event before, anywhere. The very thought was frightening and exhilarating. A social event, at what I assumed was the Henderson home . . . If that coach was anything to go by, their home could be grander than all the hotels in Yellowstone put together. I put my hand to my chest and felt my heart gallop.

At the Henderson home . . . that meant I'd see Will Henderson again. His eyes were drowning eyes, deep brown and forever.

And he had money and social standing—respectability. Now here was my dream, walking and talking. Despite Miss Everts's assertions, I found nothing wrong with desiring the comfort of money. Only the wealthy said money didn't matter—those of us who worked for a living knew better the comforts money supplied. My soul would survive such pampering, thank you.

Yet I hadn't spoken a word of my desires to anyone in San Francisco, so how was it that Miss Everts read me like a book? " . . . if money is your object, why, there is your solution." Money had always been my object and no mistake; it had not been a hard lesson for me to learn, want having instilled it early. If I had to bet, I'd bet Miss Everts had never been left wanting.

I thought again of the overheard conversation. What had they been discussing that Miss Everts found so distasteful? What was so secretive that had William Henderson worrying over spies?

There was much to ponder here. My curious nature gnawed

on the bones of these peculiar doings. But as distracting as the Hendersons may be, I had to focus on my purpose here in San Francisco: helping Pa.

Though, if I could help myself along the way, say by attracting such a one as young Will Henderson, that may do more to help Pa than any mysterious box could. The chance of allying with such a young man, one of wealth and power . . . I could truly aid Pa and myself at the same time. And Will, with his drowning eyes . . . I shook my head clear.

Kula Baker knows that to get what she wants, she must not lose her wits.

I found myself a soft chair by the fire in the drawing room, and Jameson brought my meal. I gave him the carefully folded telegram—hiding it from his prying eyes—to send to Mrs. Gale, and he left me to ponder all these doings for the remainder of the night.

Chapter THIRTEEN

April 3, 1906

"Notwithstanding all that has been done . . .
San Francisco is still remarkably hilly,
and may properly be termed 'the Hundred-hilled City.'"

—*A Guide Book to San Francisco,*
John S. Hittell, 1888

IT WAS A CLEAR, BRIGHT DAY, THIS, MY SIXTH DAY IN San Francisco.

"Jameson!" Miss Everts commandeered from the hall, as she donned her gloves.

He was right there, in an instant. Did this man live in the air, like one of those djinns from the tales of Arabia?

"Bring the automobile around front. We're going for a drive."

I tried to quell my nerves. We were about to be off in a horseless, and I could scarce believe it. My first experience in such a contraption.

Miss Everts lent me gloves, and had given me a hat from her own closet—"far too young for my aging face"—that had just the perfect, most fashionable large and rolling brim and a trimming of the softest feathers.

"It suits you." She pushed the feathers back so they rested

within the crown. The kindliness of the gesture only added to my befuddlement. I stared at my reflection, noting the surprise that lit my face. Six days in San Francisco with Miss Everts. Cleaning and tidying after her. She came and went at odd hours and kept to herself the rest of the time, making it difficult for me to press further on Ty Wong. I couldn't read her on anything.

My second morning there I'd caught her in her drawing room and begged for help in finding Ty Wong. She'd raised her hand to silence me. "I do not wish to speak of this now."

"But that's why I'm here!" My impatience wore a sharp edge, and I clenched my fists. Anger unleashed my tongue. "Ty Wong knows about something of my pa's. The whereabouts of a box. I need to find Ty Wong and that box."

"Box! Containing what?"

I'd forgotten I'd said nothing about the box to her before this. I still wasn't sure if I could trust her, and yet I had no choice now but to confess all. I took a deep breath. "I don't know. But whatever it is, it must be something valuable." It surely was to Josiah Wilkie. "Valuable to my pa, at least. He said the only way to help him was to find it. Please, Miss Everts. Time is of the essence."

She tapped her fingers against her lips. "I understand your time constraints, Miss Baker. You've told me enough. But you meddle in things you don't understand. Your father's situation will not be improved if you rush headlong into a fiery pit."

Rush! And a fiery pit! My pa rotted in some miserable cell awaiting trial and a hanging for a murder I was sure he didn't commit. But Miss Everts only turned her back on me.

I wanted to take her by the shoulders and shake her until her perfect, coiled-up hair fell about her. But I didn't. I bowed my head. I was at the mercy of her kindness. I bowed my head, but my fists were still balled up.

Then, as if she read my mind, she turned right back around to face me.

"Kula. We shall tackle this situation. But not today. I have other business to complete." And then she swept off with Jameson, leaving me stewing for the rest of the day.

In an attempt to distract myself, Mei Lien and I had walked down the hill to purchase thread and fabric so that I could occupy my restless hands with embroidery. We stopped in a shop at the edge of Chinatown filled with silks and other fine imported fabrics. The shopkeeper was a well-fed Chinese man who was eager to show me all his wares.

I'd asked the shopkeeper if he knew a Ty Wong, and he shook his head, throwing his hands in the air, and repeating, "Wong? Wong? Many people named Wong. All over Chinatown."

Mei Lien flat refused to lead me into Chinatown on a search. She shook her head and planted her feet, and tugged me hard in the opposite direction, saying, "No, no." Finally, I had to relent.

That evening, I had received a return telegram from Mrs. Gale. Pa was to stand trial for the murder of Mr. Black, the trial to commence on April 20. She would try to see him within the next few days—she would have to travel to Deer Lodge and the state prison and beg for an interview.

Mrs. Gale also answered my question, put to her in my telegram. She and Phillipa Everts had had a "falling-out."

And so there I stood on this sixth day here, in Miss Everts's hallway, wearing a hat she'd planted on my head, her kindness and meanness and peculiarities all mixed up. Mixed up! Just like the thoughts tumbling through my mind. I thought of Pa, the last time I saw him, all gaunt and cornered, there in the snowy street. My eyes welled, and I blinked to clear them.

I should be in Deer Lodge, fighting for my pa, and not here in this odd city.

I'd denied him on the streets of Bozeman in order to flee Josiah Wilkie and his snake eyes. I'd run away: fled Montana, run away to San Francisco. I shook my head. No. I'd come here because Pa had asked me to. I'd come here because he needed me here, to find Ty Wong, to find that box.

I could not allow myself to feel guilty for being in San Francisco. Pa'd sent me to San Francisco to find him something that would buy his freedom.

And if I also happened to find something for myself . . . say, the security of the right marriage—well, that was just a bit of good fortune. Meeting a Will Henderson, who it seemed right off took a fancy to me, that was extra.

I lifted my chin and admired Miss Everts's hat that sat perched on my head, and strived to ignore the warring voices within me. Kula Baker does the right thing.

Yes. Kula Baker does the right thing. For the right reasons.

"Kula." Miss Everts gestured at the door. I went to hold it for her and followed her into the bright sun.

The automobile waited for us by the curb. It was shiny black with little brass lantern headlamps and a leather top as on a buggy, only the top was rolled away, considering the fine, cool day. I circled around the thing, nervously eyeing it from every angle.

Put me on the back of a pony, even one that was barely green broke, and I wouldn't blink. I could ride bareback all the way across Montana on a four-legged animal. This was another thing altogether, putting my life in the control of a machine. It was both a fright and a thrill.

"Who guides it?" I asked.

"Jameson will be doing the driving," said Miss Everts. "Jameson, I should like to give Miss Baker a view of Mount Tam. Please drive out to Telegraph Hill."

Jameson held the door open, and I followed Miss Everts into the backseat. Jameson started the crank, and the two or three pops the engine made as it fired gave me a bigger fright, and I found myself with my hands covering my ears, wincing at the sound.

As soon as we were under way, I hung on for dear life, especially on the hills. We could carry on no conversation; the thing made too much noise, and Miss Everts seemed lost in her own world.

Then we started up the steepest hill imaginable. The automobile engine strained. I couldn't look. My stomach did somersaults, and I leaned forward to put my head between my knees. As I did so, something on the floor by my foot caught my eye.

It was a small black shoe. Being black, it all but vanished in the shadows, but I leaned over and picked it up between two fingers while holding tight to the door handle with my other hand to try to keep my teeth from rattling loose. I sat up and caught my breath. The shoe was embroidered with thick black thread along the sides and toe.

We reached the top of the hill, and Jameson pulled the

automobile to a stop and cut off the infernal noise. I held the shoe toward Miss Everts.

She looked at it and then met my eyes. "Mei Lien," she said in a clipped tone, and turned right away to accept Jameson's help leaving the automobile.

Well, I supposed it made sense. Though Mei Lien wore Western-style clothing, I was sure this shoe was Chinese made and for a delicate child-size foot. Mei Lien could certainly own such a shoe, and she was a tiny little thing. I could return it to her myself. I placed the shoe on the seat.

As I put it down I marked a smudge of black—shoe-black, I guessed—on my beige glove fingertips, and where the blacking had rubbed away on the shoe, the thread beneath was gold. Gold thread on such a shoe. On Mei Lein's shoe.

"Kula?" Miss Everts called, and I hastened out of the car, rubbing my blackened gloves clean on my handkerchief. I was thankful to stand on my own two legs again and leave that swaying, chattering, and clanking behind.

We were at the top of a hill overlooking the bay. I saw the map of San Francisco in my mind; now I saw the beauty of it all laid before me.

Everything sparkled, flashed, shone. The bay shot a million bright sparks. Ships in the harbor flashed where their glass panes turned in the sun. Sails on smaller vessels ballooned, and the air was fresh and salty and hung with morning moisture. The streets flanking the hill were packed cheek by jowl with houses, tenements, workplaces, and their east-facing windows, too, caught the light and dazzled my eyes.

This was my first view of the vast spread of San Francisco. What an enormous place it was.

"That's Mount Tam." Miss Everts pointed away to the north and west, and I turned, expecting a snow-covered peak, like the Rockies of home. But I was disappointed.

"That's a mountain? It's nothing but a lump."

Jameson, standing by the car, cleared his throat.

"This is a mountain that you can ascend to the top," said Miss Everts. "There's a train that goes right to the top, and a place to dine and admire the view. And the landscape and scenery are breathtaking."

Miss Everts pointed again, slightly to the east of Tam. "I have another home just there. Just across the bay."

Another home—two houses. I was sure the second was as grand as the first. "Do you go there often?"

"In the summer. When it's too dismal in the city. I do not care for the damp weather that accompanies the summer fogs."

I stared across the bay at the green slopes where her second home lay. So much for deprivation; Phillipa Everts was unimaginably wealthy. "And your house sits there, empty, all winter?"

"Of course! Isn't that what I just said?"

"I didn't mean—"

"Jameson." She turned away, and Jameson helped her back into the automobile.

I followed slowly. Maybe she sensed my skeptical reaction to all this talk of souls and the unimportance of possessions when she had more possessions than humanly necessary. She was an odd one, and no mistake.

When I climbed into the backseat, I looked for the shoe, but it was gone. Jameson cranked the engine, and we were off, and I was too fretful about Miss Everts to be as bothered by the automobile and the slope on the way down the hills as I had been on the way up.

By our next stop half an hour later Miss Everts was friendly again, which was happy news to me, for we'd arrived at one of San Francisco's grand department stores on Market Street.

"You'll need a gown," Miss Everts said. "We must attend the Henderson affair. I've created a ruse about who you are, and your presence is now required. You can't go to an evening event in day wear."

It was the first time I'd ever been measured or fussed over. It was embarrassing. At first, I pushed the woman's hands away. Even when I'd helped a lady dress, I'd never been so familiar. Miss Everts shushed me and pulled me aside to educate me, and after that I submitted . . . but not without shying like a spooked horse from time to time as I was touched so by an utter stranger.

In the end it was all worthwhile, for a gown of fine scarlet-colored crepe, all tiers and gathers, would be delivered to Miss Everts's house in four days' time, along with proper gloves, stole, shoes, and my first-ever corset. The last, I confess—since I had laced a few of those up the backs of unhappy employers—I was not looking forward to wearing. Yet the sacrifice of wearing one for the pleasure of donning that rosy-colored gown was necessary, and I'd be willing.

And again, Miss Everts paid for everything. I would owe her so much after all of this.

I hoped that once I found my pa's treasure it would be enough to secure his freedom and repay her, too. For I'd begun to think it must have been a treasure I was seeking. What else could it be? Nothing else would be of use to freeing Pa but money. If I could pay for a proper lawyer, Pa was sure to have a strong defense. I could even hire a Pinkerton detective to investigate and find the true murderer. I imagined what would be inside the box once I'd found it, the "box the size of a badger." It had to be filled with gold.

The idea grew in me as we left the department store. It must be gold—the rush was only back in '49, and in California. Gold from California. It only made sense.

Ty Wong was the connection.

On leaving the store, Miss Everts and I paused on the avenue beside the automobile where Jameson waited, making slow circles with a rag, polishing the contraption's already-gleaming exterior. There Miss Everts turned to me. "I must go on an errand on my own, Kula. You will stay with Jameson."

She turned on her heel and stalked up the avenue, leaving me standing next to the horseless with Jameson, surrounded by the noise and the confusion of trolleys and horse-drawns and people scurrying to and fro across that broad avenue framed by monstrous buildings.

"But . . ." By the time I'd sputtered out my protest, she was away, out of earshot. But I needed to get on with my own search. Generosity or no, I'd had enough. I turned to Jameson. "Take me to Chinatown." I had to start somewhere.

He shook his head. "I must wait here for Miss Everts."

"Fine. Then I'll go on my own."

"Miss Baker, you must not."

"I have to! I need to find Ty Wong!" My frustration broke through my voice.

"Miss Everts will take care of that."

"What? Has she— Is she looking for him? How do you know . . . ?" A sudden suspicion planted itself in me. "She means to find Ty Wong without me?"

Maybe she wasn't being kind at all. All that talk of possessions and souls and her generous purchases was just to throw me off the scent. Perhaps meanness was her true nature. Hadn't Mrs. Gale said they'd had a falling-out? Miss Phillipa Everts had lost her very own soul and was planning on finding Ty Wong to retrieve my pa's box for herself. That I could not allow.

I started down the street after her.

"Miss!" Jameson called to me.

I whirled around to face him. "Leave me alone."

He shook his head. "You should not follow her, miss."

"I'll do as I please." And I turned back again, in time to see Miss Everts turn a corner in the distance. My, but she was a fast walker for someone her age. I picked up my pace and my entangling skirts to try to catch her. It was not the first time I longed to wear a man's trousers, and it wouldn't be the last.

At the first corner I nearly got myself run over by a trolley. By the way the conductor jangled that bell you would have imagined he thought I was deaf.

After I scurried back to the curb from that close shave, I tried crossing again, only to encounter further terrors. The driver of a horseless blew his honker at me—it sounded like a sick goose—and then I was knocked about by crowds until I'd lost sense of the corner down which Miss Everts had turned.

But no mind—I would find her. I pressed on, holding my hat in one hand against the buffeting cross breeze and my skirt in the other to free my feet, and now eyeing the traffic as I came to each new intersection.

I came to the corner where I suspected she'd turned, and I turned as well down a street that was more of an alley. But she was not in sight; the alley was empty. Perhaps she had gone into one of the buildings here. Ramshackle brick warehouses lined this byway. Garbage blew along the gutter. I walked deeper in, feeling lonelier by the second. After half a block I had to give up. I must have been mistaken about where she'd turned.

I'd have to confront Miss Everts later. Once again anger filled my gut. I'd grown soft in my five months in Bozeman, in my dependence upon others. It was one thing for me to want a fine man to take care of me right. It was another thing altogether for me to let myself be duped out of my rightful belongings. That was twice, now, within one miserable week.

Kula Baker does not like being taken for a fool.

I made my way back up the street, to find Jameson and return to Miss Everts so that I could confront her truly, when from behind me I heard a voice.

"Why, if it isn't Miss Kula Baker."

I whirled around and found myself face-to-face with the man whose leering smile had haunted me for months: Josiah Wilkie. Snake-eyes himself.

Chapter FOURTEEN

April 3, 1906

> *"On my return to San Francisco it did not take me long to discover that the city was wide open to all sorts of crime from murder to petty theft."*
>
> —*California: 1849–1913,*
> Lell Hawley Woolley, 1913

"YES, MISS BAKER. I KNOW WHO YOU ARE. YOU ARE LOOKING fine, yessir." Wilkie's eyes roved over me, and I took a step back. "Mighty fine." He was duded up himself in those nice togs of his—complete with a felted bowler hat and wool suit. A wolf in sheep's clothing.

All my determination shook out of me. I kept my mouth shut. I didn't want a tremor in my voice to give me away.

"What, don't have a greeting for your old friend?"

How had he found me? How did he know who I was? I tried easing back without looking behind me, one slow step at a time.

"Your pa hereabouts, somewhere?" He took a step toward me and smiled. More exact, he sneered. "No. I imagine not. Why, that's right. I do believe he's in prison. I do believe you took leave right after he was arrested. Hopped right on that train to San Francisco, you did." He shook his head. "Not much loyalty from you, girl."

His accusation made me clench my fists, useless gesture though it was. He had followed me. He had to have followed me on the train right to San Francisco.

We were engaged in that slow dance of predator and prey, my taking one step back, his taking one step forward, all the while knowing which of us had the upper hand on this forgotten back street; which of us had few—or no—friends in San Francisco; which of us had something that the other wanted.

"So where is that key, Miss Kula? Is it, perhaps, on your person?"

My hand twitched, and he saw that at once and gave me a broad grin.

"Yes, indeedy."

How many steps were there to get back to that infernal intersection?

"You know, Miss Baker, this is my home, this city. I have a commission here. I have a job to do."

I found the nerve to speak. "Your job? Your home?"

"That's right. I am a respected citizen of the city of San Francisco. I've been appointed a marshal here, and I work for a powerful outfit in this town. And part of my job involves one Nathaniel Baker. Now your old pa, he got in over his head with something, didn't he?" He raised his eyebrows. "And you deserted him, now, didn't you? Shame."

My jaw clenched, and I edged closer to the avenue, closer to safety. "He asked me to come here."

"You want to know why? You want to get the whole picture? Your pa thought he could save you. But he made one mistake after another. See, that box I been looking for, that one for which you have the key, I already found it. Right before I put your pa in jail. And you, you've got nothing. Course, your pa, he don't know that." He examined his hands, turning them to pick at his fingernails. "I think you need to head back to him, now, don't you? I think maybe it's time you left San Francisco."

The box—my reason for being here, my only hope to save Pa—was in the hands of Josiah Wilkie. My thoughts swirled. Snake-eyes Wilkie had found it. He was right—it was time for me to go home. But to what home? And why did he care if I left San Francisco? I pulled my shaky self together. "That's my pa's box, and I'll go to the authorities to get it back."

"I *am* the authorities," he said. "Remember?"

"You got yourself a shiny pin, that's all." I practically spit the words at him.

"I got me some powerful friends. And I turned that box over to them, just as I was hired to do." He leaned toward me. "Time for you to run along home. Before you step in something . . . nasty."

He wanted me out of this town—he wanted me gone and bad. But why? If he already had the box, had already turned it over to . . . who? I was of no use to him. He was setting me up, this Wilkie, but for what, I didn't know. I knew my pa wasn't a killer, but Wilkie. . . I took a chance. "Pa didn't commit that murder. He didn't kill that man Black. You did."

Wilkie eyed me for a minute. "Maybe I did, and maybe I didn't. Either way, you'll never prove it."

I was right. Kula Baker has a good sixth sense. "Watch me." Brave words, backed by nothing but air.

He shook his head. "You have no idea what you've stepped

into here, girl. This is bigger than you; there are things you don't understand. Why, this is even bigger than me. Your pa's in the way, and he's a problem. I solve problems."

What Miss Everts had said—"things you don't understand"—echoed in what he said. "I don't care. I'll find a way to bring you to justice. You'll see." My legs shook; my strength was all gone to my brave words.

"Now, I'm sorry you feel that way. And so it looks like we got us another problem. You keep meddling where you don't belong." He took a step closer again. I clenched my fists and set my legs to run. "But we can fix that."

A rush of fear ran up my spine. "Get away from me." I turned to dart off, but he was too fast for me. His hand gripped my wrist hard, twisting it.

I pulled, but he tightened his hold. "Let me go!"

I tried to wrench my wrist from his grasp. A movement behind Wilkie caught my eye, and I sucked in air: Min stepped from a doorway and moved swiftly toward us.

Wilkie heard her coming and turned, letting me go, leaving me so he could strike out at her. "I told you to leave!" He raised his fist at her.

I edged back away from them even as I cried, "Don't!"

Min, as fast as a cat, moved to Wilkie and dropped, right there in the alley, to her knees and then facedown, placing her forehead on the toe of his boot. I gasped, my hand covering my mouth.

Wilkie stood still, his hand raised to strike her, and Min lay prostrate at his feet, clutching his foot, a sacrifice in the filth of the alley. My heart pounded. I knew I should run for safety, but I couldn't leave Min . . .

And then, for an instant, an expression crossed Wilkie's face that I wouldn't believe, couldn't believe—something like affection, a softening of his features. But it was fleeting, and it vanished as he lifted his foot away from her, his rough gesture kicking her in the face, causing her to whimper. "Go on," he said to her, his voice quiet. "Get out."

She didn't move. I crept backward toward the busy avenue. He reached down and yanked Min to her feet. As he lifted her, our eyes met, and I saw in hers a plea, but not for her. She was trying to tell me to leave, to get away, that I couldn't save her, she was already lost. Telling me to save myself, yes, get away. I backed toward the street as Wilkie pulled Min down the alley in the other direction. He lifted his chin to me, his eyes narrowed. "We'll finish this later."

I turned and made for the corner.

She was his. He owned her, or so he thought. I shuddered to think of it. She was like me, an outsider, a foreigner, judged by how she looked and not by who she was. She was Chinese, and that was enough to allow Wilkie to think that he owned her and could do as he please. That he might have felt a shade of fondness for her didn't matter to me.

I stopped and looked back. The slap of Min's feet echoed as she tripped and stumbled on the cobbles, as Wilkie pulled her away. It made me want to retch. I vowed, there and then, that I would save Min from Snake-eyes Wilkie. I wouldn't care at what cost.

Chapter FIFTEEN

April 3, 1906

> *"Of course I was in love with little Em'ly. I am sure I loved that baby quite as truly, quite as tenderly . . . that can enter into the best love of a later time of life . . ."*
>
> —*David Copperfield*, Charles Dickens, 1850

BUT FOR THE MOMENT, HELPLESS AS I WAS, I HAD TO MAKE my way out of this alley. I forced my shaky legs to carry me toward the avenue, and I lurched in that direction, when, like drawing magic out of a hat, I ran smack into David Wong.

"Miss Baker?"

I was flooded with relief, so much so that I had to hold my knees rigid to keep from collapsing into a heap right there. I looked back down the alley to see Wilkie and Min disappearing into a dark doorway, her skirt a flag of defeat.

"Miss Baker?" David repeated. "Are you all right?"

I turned back to David. "Mr. Wong. You have no idea . . ."

"What were you doing down there?" David's arm pointed down the alley.

"I . . . I ran into this, this man. Josiah Wilkie—"

"What were you doing with *him*? How do you know Wilkie?" David asked, anger storming his face.

"I wasn't doing anything with him! I wish I'd never met him!" Just what was David accusing me of? I'd never felt such hurt. "I hate that man!"

"Then you do know him." David lowered his arm, loosened his fingers.

"Yes, I do. He's making my life miserable." I caught myself. I braced my shoulders. "But wait. How do you know him?"

David's eyes went dark. "He traffics in evil."

I thought about Min. "Yes. Indeed he does." I still breathed hard.

"I don't think you can imagine. He—or those he works with—they . . ." He couldn't finish and looked away, hiding his face, before turning back to me.

We regarded one another in silence. My heart eased, just seeing him there. And then something passed between us. I reached my right hand out to touch his left, a brief touch of my fingers on the back of his hand. And still we stood there.

I spoke softly. "This is the second time you've come upon me in distress, Mr. Wong."

"I wish you'd call me David." Warmth flooded my skin, a swift and bracing change of mood from fear to longing. David Wong reached right into my heart.

"David. Do you make a habit of showing up when I need you most?"

"I wish even more you'd tell me your given name."

"Such presumption!" But I was smiling now. "It's Kula."

"That's a beautiful name."

My cheeks burned. "It comes down from my father's side. I don't know the whole story of it."

"Why not?"

"I . . ." Why not. I examined the ground, mining the road for pebbles with my toe. I fidgeted with my jacket. I was ashamed, I could have said. My grandmother was native, an Indian. But to say this to a Chinese man, to admit my fear of the stigma attached to someone who looked like me, whose blood clearly ran with the taint of native blood, to admit to David that I was ashamed, why, he might not forgive me. And I'd discovered how much I wanted him to like me. "I never pursued it."

"Miss Kula, it suits you."

That blush crept right down my neck, and all my skin tingled so, and I met David's smile. "Thank you." I cocked my head. "And just how did you happen to be here?"

"I was meeting someone. And you?"

I adjusted Miss Everts's hat, fiddled with the ribbon under my chin. "I was shopping."

"Did you recover your other things?"

"No."

"That's a shame." His gaze strayed from me to the alley behind me, to where Wilkie had disappeared. "Stay away from him if you can."

David's words reminded me of Pa's words. "I didn't come looking for him. He came looking for me."

His eyes shot back to meet mine. "Why?"

"He . . . knows my pa." I didn't know what else to say.

"He's dangerous."

"I know that already. What exactly do you know?"

David's voice came out low and deep, thick with emotion. "There's another side to San Francisco. Other than the stores on Market Street and all the wealth of Nob Hill. San Francisco is an old seaport. Lots of sailors come and go. And with the gold rush came other types. And those types brought their new wealth and a desire for pleasures of all kinds." He dipped his head. "I shouldn't speak of these things to you. They're ugly."

"And Wilkie is mixed up in them."

"Yes. I hate what he's done. Everything."

"Well." I reached my hand to him again, this time letting my gloved fingers rest on his arm. "That makes two of us."

A silence settled over us. Then David shifted, his hand covering mine. "May I escort you back to a safer place?"

"Please."

We walked back toward Market Street. When we reached the intersection, we stopped again. "Which way are you headed?" he asked.

Back on Market we were again in crowds of people. Right away scathing looks met us as David and I stood together, arms linked, on the sidewalk. I glared back at them, but I didn't want David to bear insult for my sake. "I have to walk in this direction. There's an automobile waiting for me," I said. "I'll be safe now."

He squeezed my hand. "I hope the next time we run into each other we'll be somewhere we can talk without feeling that the eyes of the world are watching." He smiled, a shy smile.

I returned it, shy myself. Then, seeing a scowl on a passing gentleman, I lifted my hand to David in a quick good-bye, slipped my arm from his, and turned away.

And I promptly stopped. I turned around; David was still watching me. "I'd welcome a visit. Should you wish to pay that call you mentioned last time we met."

"Can I call on you the day after tomorrow?"

I nodded, my tongue having become tied up in unaccustomed fashion. I did so much like that David Wong. He was not the right man for me; he wasn't what I was looking for. Still and all, I liked him. I turned away again and left him watching me, feeling his eyes on my back. Liking that feeling.

Now I had to face Miss Everts. Had she played me for a fool to recover my pa's box for herself?

Chapter SIXTEEN

April 3–4, 1906

"Angry words, much strife, and perhaps some bloodshed, were generated . . . and the hapless Chinese were driven backwards and forwards and their lives made miserable."

—*The Annals of San Francisco,* 1854

THE AUTOMOBILE SAT IN THE SAME SPOT AS WHEN I'd left it. Jameson stood stiff as a rail by the passenger's-side door, scanning the street. When he saw me coming, something passed over his stiff features before he was once again a closed book. Was that relief? Why should he care even one whit about me? He leaned over the door and spoke to Miss Everts, who sat waiting in the back of the conveyance.

Jameson opened the door. I stood on the paving, shifting from one foot to the other, trying to form whatever words I could pull together to express my jumbled thoughts.

Miss Everts leaned forward. "Well? Does it please you to so upset an old lady with your whimsies?"

"Whimsies?" I stopped shifting. "Upset you?"

"Jameson tells me that you ran off down the street without a thought to your own safety or the worries you'd impose on me."

Now I was mad, and my tongue flew off by itself. "Oh, that's rich. You leave me out of knowing what you're up to . . . I think you've been using me." I planted my hands on my hips and glared.

She leaned close to me, gazing at me with wide-open eyes. "Kula. Get in." Concern and sadness all rolled together in her. I hesitated; but at last I slipped into the seat next to her as she made room. "Jameson, if you could give us a few minutes to converse, we'll sit right here."

Jameson moved down the paving and out of earshot.

"Kula. Now, listen. I went to discover what I could. There are parts of San Francisco that you know nothing about. People in San Francisco who would be a danger to you. I did not wish to risk—" She stopped and pursed her lips. "I knew even when you arrived about Ty Wong, but I couldn't bring myself to tell you." She paused again, and her eyes grew bright. "He's dead."

I groaned. She raised her hand, flat, for my silence. "He was murdered a few weeks ago."

"You knew Ty Wong was dead even when I arrived?"

"Yes." I realized then that her eyes held tears. As if to keep me from seeing them, she adjusted her broad hat so that her face was thrown into shadow. "We were old friends. He was very dear to me."

Her emotion shattered my defense. I placed my gloved hand over hers and tried to make sense of what I heard her say. "Miss Everts. What are you trying to tell me?"

She dropped her head. "It isn't easy, loving someone when it's forbidden." Her fingers moved under mine like a fledgling bird. Her voice was hushed and faraway. "You must understand. You would have suffered this kind of discrimination all your life, I expect." She lifted her chin until I could just see light reflected in the two pinpoints of her eyes again. "Parts of San Francisco are lawless. There are gangs about, mostly young men distinguished by poverty and ignorance. They hate the Chinese."

I couldn't say anything. I understood the looks David and I had received.

She removed her restless fingers from under mine. "But it was not an accident. I believe someone has planned all this."

"Josiah Wilkie."

She turned to me, surprised but not shocked. "So you know him?"

I nodded. Before I could tell her I'd just seen him, she went on.

"I'm afraid he's only a henchman. Someone else is guiding his hand. And for much larger purposes."

My only purpose here in San Francisco was my pa. And my pa had been framed for murder. As far as I was concerned, Wilkie's connection to anything else was of no matter to me.

Ty Wong was dead. The box was in someone else's hands, if I was to believe Wilkie. All my reasons for being in San Francisco were gone. "What will I do now?" My voice was soft. Then, louder, "I should go back. Be with Pa before . . ."

"No!" Miss Everts turned sharp. "No, absolutely not!"

I squared my shoulders. First Wilkie had wanted me gone; now she wanted me here. I hated this, being ordered about, back and forth. My stubborn nature reared up. "I think that's my decision, Miss Everts."

"Kula, you must not leave San Francisco."

"Why not?"

"There is a reason. You'll have to take my word for it. With Ty's murder, Kula, things have become even more complicated. I've just uncovered some new information. I believe this information will eventually help your father."

Maybe this was why Wilkie wanted me to leave. I was tired of all the secrets, tired of playing guessing games. I leaned toward her. "And what is this new information?"

Her lips pressed together. "I can't tell you just yet."

"Whyever not?"

"If I told you now, you might find yourself in a situation not unlike your father's. There's real danger here."

"Danger, here! There's danger everywhere. I can't abandon my pa."

She turned to me pointedly. "You aren't. You will have to learn to trust your friends, Kula."

I drew back against the leather seat, confused and weary and frustrated. I didn't ask her if she was my friend.

She lifted her voice. "Jameson, time to go home."

He came at once, cranked the engine, and drove us back to Miss Everts's. I glanced sideways at her. She was the most cantankerous and complicated person I'd ever met.

But I also couldn't help the sorrow that filled my heart, the sadness that she must have known. There was that David Wong who took away my breath, yet we couldn't even stand next to each other on the street without drawing ugly looks. I couldn't imagine how she'd befriended Ty Wong without incurring public wrath.

The number of mysteries in San Francisco was growing. Miss Everts was connected with Ty Wong, something I hadn't imagined possible. Ty Wong was dead, and Wilkie said he had found my pa's box. Pa was in dire need. All my aces were gone, and time was my enemy.

I woke in the night to hear the wind howling like a thousand coyotes, and my shutters slamming against the wall outside my window. It took every ounce of my strength just to open the window and pull the shutters closed so that I could lock them, and my nightgown was soaked through with rain by the time I shut the window again.

And then I was unable to return to sleep. Wilkie's face leered, and I heard his guttural voice in my head. I tried to still my beating heart by thinking about David, but my heart yet thumped, just in a different way.

The storm raged, the wind shrieked, and the rain pounded like nails into the roof. It was hours before I fell asleep again. When I woke at last, it didn't feel like morning, the sky was so dark even through the other unshuttered window.

At breakfast I found Jameson and Miss Everts had gone out yet again. I paced like a caged lion. Every time I thought back to Wilkie and Min, I wanted to scream. I could not sit still and let this evil man do his work.

Perhaps Min knew something. If I could find her, free her even from the clutches of Wilkie, I might also be able to learn from her what he was about, and where my pa's box had gone, and how to snare Wilkie in his murderous guilt. For if Miss Everts's suspicions were right, Wilkie had murdered not just Black, but also Ty Wong, all to keep that box from my pa.

I touched the key hanging round my neck. Free Min, and discover answers, all at the same time. Then I'd finally be free myself, to get on with my life. But how could I accomplish that?

I went to attend to my chores in Miss Everts's rooms, more and more frustrated at my helpless state.

Her jacket lay draped across her bed; I picked it up and hung it in the wardrobe. I tidied her shoes. I straightened the things on her dressing table, letting my hand rest for a moment on her silver-backed hairbrush.

Mei Lien did her hair, helped her with dressing. I must not be good enough for these truly personal attentions.

The hairbrush was a beauty, decorated with a raised floral pattern. I looked up at my reflection, then pulled my braid over my shoulder and untied the ribbon and let out the woven strands. I picked up that hairbrush and ran it over my hair in long strokes from top to bottom, brushed my hair smooth and shiny, letting my hair float over my shoulder until it was a river of dark silk.

There were strands of my black hair in the hairbrush now, and I laid it back on the dressing table without plucking them out.

I finished her room with the hair on my head all scattered and loose. At the door I paused.

The hairbrush was boar bristle and the black strands were hard to pull out, but I managed and held those hairs tight in my fist as I replaced the brush just as I'd found it, and shut the door soft and gentle, like a servant should.

I tossed my loosed strands into the fire in the drawing room and watched them fizzle and crack, and I set my teeth, like a servant should not.

I was coming to a decision that Miss Everts and David Wong most assuredly would not like. I found my worn plaid jacket and my old boots and a cloak of Miss Everts's, and set out on my own.

I went to find Min.

Chapter SEVENTEEN

April 4, 1906

"The refuse, consisting of 'boat-girls' and those who come from the seaboard towns . . . is sold to the proprietor of the select brothels . . ."

—*San Francisco Chronicle*, December 5, 1869

WHERE TO FIND HER?

As if Chinatown was an ancient puzzle box, I felt pulled to start there. Min was Chinese, but that wasn't why I thought I might find her in those narrow streets. It was where I'd first met David; it was where I thought Ty would have been. An aura, a magical hue, hung over Chinatown the way rainbow hues hung over the geysers of Yellowstone. Chinatown drew me, inexplicably and irrevocably.

I huddled against the driving rain and wind as I marched down Clay, scarce able to see my way down the hills. I'd been to the edges of Chinatown twice and before too long found myself once again in those narrow streets packed, despite the rain and chill, with vendors and black-suited men wearing waist-length queues.

The stalls were covered with tarpaulins that shed the rain in sheets. I leaned over their wares, gazing from side to side in a furtive attempt to see inside. I came to a stall selling shoes and bent to examine the small black slippers, reminded of the tiny slipper I'd found in Miss Everts's auto.

Blackened gold thread on a delicate slipper. A slipper that had vanished before I could discover the mystery behind it.

Next to the shoes was a tray of embroidered envelopes, made for holding small things, fastened with loop knots. The silk was embellished with flowers, scrollwork, and dragons, dragons with tongues coiled and wings unfurled.

Embroidery I knew well. It was an art that required patience and careful fingers. Threads weave in and out and reappear, and while they are being worked, the meaning of the whole is unclear; it's only when the design is complete, all the threads drawn and tightly knotted, that the pattern is obvious. I loved the feeling of the needle as it slipped in and out of fabric. I loved creating designs from seemingly meaningless single stitches. Finding patterns in the noise.

The fruit seller, rain dripping onto his apples, called out only paces away from me. And there, again, like I'd called to her through some magic, like I'd drawn her to me, I saw Min. She hovered over the fruits, her head covered in a shawl to ward off the rain, but I knew it was her. She lifted her head; her face sported a black eye. I grew hot with anger.

And there was Wilkie, stepping right behind her. I drew the hood of my cloak over my cheek.

Min discussed the fruits with the seller, pointing and questioning, arguing in rapid Chinese. Wilkie moved on, away from the stall. This was my chance.

I slid along the stalls to the end of the tray of embroideries. I did not know what I'd do when I reached her; I imagined some kind of slip, and off we'd go. I hadn't planned. It hadn't seemed important to plan.

"Min!" My voice was low, a hoarse whisper. "Min!"

The rain battered the tarpaulins and splashed noisily on the cobbles.

"Woman!" Wilkie's voice, harsh and loud, unlike mine, overcame all the noise. He marched right up behind her, and I bent almost double over the embroidery, huddling beneath my cloak. "Let's go." He took her arm; I could see his thick fingers out of the corner of my eye, wrapping those fat knuckles around her thin arm, tugging her away.

I stared hard at the embroidered dragons, their flames and tongues darting. I examined the silks as if I was picking out individual stitches. I didn't reach out and grab Min and run. I didn't dare stop Wilkie, whose hand gripped her like a manacle. I let her go. I let her go with that devil.

My fists curled into balls and my lips made flat planes, and the anger that I felt against myself burned in my throat. I'd failed, yet again. I'd been lucky enough to find her, and still I let her slip through my fingers. It was my fault, and I had no business feeling sorry for myself. I bit down hard as I could on my lip, closing my eyes.

I knew I couldn't face Wilkie. He was far too strong for me, a killer even. He was the wolf; I was the crippled doe.

Wilkie and Min pushed away from me through the driving rain, disappearing into the crowd. I pushed away, too, in the opposite direction, the tears flooding my eyes as the rain flooded the streets. My feet and the hem of my skirt were soaked, but I didn't care. I didn't watch where I walked. I didn't watch where I was going.

I walked down one street and then down another, twisting and turning, twisting in a rage against myself. The rain dripped off my hood and blinded me. I reached a narrow alleyway and realized I was deep in the heart of Chinatown, in a place I hadn't seen before. I stopped, trying to get my bearings.

Through the pattering of the rain I heard whimpering, as of a wounded animal. Instinct told me to flee; instinct told me to help. The two sides of me were at war.

The sound came from one of the darkest of the little passageways, off to my left. A stench emerged from the passageway, and other sounds that gave me chills, and a sense that if I went in there I might never come out. I took one step closer and sucked in my breath.

Small windows with iron bars sat right at ground level, and at each of these windows faces pressed against the bars, the faces of Chinese girls so young they looked like tiny children, all dirty, all wide-eyed, all blank-eyed, as if feeling had been stripped from them, as if they were draped in a self-protective blankness of mind. Some of them wore so little clothing they might as well have been naked.

I gripped my hands tight to my chest. The rain ran down my face as I tried to grasp the horror.

I knew what I was seeing. I hadn't lived a completely sheltered life. Pa had protected me, but I had eyes and ears. This was slavery in its worst form, humiliating and degrading, painful and frightening. And they were children, these slaves, all girls. They were all so small. Tiny fingers, gripping bars, slender fingers made for playing childish games. Oh, my heart. I thought I would die from the ache. I slumped against the far wall, staggered and sick.

Kula Baker . . . Kula Baker . . . doesn't know what to do.

From the shadows at the end of the alley came a woman. She carried an umbrella; she was dressed in Chinese fashion. Her face was painted, her lips garish red against all the gray misery. She beckoned to me to come, come.

"Pretty, pretty girl," she sang. "You pretty, pretty. You come, my house."

Panic rose in me as a wave of nausea. I was rooted to this spot, chained by the tangible misery, by those blank eyes. The woman came toward me, beckoning, moving past the girls like an evil genie.

One of the girls cried out. And another, and another.

Awakened from my stupor by their hysteria, I didn't hesitate. I yanked myself out of my nightmare and moved fast away from the alley, into the street and up, hoisting my skirts, and I ran, their cries following me; I ran, my skirts heavy and cumbersome, wet, tangling around my knees. I tripped; I almost fell; I pulled up twisting and limping. I sobbed, a single deep sob so that my chest heaved, my lungs ached.

The end of the street was only a hundred yards. Market Street—I knew where I was now. I pulled my skirts higher, running like a deer runs in the woods, not caring how I looked, my hood falling open and my hair coming loose, until I reached Market and ran full into the street.

I ran smack into a gentleman.

"Hey! Watch yourself!"

I pushed away from him, breathing with coarse, choking swallows, and turned, nearly running into another man. I ran up Market. An automobile pulled up alongside me.

"Here!" A voice, addressed to me.

I raised my arms in protest. My voice came out a croak, broken, choking. "No! Leave me be!" I feared being trapped, feared the bars, the tight space that I could avoid but those girls could not, feared what I'd just seen and its horror, feared what was happening to Min that I could not help.

I rushed along Market, thrusting this way and that, heedless.

"Miss Baker!"

The automobile again. But this time, my name. I stopped and looked, peering through my wet hair that was matted and fallen and covering my eyes. The rain that mingled with my tears, the wet that threaded my face, clung to my cheeks, my throat, my aching throat.

The soft, smiling face of young Will Henderson leaned toward me from the driver's seat of a sleek black machine. "Come on, get in out of that rain." He reached across the seat and opened the front passenger's-side door.

I slid into the seat, shaking like a quakie in a blue norther. I had no clue whether Will was friend or foe. Miss Everts did not like his father, that I knew. But me? I was no longer sure that anything I did would make one whit of difference to anyone.

Chapter EIGHTEEN

April 4, 1906

"Nothing about his betrothed pleased him more than her resolute determination to carry to its utmost limit that ritual of ignoring the 'unpleasant' in which they had both been brought up."

—*The Age of Innocence*, Edith Wharton, 1920

WILL PULLED THE AUTOMOBILE TO A STOP UNDER AN arched portico. Rain still hammered down, a curtain veiling the outside world, but beneath the shelter of the portico it was dry.

I straightened and rubbed my face hard, as if to wipe the rain that dripped from my hair. He cut the engine. I found my voice. "Thank you." Sheets of rain shrouded the portico. "Where are we?"

"My house. Come on inside. Let's find you a towel or two. I'll have Xue make you some coffee."

I'd managed to swallow my grief, but I was soaked through and still shook from head to toe. "Maybe I should get back to Miss Everts."

He smiled that stunning smile. "Not to worry. My father's at the bank. He rarely comes home before supper." It was an odd thing to say, but in the face of my terrible experience I couldn't worry over it. Will left his seat and came around to my side to help me out of the automobile. When he opened the door, the noise of the rain was deafening and the cold air made me shake.

He led me inside. "So what were you doing out there in the rain? Getting a feel for San Francisco at her worst?"

"I got lost."

"You must be freezing. Come on." I followed him into his family mansion through the kitchen door, where my jaw dropped.

The kitchen alone was enormous, gleaming black-and-white tiles, shining copper and brass pots hanging above a long worktable, glass-front mahogany cabinets filled with white china. At one end a fire snapped in the stone fireplace, and as Will directed me to a chair by the fire I could see through swinging doors into the hallway: marble floor, dark polished wood walls, heavy brass door hinges, crystal chandeliers, artwork.

Xue—a slender, silent Chinese man wearing a starched white smock—brought me coffee and towels. I alternately toweled my hair and warmed my hands by wrapping them around the hot cup. Will leaned against the fireplace, that smile playing on his perfect face.

I blew on the coffee, sending up swirls of steam. "You stare at me as if you've never seen a dripping wet girl before."

"Do I?" He shifted. "Sorry. Do I make you uncomfortable?"

"No," I lied.

Xue bustled about at the other end of the kitchen. He seemed oblivious of us. His slight figure made me think again about the girls. I shivered.

"I hope you haven't caught a chill," said Will, and he moved to sit in the chair next to me. His face was now creased with concern.

"I was just thinking about something, that's all." I worked

the towel on the ends of my hair. "What do you know about Chinatown?"

He sat back. "They have their own lives, there. I don't pay much attention to them."

I stopped rubbing. *Them*. "They" were not like him, so he paid no attention.

He shrugged. "I've been on the East Coast finishing a bit of college. I'm only just back in town a few weeks. I haven't been into Chinatown since before I left." He shoved his hands deep into his pockets. "I don't pay much heed to what people do there. What I'm interested in is the art."

"Art?"

I leaned forward, warming my hands before the fire. He didn't know what went on mere blocks from this grand home. He lived a fine life, sheltered from the horror of what others did. It shouldn't surprise me; after all, wasn't that the kind of life I wanted to live someday? Sheltered and content? I couldn't let myself believe that he wouldn't care if he did know. He was ignorant, that was all. Most rich folks were.

"Art is my father's business. Import, export. He wants me to take over that part of the company. But you must know that already. Father deals with Miss Everts, and that's why I was at that meeting—he wants me to work with her. Miss Everts provides the clients through her connections, and we provide the art. It's all very important, you know."

"Of course." I toweled my hair again, hiding my face from him.

"Here I am going on and on about it. I'm sure you already know something of it, being a model and all."

His knee brushed mine, and the sensation sent a shiver right up my spine and set my scalp tingling. "I haven't paid much attention." I floundered, trying to find a story. "You know, to the other side of the canvas." Heavens, I surprised myself with the things coming out of my mouth.

Will laughed. I peered out from behind the terry cloth. That blond Adonis hair, his silky eyes. He was really perfect, his legs sprawling and easy, his manner that of one so comfortable with himself. He occupied space like it was made to fit.

He leaned toward me, his eyes sparkling. "Maybe I can find something for which you've posed. I'll add it to our collection."

Kula Baker doesn't often blush.

"I'd like to find something new. Something impressive." The sparkle faded a little. "My father . . I actually would like to make some finds on my own, you know? He's difficult to impress . . ."

"I'm sure he's most proud of you."

Will brightened again, and then took my free hand. Now a current ran from my fingertips right through to my toes. He examined my hand, turning it this way and that, as he said, "Your last name. Baker. I'm familiar with a Baker family. Where did you say you came from?"

I hadn't, and I didn't want him to know. A clock somewhere in the house chimed. I withdrew my hand from his, slowly, reluctantly. "My. Listen to the hour. Miss Everts will be most upset if I'm not home soon."

He jumped to his feet. "Oh, of course. I'll be happy to take you."

As we left the kitchen, I stopped to thank Xue. He looked startled before his eyes crinkled with pleasure, and he bowed. And

I noticed his smock: it bore an emblem. A dragon. That dragon. Which also hung above the door.

"Mr. Henderson . . ." I pointed to the dragon.

"Miss Baker, please call me Will."

"Will. What is that sign?"

"That's the family crest. Something about when the Hendersons arrived in San Francisco. They had luck finding gold, and then formed a relationship with a Chinese outfit and picked up that dragon thing. Something like that. I have to be honest, I never paid too close attention when those stories were told."

I had the feeling there was something he wasn't saying, something he didn't want me to know. I shook it off; he was so charming.

He helped me into the automobile and closed the door. I glanced back at the house as he cranked the starter. Such a house—the house of my dreams, really. And Will—he could be the man of my dreams. I did like him, even though there were some things that bothered me; he was so very charming. And he seemed to like me. Why, he liked me even with my hair all wild and loose and soaking wet. Perhaps if I kept his interest . . .

Will jumped into the automobile next to me, and as if to confirm my thinking, he leaned across the seat and in one swift move kissed me, hard and sure, on the lips. I was so startled I put my fingers to my lips as he drew back and smiled.

It was forward, brazen. Unacceptable, really, and I shouldn't have allowed it. I had never been kissed before, but that kiss warmed me right through.

I said nothing, but left my fingers on my mouth on the short drive home. I tried to ignore that stuffy little voice inside me reminding me about Pa, about who I really was. What Will would think about me as Nat Baker's daughter. I was no artist's model, I was the daughter of a criminal.

And then there was David. Oh, sweet David. They couldn't be more different, David and Will.

I shoved those images, those doubts aside, and watched the handsome, wealthy Will Henderson drive me home. And his soft lips brushed my hand in an oh-so-sweet way as he left me at Miss Everts. The charming Will Henderson and the possibilities he presented occupied most of my thoughts for the remainder of the afternoon.

Most of my thoughts. Because no matter how hard I tried to forget what I'd seen, the image of the girls in their cages—their eyes—would not leave me alone. That image would forever haunt my every waking moment.

Chapter NINETEEN

April 5, 1906

"The air is chill, and the hour grows late
And the clouds come in through the Golden Gate
Phantom fleets they seem to me
From a shoreless and unsounded sea."

—*"Evening,"* Edward Pollack, 1870s

A TELEGRAM FROM MRS. GALE GREETED ME THE NEXT morning.

> YOUR FATHER WELL TRIAL MOVED UP TO APRIL 12 STOP YOU MUST FIND BOX CONTENTS CRITICAL STOP DO NOT RETURN TO MONTANA WITHOUT IT STOP MY THOUGHTS WITH YOU HG

Trial moved up. I stood in the hallway, holding the damp paper in trembling fingers. How was I going to get that box when Wilkie already had found it? Turned it over to someone else? And I didn't even know what was inside.

Wilkie knew where it was. If I confronted Wilkie . . . or found Min . . .

The rain sheeted the window so that across and down the street the other houses looked like ruins, gray and ghostly and vanishing. The street cobbles appeared to flow like the Yellowstone. If I was going to save my father, I had to get that box from whoever had received it from Wilkie. And Min. I had to free Min. So much depended on me; their futures depended on me.

I straightened my shoulders. Kula Baker does not back down.

I would uncover the whereabouts of Pa's box. I would take the box back to Montana—and I would do this before April 12, when I knew Pa would be convicted and then hanged for a murder he did not commit.

A murder that I felt sure Wilkie had committed.

I paced the hallway, once more a caged cat, imprisoned by the weather and my fears. Time was of the essence, and yet I had no plan. No plan to go up against a murderer and an evil man. That's what David had said—he traffics in evil.

David—David was to come calling today. Was it only two days ago that I'd seen him? And just yesterday had been kissed, so unexpectedly, by Will. Anxiety gnawed at me. I had promised David nothing, yet why did I feel guilty for even thinking about Will? How would I feel when I saw David, after my encounter with Will?

I asked Miss Everts for some sewing, knowing that keeping my hands busy was a good remedy for worry.

She gave me a linen napkin to work. After a time she asked to see it, and I showed her the embroidery I made on the corner of the napkin. I'd done up a ribboned bunch of wildflowers from memory: yellow black-eyed Susans, red paintbrush.

She examined it in silence for some minutes. "This is fine craft."

I sat up a bit straighter. "I've had lots of practice." I'd taught myself embroidery and sewing when I was young, so I could hire out to do mending while I learned the finer arts. A good seamstress always has work.

"Could you teach it?"

I looked at her stiff fingers. "You could learn some stitches, I think."

She waved her hand in the air. "No, not me. But could you teach this kind of work to willing younger hands? Could you teach Mei Lien?"

Without waiting for my reply, she left to fetch the girl. They were back together in minutes, and Mei Lien pulled up the chair next to me so that we were sitting in whatever gray natural light came through the windows, which was always better than light from the electrics.

Mei Lien looked at my work, a tiny murmur of delight escaping her lips. I could read her feelings better the more time I spent with her. "I'll teach you," I said. "It's not so hard."

Miss Everts brought us old linen scraps to work on, and then left us alone. I started Mei Lien on simple stitches: chain, blanket, satin. I made her work over and over. She was a patient one, willing to repeat those boring practice stitches until they were decent. It was good distraction for me to instruct, and shy Mei Lien began to open like a spring bud as we worked.

"You teach me the flower?" she asked, pointing to the forget-me-not I worked on now.

"Yes. Here. Watch me. Try it on the scrap first."

Thunder rumbled, causing me to lift my head and purse my lips and scowl. I looked back at the stitching as she'd started it.

"That's good, Mei Lien. That's lovely."

She lifted her head and smiled. I sought to make friends. Mei Lien knew the workings of this house and Miss Everts.

"She confuses me, Miss Everts does. What is she like to you? Does she treat you all right?"

Mei Lien drew up. "She saves me."

"She saved you?" I stared. Mei Lien's face had gone as red as a poppy. "Saved you from what?"

Mei Lien shook her head. "Cannot speak. All shame."

All shame. I pulled my needle through the linen, concentrating, keeping my face a mask. "She saved you."

Her grave eyes met mine. "I come here on ship. I come here to be bride."

"Bride! Why, how old are you?"

"Fifteen."

I was staggered. She was younger than I was. "Well, I hope you like him. Or that he's rich at least."

Her face darkened. "No husband. Many husbands. Miss Everts save me."

I understood then. Those girls in the alley who would not leave my mind. My eyes filled, and I looked away. "I'm sorry."

Mei Lien stood up. "She saves me. She saves you, too." A tiny accusation lay in the way she said that. I heard the tremor in her voice.

"Me?"

"Yes."

I wanted answers, but I couldn't bring myself to be direct with her. I thought of Miss Everts's odd behavior the day before. I examined my work, pulled on a stitch. "I found one of your shoes in the back of the horseless yesterday. I think Jameson must have it, or maybe Miss Everts. So it isn't lost after all." I hoped she would explain it, explain the blackened thread.

But her hand flew to cover her mouth as she whispered, "You found . . ." She dropped the stitching and ran from the room in a fast swish of skirts. Now I was as perplexed as anything. It was the shock of pushing the needle into my own finger, and seeing the fat drop of blood that bloomed there until I stuck it in my mouth, that jerked me back to sense.

In the afternoon, David did call, and his presence brightened this gloomy and confusing day. I met David at the door and edged Jameson, all arched brows, out of the way until he performed his ghostly disappearing act. I brought tea into the small parlor. As I sat with David I knew that we shared something inexplicable. How could this be? He was not the man of my dreams—not the one I'd hoped would come and provide me with the means and the opportunity to rise above having been brought up an outlaw's daughter and a lady's maid. He was not rich, he had no social standing that I knew of. And though handsome, he was not so beautiful as Will. David was an outcast.

He was like me. We understood one another. We sat without speaking; I could almost read his thoughts.

Sitting there in that quiet parlor with our tea, I knew he would understand things that Will, sweet Will, would never fathom. Even if Will could give me everything I wanted.

I sighed, and turned my thoughts to what now plagued all my waking moments. "Would you answer me a question?" I asked.

"Anything."

"Don't mock me."

He set down his cup.

"I was lost in Chinatown yesterday."

"Kula, I begged you to be careful. You should never have gone there."

"But I did. I'm fine. That's not why I bring it up. It's about what I saw there."

His face grew solemn, his lips drawn tight.

"There are children." My throat contracted—their eyes. I couldn't say more, but I knew he understood my meaning. "What can be done?"

He stood up and paced away, then came back to sit. "Kula. Things *are* being done."

I leaned over and put my two hands on his arm. "Truly? But . . . how?"

"You have to believe me. As much as possible, things are being done."

My throat burned and I turned, trying to swallow. "Can I do anything?"

"You can stay out of Chinatown. And away from the Barbary Coast."

"But—"

"No, Kula." He placed his free hand on mine. "You must not go into these places. Promise me."

I didn't answer. Much though I felt a kinship with David, I did not like anyone telling me what I could do. And I had to find Wilkie. Min. The box.

The door opened—Miss Everts. David stood at once. Either she did not see us in an intimate setting, or she chose to ignore the obvious.

"Mr. Wong, I did not know you were here."

I looked between them, surprised. "You know one another?"

Miss Everts said, "We are long acquainted. This is a small town, as I once told you. San Francisco has many overlapping layers. Wouldn't you agree, Mr. Wong?"

"I didn't have a chance to tell you what I do for a living, Miss Baker," David said.

He didn't call me Kula; he still stood, formal and polite. I played along. "That's true. So what do you do?"

"I import things from China. Art, tea, things for the Chinese people."

"It is the art that most interests me," said Miss Everts. "Mr. Wong's family has a long history of importing art. There are people the world over who love the Oriental art. I help Mr. Wong find a home for his collections."

"Ah." I took a chance. "It would be a family business, then." I looked up at David.

"Yes."

"And your family has been in business for some time."

He nodded. That settled it in my mind. He was, in fact, related to Ty Wong. And the Hendersons, too—there was another connection here to Will and his father.

"Kula, Mr. Wong and I have some business to discuss." Miss Everts gestured at the door.

I exchanged a look with David, then I left them alone. I headed upstairs to my room. It was time I took a closer look at my Blue Boy wearing the ring in that painting on the wall of my bedroom.

Safely in my room with the door shut to prying eyes, I dragged the heavy upholstered chair over to the wall and removed my boots. I hiked my skirts and stood on the chair in my stocking feet, pulling myself up to try to read the words on the rolled-up paper in his left hand, where he pointed it toward heaven.

The printing was tiny; I had to tilt my head until my neck ached. Some of the words were illegible, but what I could read by squinting was this:

> *Everts, Baker & Henderson. Saus . . . o, 1849. Merchant S . . . Dragon. Wong Brot . . . s Imp . . . rs of Fine Oriental G . . . ods. "Brothers in the Land of the Golden Mo . . . tain."*

I read it several more times as my chest grew tight.

Baker.

It was a common enough name, I told myself. Why, there were Bakers all over the world, in all likelihood.

Everts, Baker & Henderson. Wong Brothers.

I plopped down in that chair and stared across my room at the window, through which I could see the rain slashing down as the dusk grew. The house groaned and whistled around me like I'd imagine a ship would sound as it bounced on a storm-wracked sea. Baker. Everts, *Baker* & Henderson.

I knew Pa hadn't always been an outlaw. He spoke so rarely of his upbringing, and never in front of his men. I tried to remember what Pa had told me of his family and of where he'd come from.

I knew my given name was his grandmother's given name. And I knew that she was native, but that's all. I had never inquired as to her people, where they had come from, where *she* had come from. Why I was reminded of her every time I saw my reflection, every time someone commented on my native looks.

But what of Pa's other side? He'd said he'd been an unhappy young man. That he'd made his way to Wyoming and Montana in search of adventure and had fallen in with a gang of hold-up men, and that life had been a thrill to him until he met my ma. From then, and from when I was born and Ma was taken from us, Pa did what he had to do to survive. I lost her before I ever truly knew her. He did what was needed to keep me in food, to raise me up, to teach me my letters and numbers.

And that was all I knew. I hadn't known whether Pa hailed from east or west or north or south, or who his people were.

Henderson and Everts, clearly mixed up together long before Miss Phillipa Everts and Mr. William Henderson had dealings with art. And the Wongs. All the families were mixed up together.

I thought about what Will had said when I asked about the dragon symbol. That the family crest was the result of their relationship with a Chinese outfit—surely the Wongs—and gold.

Me. Miss Everts and Mrs. Gale. David. Will. All of our families mixed up together—mixed up with gold. Such a long history together, long and complicated. A history that I knew nothing about.

Chapter TWENTY

April 6, 1906

"Miss Menken, stripped by her captors, will ride a fiery steed at furious gallop onto and across the stage and into the distance."

—Advertisement, Maguire's Opera House of San Francisco, August 24, 1863

THE STORM HAD NOT LET UP EVEN THE NEXT MORNING. Miss Everts did not make an appearance at breakfast.

Around noon, my new gown was delivered. I had to call upon Mei Lien to help me try it on with the corset and all, for she had to lace up the strings that would hold me in. Pulling corset strings was a job I had done many times, but this was the first time I'd be subjected to compression of my own innards.

When she arrived in my room, she kept her eyes downcast. I took her delicate hand and held it between my own.

"Mei Lien, whatever I said yesterday to disturb you, I'm humbly sorry for it."

She was still and silent.

"I wish you would forgive me."

Mei Lien nodded. She seemed to accept this. I changed the subject.

"Will you help me with this dress?"

She smiled a little for the first time. It was a relief to have something pleasant to occupy us.

Yet after struggling with whalebone and starched fabric, I wondered why I thought anything involving corsets would be pleasant. Corsets, in my opinion, were a curse to womankind. Why, it was impossible to bend over. No wonder rich ladies dressed in their finery needed someone else to lace up their boots. I hated feeling as though I could not move in that contraption. Even if I was astonished when I regarded myself in the mirror, my waist narrowed to almost nothing. It took my breath away in every sense.

But the scarlet-colored gown was the most gorgeous thing I'd ever seen. And now that I wasn't being poked and prodded by the overly intimate and unfamiliar hands of the seamstress, I could take the time to admire the work in that gown.

It was of crepe, and adorned across the bodice with embroidered flowers in silk thread of the same color. The skirt sported layer upon layer of fabric plummeting to a train. I studied the embroidery and then showed it to Mei Lien, describing how I thought the flowers could be made, and what stitches would work best. The neckline draped across my not-quite-bare shoulders—they were covered with more ruffles. It was a minimum of modesty.

My olive skin had never before been so exposed, and I ran my fingers up my arms, feeling the goose bumps.

I'd never spent such time before a mirror. Here and there in the past, yes, while I worked in the homes of my employers I'd sneaked a look at my reflection. But I'd had no proper looking glass at camp, and even if there had been, I knew what I'd see looking back at me: a part native, plain-faced girl. But this, this was different. It felt peculiar. I looked at the girl who looked back at me, and I saw not myself but someone exotic and fancy, with my crow-black hair all done up at the hands of Mei Lien in ringlets and swirls that trailed down the back of my neck.

I saw my features clearly, and had a sense now what people here in San Francisco must have thought when they looked at me, for I was not a fair-skinned delicate creature. My dark eyes burned out from that angular face in the mirror.

For so much of my life I had wanted nothing more than to have what those rich girls had growing up. Pretty things and parties. I imagined seeing myself just like I looked now, dressed up and fussed over, in a mansion, and in my imaginings I was blissful.

Well, here I was, dressed up and fussed over, except that my stomach was in knots. There was no bliss for me, only knots over my situation. Pa. The future. Without Pa I'd be an orphan, and maybe a servant forever. Even if by some means Pa didn't hang for that murder, where did that leave me? The daughter of a thief, an outlaw. What kind of future did that hold for me? I couldn't work my way out of servitude—I could only marry my way out, but only if my intended never discovered my past. Someone like Will Henderson might answer my dreams. He would raise me from my station if he married me, that was sure.

But would that be what it took for me to find bliss?

My glance strayed to Mei Lien and back to my reflection. Mei Lien fiddled with my petticoat, training it out behind me. "Pretty."

"Yes. Well, we'd best take it off now so I can wear it on Thursday next. And so I can suck in some good air."

Once I was back in my everyday clothes, I turned to Mei Lien.

"Would you like to learn more stitches? Maybe we can figure out how to make rosettes like these."

She smiled at that, and we went down to the parlor and sat by the fire for the rest of the afternoon.

At teatime, Miss Everts appeared.

I went to her. "I've been harsh." It was the best I could do in the way of apology for some of my behavior. She was my employer, after all, and I needed to be in her good graces. But I also admitted some grudging respect for her. For what she might have done for Mei Lien.

But she brushed me away. "It was not you." She straightened her back. "I've allowed myself to drift into sentimentality. Compassion is an acceptable emotion. Sentimentality leads to regret, and regret is dangerous."

I certainly knew about regret. Regret that I hadn't stood up for my pa. Regret that I hadn't made him leave Yellowstone sooner so we could have a respectable life. Regret that I hadn't rescued Min. Regret all the way back to not having my mother with me as I was growing up.

"I see you and Mei Lien have resumed lessons? Oh, that's lovely work, my dear. Yes, this will do very nicely, don't you think, Mei Lien?"

The two exchanged a look I couldn't fathom: Mei Lien nodded and smiled.

Miss Everts turned to me. "I take it the dress has arrived. Well. Now that you're ready to attend, we'd best discuss our little ruse before the Henderson affair."

"Ah. My so-called career."

"You are an artist's model. That accidental pretense has given me an opportunity. Mei Lien, would you mind getting us all some tea?"

Miss Everts shut the drawing room door behind Mei Lien. She wanted to speak to me alone. Indeed, her next words were a rush of confusion to my ears. "I know your primary concern is for your father. But we can do nothing for the moment, and I have something else to attend to. You can help me. I need you to play the part."

Phillipa Everts had no clue about the part I already played with respect to Wilkie. But there was, in fact, nothing I could do until I'd uncovered more about the intertwined relationships—that brotherhood of families—and figured out how to get to Wilkie. "I'll try."

"It's simple. We must create a story for you. Say, you have come to visit me after having been discovered in Santa Fe. Will that suit? I've brought you here. There will be many patrons of the arts at this social gathering. In the next few days, before the party, we shall visit one well-known artist."

A knotty fear wormed inside me. "Will I have to do anything . . . peculiar?" I didn't know how else to put it.

She looked at me, sharp. "No. Nothing. And that is my sincere promise. I only need to buy a little more time. Create a diversion."

"For what?"

She turned away, silent for a moment. She continued. "With you adding the new element of distraction at that event, I should be able to slip some things by—"

"Miss Everts, I wish you'd explain this more plainly."

She fixed her gray eyes on me. "If I did, I'd be afraid you'd give it all away."

Now she had me peeved again. Give what away? And if anyone could hold a secret, it was me.

"The artist's name is Sebastian Gable. He's a good friend. I'll try and arrange things for Monday."

I nodded, biting my tongue. Secrets and more secrets, and I was tugged in two directions. I put my hand on my throat, felt the key that lay hidden, touched the cameo at my collar. From a scarlet-colored silk gown and rich Will Henderson to David Wong and Josiah Wilkie. From Nat Baker's daughter to Phillipa Everts's protégé. Art to artifice. I didn't know anymore who I was, or where I'd come from, or where I was going.

Chapter TWENTY-ONE

April 9, 1906

> *"The civilized world is trembling on the verge of a great movement. Either it must be a leap upward, which will open the way to advances yet undreamed of, or it must be a plunge downward, which will carry us toward barbarism."*
>
> —*Progress and Poverty*, Henry George, aka "The Prophet of San Francisco," 1879

"KULA," MISS EVERTS'S VOICE BELIED HER IMPATIENCE with me. "It's perfectly all right. He wants to do a series of studies of your face. Normally, he only paints landscapes. But he's working on something different." Miss Everts pulled on her gloves as I waited by the door.

"And you said he'll pay?"

"Handsomely. Which you could send to your father's defense."

Jameson drove us to the home of Sebastian Gable. I wasn't sure what I'd been expecting, but my nerves were calmed the minute we walked through the door and stood in his broad entry hallway. His paintings were everywhere, and what a collection they made.

I'd never seen the like. These landscapes were not dreamy or dark. They were so colorful and riotous that I had to whisper to Miss Everts if he painted real, actual places.

"Yes. Why, that one's Goleta Point, and there's Mount Tam. In a few weeks, when the wildflowers are out in all their glory, you'll see. This is the way it looks here later in the spring, and in summer and fall."

Mr. Gable appeared from the end of the hall. He greeted Miss Everts, and turned to me. He made a slight bow. "Miss Baker. I'm delighted. And happy you've given me this opportunity. Phillipa has told me so much about you. Come." He pointed down the hallway to an open door through which intense light spilled.

All that light came from a bank of windows that formed one wall of his studio. Even in the gray weather—rain had finally given way to dull and damp—the light in this room was rich and cheering. Paintings in various stages of completion hung or stood or leaned on the other surfaces. He'd set a chair in the center of a low dais.

"Would you like anything? Some tea?" His courtly manners settled my nerves once and for all.

I sat and posed for him for over an hour while he sketched. Every so often he would ask me to move or turn and look in another direction. Miss Everts sipped tea and watched him work. When he finally seemed satisfied, he let me see what he had done.

There were three or four studies all done in pencil, and I felt both embarrassed and thrilled. It was me, but it was not me, and he'd captured something else, something inside me. Obstinacy. Pride.

"What will you do with these?" I asked.

"I am working on something different. A large work, a series of murals. It's a commission for the State Capitol. I want to represent California in a new way. The new California. All of her people, waking to a new century." He paused. "Would you care to see what I've begun?"

"I'd love it."

He led me to the back wall and pulled a cord, revealing from behind a curtain a series of three huge panels, eight feet high and ten feet long, in various stages of completion. He led me along, pointing out places and people, the snowy Cascades, the southern deserts, the industry and commerce, and the great bay of San Francisco, its fleets of ships and flower-studded slopes and bustling thoroughfares.

"This is beautiful." I paused. I followed with my finger his representation of Market Street. "But you've forgotten something."

"Really?" He seemed interested, leaning toward the painting first, and then turning to me, puzzled.

"You've left out the cruelty."

I heard the sharp intake of breath from Miss Everts. I felt Mr. Gable's eyes on me.

I didn't care. "You've left out the alleys in Chinatown. The bawdy houses in the Barbary Coast. Did you mean to leave them out?"

"Kula." Miss Everts's tone was sharp.

"No, Phillipa, she's quite right. I shall make amends for it, shall I?"

We exchanged a glance, and he gave me another slight bow. "I believe I know where to place you in this work. I would like to make new sketches. Would you be willing to return?"

I nodded.

In the hallway at her house, Miss Everts handed me an envelope with twenty-five dollars. Twenty-five dollars! For one hour's work, if you could call it that. Why, twenty-five dollars was a fortune for so little effort.

"Your comments were quite forward," she said.

I knew they were. I didn't know what came over me. Why should I care about the lives of these girls, these unfortunates—what did they mean to me? I'd been looking after myself for long enough, and all I wanted was freedom from what I'd seen as my own slavery. All I wanted was to free my pa so that we could then make a life for ourselves. And a life for me with a rich husband and a high station and pretty things all around. What did the lives of these girls—the ones behind the bars—matter to me?

They mattered. They did. I would never forget their eyes, their thin fingers. Oh, I still wanted a decent life for myself, but maybe I could have everything I'd always wanted, and more besides. Maybe I could have something more, something larger than even my dreams.

"But it was also quite right that you spoke up," Miss Everts murmured, her words an echo to my thoughts. Her steel eyes met mine. I squared my shoulders. "Now. On Thursday night, you will have to pretend you know nothing of that side of life in San Francisco. You will have to put on a show. Can you do that?"

I nodded, once.

"Only a little while longer. That's all. Then you'll understand. Then I'm confident you'll be able to help your father. It will all come out right." She turned to remove her hat and left me fingering the envelope.

Chapter TWENTY-TWO

April 12, 1906

"If you would slay the Social Snake
That brings the Bosom grief and ache
Dance while you may, dance while you may
For heaven comes forth in Social Play."

—Thomas Lake Harris, founder of
Fountain Grove in Sonoma, 1875

THE WEATHER CLEARED AT LAST, AS A BRISK, STINGING wind blew in from the ocean, blustering all those rainy clouds off to the east to make way for a robin's-egg-blue sky behind. By noon on Thursday the sun threw glinty sparks off all the rain-washed trees and streets and houses. By the afternoon the breeze had all but dried out the city.

Either way, change was in the wind. On that Thursday it was time for me to play my part and attend the Henderson party, the first social affair of my life.

On that same Thursday my pa would stand trial, far away in Montana. I had to trust Miss Everts's assertions that playing my role at the party would bring me closer to freeing my pa.

Dress, shoes, gloves, delicate underclothes all laid out across my bed for me.

Here was a thing I'd waited for all my life, had envied other girls for—a social occasion at which I was a guest and not a servant.

And my mind was a whirl of mixed-up fears and longings and confusions. The butterflies in my stomach carried on so I couldn't tell if it was excitement or nerves. I knew I'd see Will Henderson tonight, and yet I could not stop thinking of David Wong.

As Mei Lien helped me into my corsets, I thought I'd ask her. "How well do you know Mr. Wong?"

It seemed an innocent enough question. But maybe I'd asked it at the wrong time. Mei Lien was in the midst of tugging those laces. She gave a yank that nearly pulled me off my feet.

"Not know him," she said. "Never see him. He never come here."

"But he was here just the other . . ." I wheezed, and gave up as Mei Lien yanked again. It was all I could do to breathe, let alone pry further.

Jameson drove Miss Everts and me in the horseless—its bonnet pulled up snug against the breeze so we wouldn't end up with hair like a rat's nest—to the Henderson mansion.

My. Such a grand place. I'd seen the back entry; now we arrived in full splendor at the front. Unlike Miss Everts's house, the mansion was made all of stone, white and gleaming in the electrics that flickered along the front. Horseless carriages and fancy traps drawn by well-groomed ponies lined the street up and down. Jameson had to pull around and leave us in the hands of the doormen, who guided us inside.

An orchestra played music in one corner. Along the wall sat a table spread with small packages—gifts for us guests to take home, Miss Everts whispered. Gifts for us!

I began to yank off my long kid gloves—dyed to match the dress—before Miss Everts stopped me. Even though they chafed my upper arms, it seemed I had to keep those gloves on all evening.

I wished that I knew more about how this socializing was done. One thing was certain. I wouldn't be slouching in that scarlet crepe dress. Thanks to the whalebone, my back was ramrod straight and my stomach tightly cinched. I didn't think I'd be eating much, either.

Mr. Henderson greeted his guests at the entry to a room big enough for a small town. I shook his hand and made a little curtsy.

"Young Will is visiting with other guests," Mr. Henderson said. Was he excusing his son or suggesting I leave him alone? I didn't like the way Mr. Henderson looked at me. I was being inspected, his eyes looking me up and down. I almost thought he'd ask me to open my mouth so he could see my teeth.

As we moved away, I whispered to Miss Everts, "Where's Mrs. Henderson?"

"Dead."

A widower. Maybe that accounted for the examination. Still, I felt like an object, pure and simple.

Miss Everts and I made our way through the throng. Right and left I was introduced as her protégée, an artist's model. All according to her plan. I remained silent through much of it, fearing I would give myself away by saying something foolish.

Thin-lipped matrons and their goggle-eyed husbands swirled through the room. A clutch of young women gathered in the chairs along one wall. Single men slipped in and out, stealing to the back terrace for what I presumed was a puff on a cigar. Inside grew warmer and warmer due to the press of bodies.

The mansion stretched from one exquisite room to the next, all furnished in grand high style. The central hallway featured a stair that curved up and then split in the middle, and I imagined going up one side and down the other, like the grand entrance a lady could make. Statues stood rank on rank along the hallways to either side of the stairway. I wandered off from Miss Everts's side and peeked into this room and that for at least half an hour until she found me again and tugged me back into the ballroom.

The orchestra played waltzes, and waiters slid through with trays of delicacies—a seafood (shrimp, according to Miss Everts's whisper), a pastry filled with small black nubbins (caviar, Miss Everts called it), and, of all the awful things, snails. Due to my constrained condition and the peculiarity of these dishes, I declined to eat.

Will materialized in front of us.

"Miss Everts! And you've brought your lovely guest. Hello, Kula."

He bowed over my hand, his eyes lifting to mine the lower he went. Right off the bat, I was flustered. Back in Yellowstone, one of Pa's men told tales of magicians who could enchant a subject with a mere look, put her to sleep or make her do silly things. Mesmerizing, after the doings of a Dr. Mesmer, he'd said. I'd scoffed—surely that wasn't possible. But now I knew it was true. I wondered what silly things I might do under the gaze of that Will Henderson.

"May I get you something to drink, ladies?"

Miss Everts glanced at me and spoke up. "Kula, I shall socialize. Will." She slipped right away, leaving me alone with Will, who looked at me.

"Some punch?" he asked.

"Yes," I said. "Punch." I followed him across the crowded space, slowing to regard the artwork on the walls as we passed.

There were the usual landscapes and portraits, but there were also paintings the likes of which I'd never seen. I confess that the naked ladies made me blush, and I moved past them with a quick step. Heaven forbid I—the "artist's model"—should ever pose as such. But there were also two panels of work that captured me. They were in gilt frames around painted images that progressed as if the subjects were on parade, from top to bottom: ladies in their odd robes cinched at the waist with their hair tied up in wide ribbons, wandering in gardens with arching bridges, passing through willows that wept over rippled ponds, serving tea in tiny shelters with wing-tipped roofs.

I stood before these panels long enough for Will to fetch my punch and return.

As I took a sip he asked, "You like Chinese art?"

I nodded. And then drank a few swallows of the punch, my thirst making up for my lack of appetite. There was alcohol in that beverage; I recognized the pungent taste from sips I'd stolen while working in a steamy kitchen. "I've never seen such work before. I had no idea it could be so lovely."

"There is nothing lovely in this room. Except for you."

I was in the middle of another sip and gulped it down in surprise. On top of what I'd already drunk, the alcohol went straight to dizzying my brain. I choked out, "Ah . . . thank you."

"It's true, you know. You're turning heads."

"You are blunt, Will Henderson. Is it warm in here?" I suddenly knew the reason for the fan that dangled from my wrist. I snapped it open and waved vigorously.

He lifted his hand to push that thicket of wavy hair off his face. I dared not look him in the eye, and instead examined the other guests more carefully. There were any number of girls my age about the room. Most of them had eyes planted firmly on Will. I could certainly understand why. And yet Will was here next to me.

I took another swallow of punch. "You know," I said, tilting my head at the other girls, "I believe many of those heads turn this way for you, not for me."

He smiled through his teeth. "They're waiting like vultures."

I had to laugh. "For what?"

"For me to make up my mind."

"About?"

"Which one of them I'll marry."

The alcohol was having a most uplifting effect. I giggled. "Oh, and do you have a favorite?"

"No." He looked in my eyes. That mesmerizing technique worked its magic on me, again. "None before now."

I drained my punch cup. "And now?" The squeaky voice must have been mine, though I didn't recognize it.

"Now I've found someone so different, so . . . unspoiled." He leaned toward me, his lips brushing my ear. "It would send all their tongues wagging, would it not? Me with someone like you?"

His words had an immediate sobering effect. I pulled back. "Someone like me?" Someone with my skin color, he meant. Of course. I pursed my lips.

"Oh yes! Why, you know what I mean. Gorgeous. Unique. Not from their silly little circles." His eyes met mine, and his seemed so genuine, so filled with sweetness, or what I took for sweetness, that I forgave his comment. I wished his lips would brush my ear again. He asked, "Would you dance with me?"

I took a breath. "I'm not practiced."

"It's not hard. I'll show you."

Which he did. When his arm circled my waist and his hand pressed my back, I thought I might dissolve. After two waltzes, during which I became increasingly dizzy—whether from that punch or the dancing or some combination—I begged for a rest.

Will asked, "Would you like more punch?"

I nodded, unable to speak. In point of fact, my tongue was a massive object that seemed to be giving my mouth a certain deal of trouble.

Will went for the punch and returned almost immediately. We sat now, in a pair of chairs against one wall of the room. I drank, trying to cool my mouth. The alcohol taste was stronger in this cup. It gave me a loose, dizzy feeling that only seemed to increase my fondness for this charming boy beside me. He was elegant, friendly . . . I remembered how he had rescued me from the rain.

I leaned toward Will. I felt so safe, so sure that I could tell him anything. "I have a secret. Shh."

He leaned toward me so that our faces were only inches apart. "Please share."

"I know about your dragon, you know. I'm not really . . . I'm really here because I'm looking for a box that belongs to my father. And, you know," I tapped his arm with my fan. His eyebrows lifted, but I pressed on. I dropped my voice to a whisper. "I think it must be full of gold."

He smiled. It was a funny smile, not one I'd ever seen from him before. It was almost cruel. But his warm eyes crinkled again. "Why do you think so?"

"Oh, the gold rush. The past. Something about that dragon brotherhood." The room spun around me. It was so warm in that grand room. "And it needs to be gold, in order to set Pa free."

"Set him free!" Will laughed, so I did, too. He laid a hand on my arm; it was soft, warm. "What, is he an outlaw? Or some kind of a captive?"

I nodded. "Sadly, yes. He's both. But he didn't do it, what they're saying. He was bad in the past, but he doesn't deserve this. Not my pa. It was that Snake-eyes, evil Snake-eyes." I shook my head, trying to clear Wilkie's looming face from my mind. I thought of my father's eyes, those sad, clear, blue eyes. My poor father. "And when I set Pa free, then I'm going to set myself free." I smiled at the thought. "Yes. Set *myself* free. Not wait for someone to do it for me."

Will lifted his hand and brushed a stray hair from my face. "Aren't you free now, Kula?"

Melt—I thought I might melt. Oh, I could be free with you, Will Henderson.

He leaned closer, and I thought for a second he would kiss me, right there, in public, in front of fine society. Me, Kula Baker. But instead he whispered, "I'll go fetch more punch." And he was gone.

I blinked. The dancers swirled about on the floor. Heavens. My brain was addled. What had I just said to Will? The room closed on me, the bodies pressing in on me from the dance floor. I lifted my fan and batted like crazy. I stood. The press of bodies around me grew like a wall. I gulped air. I had to get out, get some air.

I looked for Will but could not see him through the crush of people. I thought it best to seek reinforcements, since my brain was no longer functioning as it should. Miss Everts. I could find her;

she'd help me. But she seemed to have taken a page from Jameson's book and vanished into thin air.

I crisscrossed the great room, inserting myself between guests who increased in hearty behavior with every instant. William Henderson must have invited the entire city. The orchestra turned up the tempo; what was that lively tune? The temperature in the room grew to sweltering. I used my fan with a passion, but it did not help. Will—where was Will? I blew the lank hair up off my forehead and then mopped my cheeks with the back of my gloved hand.

What had I just told Will Henderson? Something about gold, about being free. Being free. The image of the girls, those girls, those girls behind their bars came into my mind, and my empty stomach roiled.

I reached the opposite corner of the room and still no sign of Miss Everts. And no sign of Will, either. Although I was sure I no longer needed punch. What I needed was air. I pressed one hand at my middle, hoping it would help me breathe. This blasted corset—I could not catch my breath. I fanned so hard I was sure the rice paper would split along the bamboo splines of my fan.

"Air." I think it was my voice; it sounded like my voice, but it was as though I was hearing it through a thick fog. And just as the room began to swim again, a firm hand caught my elbow.

Chapter TWENTY-THREE

April 12, 1906

"The particularly fine portions of the cargo,
the fresh and pretty females who come
from the interior, are used to fill special orders
from wealthy merchants and prosperous tradesmen."

—*San Francisco Chronicle*, December 5, 1869

THE HAND GUIDED ME ALONG THE WALL TO A DOOR. Helped me through the door and into the sparkling night.

The cool air was like diving into the lake—like gulping ice or waking to a frosty morning. I shivered, but I was revived. My head beginning to clear, I turned to my rescuer.

"Mr. Gable!" I lifted my thick ringlets off my neck, thankful for the cool night. "Forgive me. It was so hot . . ."

"Yes. And the punch is heady. Particularly when you've been offered so much." The artist smiled at me kindly.

"Yes." Noise from the party spilled out onto the balcony where we stood, filling the awkward silence.

"Kula! There you are." Will, looking disheveled, stared as if he'd been searching for me for hours. "Mr. Gable."

Sebastian Gable bowed. He regarded Will and the punch glass in his hand. "Miss Baker could do with water."

A momentary silence. Then Will said, his voice bright once

more, "Of course! I should have thought of that." He called to one of the servers, who brought water on the spot. I took it and drank gratefully.

"Miss Baker. If you're all right . . ." I nodded. "Well, then." Mr. Gable turned to leave. He hesitated. "Miss Baker, you do me a great honor by allowing me to sketch your *visage.* Your comments have made me think."

"I . . ." I was flabbergasted. "Thank you."

Mr. Gable eyed Will for a moment, then nodded to me with a smile, and slipped back in through the door.

Will leaned to me. "You've proved my point."

"Which point is that?" While now I could breathe, I confess that Will still befuddled me.

"The unspoiled one." His truly was the sweetest smile. "I knew it from the moment I met you."

My throat had grown thick again, but now it was with an emotion entirely shocking, one I could hardly put into words. "Knew what?"

"Knew you were different. Knew I wanted to get to know you."

Here, standing before me, my dream come true. As handsome as a god, as rich as a king, as sweet as butter. And fawning over me. Young, too. I hadn't expected that. Will was the desire come true of my life. My corset bound so tight and my feelings pressed so that I thought I might snap the laces.

Yet there was more niggling at me, in the back of my head. A tingle that I tried to tamp down. Oh, that punch had truly addled my brain. I took another gulp of water.

"Let me show you around San Francisco," Will pressed. "I can show you the real San Francisco. Come with me tomorrow."

"I . . ." I knew the real San Francisco, did I not? The madhouse streets, the girls in cages . . .

"Come. You won't be able to avoid me, Kula Baker."

"All right," I began, "but . . ."

"No 'buts.' I'll be at Miss Everts's house at nine."

"But . . ."

Will held up his hand to silence me, and gave me that dazzling grin again.

A chill breeze blew across the patio, and I shivered. No, I shook like a leaf, but not from the cold. It seemed that I now had exactly what I wanted. Will could give me everything—money, power, respectability. He could help me find Wilkie, find Pa's box. He could give me everything. Unlike David, David who could give me nothing.

"You're chilled. I've been thoughtless. Let's go inside," he said.

We stepped through the doorway. All eyes turned in our direction as if on cue. The girls scowled. The young men smirked. The gentlemen and ladies stared at me and Will Henderson with mixed expressions.

I lifted my chin. Those society girls would not make me feel inferior. As to the others, I knew prejudice mixed with jealousy when I saw it. I turned to Will. "It's late. I think I should go home. I need to find Miss Everts."

"Yes," said Will. "Of course."

We made our way through the crowd. This time no one jostled us; it was as if we were parting the Red Sea. On the far side of the room Will said, "Just wait here, will you? I'll see if I can find her."

I waited, with every eye upon me, or so it felt.

My scarlet dress was a beacon; that could be the only explanation for the eyes trained on me from every quarter. It wasn't long before my face grew hot and I snapped open my fan again. I went out into the vast marble hallway and looked at the artwork, which drew me like a magnet.

There were paintings everywhere—more, even, than in the ballroom. They lined all the walls, up the grand staircase and up to the second story. As I climbed, I examined the paintings. They grew increasingly odd, modern, abstract. I followed them up and then along the corridor, studying each piece as if I were in a museum.

With each painting I looked at, I grew more and more uncomfortable. No—that wasn't it. I grew frightened. The paintings scared me. Not because they were of monsters, or terror. They were peculiar and unrecognizable sometimes, yet gorgeous and emotional at others. But they were free and rambling and untethered . . . and everything that I was not.

I was not free. I was tethered to my place as a servant. And I was a slave to my desire to be otherwise, to be worshipped.

Will. He was the perfect catch—hadn't he said as much in the ballroom? All of the girls in San Francisco wanted him. I wanted him—he was my dream. This was the opportunity I'd waited for my entire life. It was up to me to seize it now. I should have felt free, to be so close to attaining everything I'd ever wanted, but instead it was as though I'd just stepped into a windowless room, the door locked behind me, trapping me inside.

I was lost in thought when I heard familiar voices issuing from a room down at the end of the corridor. The door was partway opened, and Miss Everts's distinctive voice rang out clear as a bell, then mixed with others I didn't recognize. I slipped along the hallway, thinking to signal her that I was ready to leave.

But at the door I stopped. The voices were raised—a quarrel. The door was open six inches, which was enough for me to peek through.

It was a good thing that I'd had nothing to eat. It was a good thing that my head had cleared from the punch. Otherwise, I would have become a puddle of scarlet silk on the floor.

Josiah Wilkie stood at one end of a table, William Henderson at the other. In between them was Phillipa Everts. I didn't know what words had passed among them, but I surely knew what passed between their hands. I watched Phillipa Everts hand a thick stack of bills to Josiah Wilkie.

Money.

Miss Everts gave Snake-eyes money. The man who framed my pa, the man who had destroyed my life, the man who wanted to bind me in chains, the man who held Min in torment and trafficked in evil . . . The man who had stolen the one thing in the world that could free my father.

And my patroness, Miss Phillipa Everts. My employer, my . . . my friend, even. The one person in San Francisco I'd trusted with my life and all my secrets, Miss Phillipa Everts gave Josiah Wilkie money.

I backed away into the hall, clutching my stomach and leaning against the wall for support. If they found me, I was dead. I had to leave, and fast. I made my way to the marble staircase and then fairly ran down it to the bottom, at which point I clutched the banister and tried to regain my senses. I shut my eyes, but all I could see was Phillipa Everts's hand clutching those bills.

"There you are! It's all arranged." I spun around; Will smiled down at me, with Miss Everts and Mr. Henderson arriving close behind him.

"What . . . ?"

"Our excursion tomorrow." Will shook his head. "I will not hear protests. I've spoken with Miss Everts. I shall be there at nine to fetch you for the ferry. I'm taking you to see Mount Tam."

I said nothing—how could I? Miss Everts came to my side. As we made our farewells, Will clutched my hands in his until I forced mine from his grip.

I couldn't look at Miss Everts. We rode home in silence, and I went straight to Mei Lien and begged for help in freeing me from my corset. After dousing the lights I lay in my sheets and stared through the night at that blood-red dress that lay draped over my chair, lifeless, as if a corpse. As if all hope had drained from it and lay drowning on the floor in the swamp of that ruffled train.

Chapter TWENTY-FOUR

April 13, 1906

> *"Such beauty as this was apt now to crush and break her. All her being was still sore, and this appeal of nature was sometimes more than she could bear."*
>
> —*Lady Rose's Daughter,* a novel by Mrs. Humphrey Ward, 1903

I TOSSED AND TURNED ALL NIGHT, A MESS OF sleeplessness, fears, uncertainties . . . and longings.

When I did sleep, I was tormented with broken dreams: about my father hanging for a crime he didn't commit, about finding the wealth that might buy his freedom, about David's smiling eyes, and about the rich, handsome Will Henderson. Each time I woke, I could hardly pull together more than snippets of images. At some point I ran away from an artist who kept trying to paint my *visage.* I followed Miss Everts to a secret passage. I sat alone in the horseless behind a semi-invisible Jameson.

And worst of all were the images of Wilkie. Wilkie and Mei Lien and Min. Wilkie chasing after me, but also chasing after the two of them. And I was the only one who could stop him by beating him with a rolled-up parchment that didn't feel anything like a weapon.

I didn't want to see Phillipa Everts in the morning, and I hadn't been expecting to, but for a change, she was in her rooms when I went to tidy them. I found myself slamming doors and tossing things aside and shoving my way through my chores.

"Kula! Please be careful. That mirror was my grandmother's."

I'd almost broken it when I'd thrown it down on the dresser. Exhaustion and anger at her loosed my tongue. "You disappeared during the party."

"I told you I had business to attend to. And you did provide adequate distraction."

"Distraction!" The only distraction I saw was her with Josiah Wilkie.

"Kula, I know you aren't skilled in social niceties, but I assure you it was obvious to me that all eyes were on you, my new-to-San-Francisco-and-obviously-foreign protégé."

I pursed my lips. "I'm glad to be of service."

She pointed her finger into the air. "I have told you that all will be revealed soon. You must be patient."

"Fine." I felt disgust. We two were quite a pair, her with her secrets and me with mine. I left to ready myself for Will's arrival, slamming the door in my wake. The whole house seemed to vibrate.

The day was fair and promised to warm up following the passage of the storm front. By eight forty-five I was pacing in the front hallway. Into the parlor and back, into the drawing room and back; I couldn't keep still. When the doorbell rang and Jameson answered, I was right behind him to see, to my horror, both David and Will standing on the porch at the same time, regarding each other with sidelong glances.

Jameson showed both men in, giving me that fish-eyed look that was becoming so familiar. He bowed and disappeared, probably to laugh behind my back.

I looked from David to Will. I'd gone from dreaming of one man in my life to a state of overabundance.

David was the first to say something. "This is a pleasant surprise." He didn't seem pleasantly surprised to me.

I gestured, helpless; I couldn't find my tongue.

"You're Will Henderson. We met once or twice before you left for the east. I'm David Wong." David reached out his hand to shake Will's. "My family owns Wong Importers."

"Ah! My father has spoken about Wong's." Will said. "You must be here to see Miss Everts."

"I'm actually here to pay a call on Miss Baker," David replied mildly. "I met her last week and thought she might want to see some of the sights of the city."

Will looked at me. His eyebrows were raised so high they seemed to be missing. For an instant something passed over Will's face—surprise? anger?—and then he said, "I'm taking Miss Baker on an excursion to Mount Tam."

"Ah . . ." My voice came out in a pathetic high pitch, so I smiled at them both with as much feeling as I could muster. I looked from one to the other.

"It was so nice of you to think of her, David," Will continued, then flashed his most enticing smile. "I'll bet you thought she knew no one in San Francisco. But Miss Everts introduced her to our society at my home only last night."

For a moment I was confused. Why was he being so rude to David? Then I understood. Will never imagined that I would want to be with David because David was Chinese. Even me, with my exotic looks—it would not be possible in Will's world that Kula Baker could spend any serious time with David Wong.

In that moment I regarded Will with pity. Charming, gorgeous Will, who saw the world through his own tight lens.

David said evenly, "Well, that's fine, then." He shot me a look, and then went to turn away. Did he assume I thought as Will did?

"Tell you what," Will said, clapping a hand on David's shoulder. "Why don't you come along? I have to make a stop at the end of the day in Sausalito, and Miss Baker wouldn't need to be detained with me. I hate to inconvenience her. You could bring her home." He leaned over. "Maybe we can discuss a bit of business. I'd like to do something to surprise my father." Will turned to me. "I hope that's all right with you, Kula. If not, I'll delay my other business."

"No! Yes! That's lovely!" I chirped. I looked at David, practically pleading with my eyes.

David turned his hat in his hand, gazing past me down the hallway. His face was impassive; when he did look at me, his eyes revealed nothing. He nodded and said, "Let's go then."

Will drove us to the ferry landing in his automobile. The two gentlemen sat in front at my insistence; from the backseat I observed them carrying on a pleasant if high-volume conversation.

Will Henderson. Rich, handsome, clearly smitten with me. My dream come true.

David Wong. Who stirred something in me that I didn't know existed. David, who held my heart in his gentle palm and my soul in his dark, kind eyes. David, who could give me nothing.

Whatever had I gotten myself into? I sighed.

The three of us must have been a curious sight, because the other passengers at the landing and on the ferry gave us no end of peculiar looks. Will—Anglo and handsome and a gentleman; David—a Chinese man consorting openly with two non-Chinese; and me—dark-haired and olive-skinned.

But I grew distracted by our journey. Seagulls flew overhead, crying like abandoned babies. The water stank of raw smells, a bit like the lake at home, but also with a salty tang, and it was foamy and green, with floating bits of seaweed. A brisk wind made a chop on the water, but I'd been on the *Zillah* on the lake and could stomach the tossing of this ferry. I stood at the rail, savoring every movement, the sounds and smells and chucking breeze, not to mention the sight of the sunlight sparkling off the water and the sapphire sky overhead, the color of that sky reminding me of my hot springs.

It was not a long trip. The town of Sausalito climbed stair step up a wooded hill above the bay, a sight to behold from the ferry. Once we docked, we transferred direct from the ferry to a train to take us to Mill Valley; we would ascend Mount Tam on the mountain railroad that departed at ten forty. I was glad for fair weather, for the mountain car was open, pushed by the engine up the winding slope. Will explained that the rail line had a nickname: "the Crookedest Railroad in the World."

I sat between Will and David on the seat at the very front of our car. Will on the one side pressed his shoulder against mine, and asked constantly if I minded the steep slope; David on the other side sat silent. The ribbons of my hat were tied firmly under my chin to keep it from abandoning my head in the breeze. The strings of my heart were drawn tight between these two men.

Our car clacked and climbed through areas wooded with coast redwoods and oaks and chaparral, as my companions told me the trees were; beneath the tall and somber redwoods, ferns were beginning to unfurl from the cool earth. The train climbed into the higher stretches, where the woods grew spotty. The vista opened across the peninsula to the Pacific, its blue waters pocked with chain stitches of white foam meeting the brighter blue sky, and I leaned forward to clutch the metal car frame and turned in my seat to let my eyes roam as far west as they would, into that thin dark horizon line where sky meets sea.

The hills that gathered and rolled between us and the ocean beyond were dotted with early wildflowers—purple lupines, pink and red poppies, nodding yarrows. Wildflowers in Yellowstone came so late, but these already were a carpet of color stretching as far as I could see, banks of yellow and blue shading into the dun of grasses.

At the top of the rail line, and just below the peak of Mount Tam, sat the tavern, a simple but pleasant place with a lunch service and even a dance hall and overnight accommodations.

I pressed through the light crowd milling about the tavern to the railing of the porch overlooking the bay. Will and David came alongside. Will placed his hand on the small of my back, and a tingle ran all the way up and down my spine.

And there was David, who moved away, down the railing. I wanted to reach out and pull him back.

I'd never thought to be in such a situation in all my days. Three months ago I would have been over the moon at having Will's attention. I still would, if not for David. Such confusion filled my heart.

After lunch we took a walk. A trail led down the slope from the tavern toward the west. My fashionable new shoes were next to useless. I would have given my right arm for a pair of my stiff but sturdy old boots. Will walked close enough to me that he caught my elbow each time I faltered.

Will spoke to David, pestering him with questions about the import business, about particular Oriental pieces.

Small outcrops broke through the thickets of scrub oak, and the day warmed to uncomfortable as we trailed down the slope of Mount Tam. I took off my jacket and looped it by its sleeves around my waist.

At a lookout point was a broad rock that tilted back like a ramp and gave us a view up and down the coast. David and Will scrambled up; I gathered my skirts in one fist and gave my other hand to Will who offered his to help me to the far edge.

The view fell away at our feet. We looked west across the rolling foothills. The sun had arched over and now met our eyes direct. I was grateful for the wide brim of my hat; Will and David shaded their eyes. The warm wind that sprang out of the south drove up the slopes and rattled the oak leaves and fir branches.

"Where is that?" I asked. "That point on the ocean?"

"Point Diablo, I think it's called," David murmured.

"What does it mean, that word? *Diablo?*"

"Devil," Will said cheerfully.

Devil. Diablo. The Chinese people called themselves "Celestials" and they called us non-Chinese "Demons." Devil. Demon. The demon Wilkie. The faces of the girls came back to me, their innocence and fear. There were no clouds in the sky, but to my eye the sun seemed to dim.

The Crookedest Railroad in the World took us back down the mountain using the force of gravity. I wasn't so keen on this contraption, but Will assured me it was as safe as houses. On the way back Will pressed David about a certain vase. David was tight-lipped but courteous, and they made some arrangement or other. David had said hardly a word to me. I couldn't pay attention to their business, sitting as I was between them, their shoulders pressing into mine, my mind all distracted. We arrived in Sausalito just in time for the late afternoon ferry.

"And here's where I leave you," Will said. "I hope you don't mind." He lifted a strand of hair from my forehead.

I felt like two people. The one of me couldn't stop feeling David's presence, as he moved a little way off, away from me. The other of me was right here, ready to fall to pieces at Will's feet, the feet of the man I'd always dreamed about.

Will raised my hands and kissed my palms, left, then right. "I must be off, Kula. I'll call on you tomorrow." As he walked away from the ferry landing, I stared after him until he disappeared.

"He seems to like you very much." David's voice, once so warm, was as cold and hard as ice.

I turned to David. I put my hand on his arm. He pulled away from my touch, and I didn't try again.

The ferry ride back was a silent one.

At the landing, David turned to me, stiff and unsmiling. "This is impossible."

"What is?" I pushed the words past the lump in my throat.

"I can't love you."

"What . . ." Love? Anguish filled me.

Kula Baker does not show emotion.

"You have feelings for him. Not for me."

"No—David. That's not . . ." Not what? Didn't I love the idea of being a rich man's wife? Didn't I love the idea of being able to use Will's power and money to raise myself up and save my father?

"Kula, I don't know what game you're playing. But you won't play it with me." His eyes were black pools, his lips an angry knot.

"I'm not playing a game. It was a misunderstanding. Please don't be angry with me."

He confronted me, face on. "Misunderstanding? Please. Do you love him, Kula?"

"I . . . I think . . . I mean . . ."

"You don't even know." He shook his head. "I'll bet all you care about is his shiny automobile, his big house, and his bank account."

I felt cold all over.

"Well, I don't need this," he said. "I certainly don't want to be mixed up with a girl who cares only for money."

"It's not that, David. I've been serving people my whole life. The freedom—"

"Freedom? Freedom! You don't think you're already better off than so many others? You don't think you're free to make choices, to do the right thing? Please, Kula." He waved his hand. "I thought you had a good soul. I don't know anything about you, really. I thought you cared. I was wrong."

He'd as good as stabbed me right through the heart. I was mute.

"You go on and marry a rich man who you think will treat you fine. You're well rid of me." He placed his hat firmly on his head. "Good-bye."

I was rooted to the spot, fixed, frozen, broken into a million pieces.

Kula Baker does not fall in love.

Kula Baker does not let her heart betray her.

Jameson, ever there when least expected, materialized a few feet away from my left elbow. Of course. He was there to fetch me. To bring me back to that house. Miss Everts's house.

David bowed. His next words were spoken so softly that only I could hear them, and then he turned away.

I could not see my feet as I made my way to the automobile and Jameson's open door. I leaned into the automobile's leather frame. My shoulder shook and my hands trembled as I covered my face. And my heart echoed with David's last sentence.

"I won't bother you again."

Chapter TWENTY-FIVE

April 14, 1906

". . . the only reason why the 'Celestial slaves' are not now occupying dens in Chinatown is because the arrangement of the smugglers miscarried."

—"Chinese Slave Girl Plot Foiled,"
San Francisco Chronicle, November 27, 1912

THE DAY AFTER THAT PAINFUL TRIP TO MOUNT TAM, I felt ill. I couldn't eat, my stomach was in such a twist, and yet I could not keep still. I was in the service of an employer who herself was in service to the man who had set out to ruin my family and me.

I was in a helpless state, unable to recover what Pa most required in his time of direst need.

And worst of all, I was not going to see David Wong again. A huge hole had been opened in my heart. Despite my best intentions, despite the fact that he was completely unable to fulfill my dreams, to give me what I needed most, I had come to the realization that I loved David. And I'd gone and ruined everything with him—I wasn't even sure how it had happened, but he was gone from my life.

I marched into the drawing room only to find Miss Everts in her accustomed place by the fire. I turned to leave again.

"Kula, come here."

Her tone rankled me. "Yes?" I stood still on the spot.

"Close the door."

I complied, but remained at the far end of the room, away from her. She rose and came to me.

"Events will unfold according to plan." Her fingers worked the air, as if she was playing an invisible instrument. "I will tell you something I don't know but I feel to be true. The contents of your father's box."

"What of it?"

"Don't trust to wealth. There may be something in that box that is more important than money."

"What could be more important—"

"My dear, I shall say it again. Look to your soul."

"My soul is not in that box!"

"Is it not?"

I opened and closed my mouth, and let out an exasperated sigh. Why could she not just speak plainly? I was tired of talking around things, talking in riddles. I wanted to ask her to look to her own soul, especially where money was concerned, but I held my tongue.

"What is it, Jameson?"

I whirled to see him standing directly behind me. He was a quiet one.

"It's the telephone, ma'am," Jameson said, "It's Mrs. Hannah Gale."

"Well, then," said Miss Everts. "Perhaps her apology has finally arrived." Miss Everts pressed past me toward the door.

"She's asked for Miss Baker, ma'am."

"For me!"

Jameson stood aside to let me through the door, and then he led the way to the small parlor. I picked up the handset that was attached to the base by a long stiff cloth cord.

Though I'd seen a telephone at Mrs. Gale's, this was my first conversation on one.

"You speak into that part," Jameson said, pointing, "and listen there."

I lifted the heavy black thing up toward my face, staring at it. "Hello?"

I heard the shouted "Hello," which Mrs. Gale and I repeated back and forth several times before she shouted, "Your father has been convicted. He'll be hanged in a fortnight, on April twenty-eighth. Kula—"

I dropped the handset onto the floor, where it landed with a thud.

I ran to my room, sat in my chair, and rocked, head in hands.

I woke still dressed, still in the chair, and well after midnight with a sore neck. I changed to my nightgown and moved to my bed. As I lay in the darkness awake, a sound drifted up from downstairs.

I slipped out of bed and threw a shawl around my shoulders and stood at my open door. Soft voices, footsteps, scraping. Years of sleeping in still forests and worrying over nasty possibilities had sharpened my senses.

The first thing to cross my mind was Jameson and his ghostly ways. I shivered, standing there in the dark doorway, leaning forward, trying to catch a sound.

Someone or something was making noise in the kitchen. And with no lights on. This was not normal, not as it should be. Robbers. I made my way down the stairs by sticking against the wall, my bare feet making no noise. As I passed through the hall I reached for one of the candlesticks I'd seen on the table there, to use as a weapon . . . only to find the candlestick missing.

That stopped me cold. Thieves were in the house for sure.

A noise came from the kitchen. I searched for another heavy object and found a nest of walking sticks; I chose the sturdiest one.

I went to the door of the kitchen. There it was again. Ghosts flickered fearsome through my imaginings.

Then came another noise, a soft thud. Ghosts didn't make noises like that.

I reached for the doorknob as I heard more, and then something that had me holding my breath as I strained to listen.

It came like a murmur of water, a faint, soft, watery whisper. Women's voices.

Whatever gave me courage after that, I don't know. I turned the knob and opened the door, just as the moon slipped back out from behind the cloud and illumined the entire dark kitchen.

Two round faces stared up at me, two women crouching, two faces etched with terror. One was Mei Lien. The other, another Asian girl, younger.

"What are you doing?"

Mei Lien gestured frantically. Silence.

I knelt down, close. The younger girl scuttered backward on her knees, fearful. "It's all right," I whispered. I turned to Mei Lien. "Tell her. Tell her I'm not going to hurt her."

The two girls exchanged a look; the younger nodded, her

swollen eyes fixed on me. She looked pitiful. Skin and bones, and so young. Face so dirty I wanted to take spit and my nightgown to it. Her hair was matted and hung to her waist in dreadful knots. My heart broke for her.

After her betrayal of me, I knew Miss Everts was not to be trusted anymore, no matter what Mei Lien thought. Whatever needed to be done here, I would do it on my own.

I gestured. "Come." I backed up, toward the door. "My room. It's safe there. Come."

Mei Lien hesitated, took the other girl's hand, said something in Chinese.

"Come!" I repeated. I didn't want Miss Everts waking up.

They followed me, silent now, and we slipped along the hallway, up the stairs, and to my room. As we passed the hall table I took note—both of those silver candlesticks were missing.

Once inside my room with the door firmly closed, the three of us sank to the carpeted floor. I pulled my warm blanket from my bed and wrapped it around the shivering girl. I turned again to Mei Lien. "What's going on?"

"This Yue. She is run."

"Run from what?"

"From the wicked man. The evil man."

"What evil man?"

The two girls exchanged looks again. Mei Lien leaned toward me. "His name is Wilkie. He steal her, so she run. He bring girls here on ship. He steal girls from Middle Kingdom. He sell girls in Golden Mountain."

I held myself still.

"He sell them to other bad men. Here, in Golden Mountain."

"Golden Mountain," the Chinese name for San Francisco.

I had lived with men in the wild; I knew the ways of men, though I'd been protected by my pa from the worst of their nasty doings. The image of the girls I'd seen in Chinatown flooded my mind. Wilkie "stole" girls in China and brought them here. Mei Lien's situation, too, all of it . . it all funneled down to Wilkie and those he was mixed up with, including, I now believed, Mr. Henderson and Miss Everts. We non-Chinese were "Demons." Yes, we surely were. I put my face in my hands. Then I bucked up; these girls needed me firm and strong.

Mei Lien's eyes searched the floor.

"Listen. You let me handle this, yes, Mei Lien?"

She looked up at me, confused. "Miss Everts—"

"You let me handle her. I'll deal with Miss Everts. We have to protect Yue. Right?"

Mei Lien's brow furrowed.

I reached over and took her hands. I wanted her to understand; I knew that Miss Everts was not as Mei Lien thought. She paid Wilkie—the very devil who stole Yue. I could not let her know Yue was here; I could not let her tell Wilkie. "You must swear. You must promise that no one knows about Yue except me and you."

Mei Lien nodded slowly.

I looked at Yue, sorrow expanding my heart. "You stay here, in my room. You'll be safe here." I moistened the end of the blanket with my tongue and wiped the dirt streaks from Yue's gaunt cheeks.

Mei Lien looked at me as if she didn't understand.

"No one will find her in my room. Only you and I come in here. She can hide here."

"Ah." Mei Lien understood at last. "Ah. Here, all right."

I draped my arm around Yue's thin shoulders. She couldn't have been more than twelve. Her eyes were like dark wells, shutting out the hurt that may have already been done. It made my blood boil to think of someone hurting her.

Together, Mei Lien and I lifted her into my bed, where she closed her eyes and was asleep almost at once. I stroked the matted hair from her forehead, pulled the crisp sheet up to her chin. She could sleep there as long as she wished.

I had to deal with Wilkie. This girl, and how many more like her . . . I had to find the will to face him. I had to confront that monster Wilkie so that he could never hurt anyone else again.

I'd rescue this girl and Min and any of the others I could find. I was done with his threats and his demon ways. And Miss Everts . . . I'd find out who was standing behind him—and if it was Miss Everts, I'd make her pay.

Chapter TWENTY-SIX

April 15, 1906

> *"Society was sore diseased.*
> *Villainy wielded the balance of power,*
> *and honesty was at a discount."*
>
> —*Metropolitan Life Unveiled,*
> J. W. Buel on the situation in San Francisco, 1856

I WAS UP WITH THE DAWN THE NEXT MORNING. IT was Easter Sunday, and so it was no surprise to me to find that Miss Everts had left the house. She worshipped alone. I made my own way to early services, expecting that she would be back when I returned, but when I arrived home, she had not. She was not back even after breakfast had been laid by Jameson and eaten by me and cleared by a sleepy Mei Lien.

Yue was still in my bed, sleeping the sleep of someone much deprived. I had to sort out how to help her. It all came down to money, no matter what Miss Everts said, and in her case actions spoke louder than words. There had to be a heap of gold in Pa's box, and now I needed it for many reasons. And if there wasn't, or if I couldn't get it from Wilkie—well, I was ready to take my chances.

I went to the drawing room, one hand on my hip. It was then I noticed that the small silver boxes that had graced the table by the fireplace were missing. There had been five, all engraved and polished to a fare-thee-well. Now there were none.

Kula Baker is not a thief. But someone else surely was.

My thought went to Jameson, that sneaky devil. But . . . as sly as he might be, I couldn't imagine he would steal from Miss Everts.

My problems were multiplying like rabbits. I had to save my father with or without his box, and now without the help of Miss Everts. I had to deal with Wilkie. I had to protect Yue. And then there was that puzzling connection between my father, the Hendersons, and Miss Everts. And between Will Henderson and David. And now a skulking Jameson stealing silver from Miss Everts?

Miss Everts. She spoke in riddles, never giving me a clear answer. I don't know why I expected an answer from her still, considering how she must be in cahoots with Wilkie. Yet I couldn't seem to reconcile her as one with a rotten heart, as one who also trafficked in evil. And then, as if on cue, I heard voices approaching in the hallway. I stood near the partly open door to hear.

Miss Everts: "Detestable business. What now?"

Mumbling; from Jameson, I presumed.

"How on earth? When?"

More mumbling.

"What about Mei Lien?"

". . ."

"We must act swiftly then. Roddy, you'll have to go." Jameson had a first name. And Miss Everts used it, familiarly.

". . ."

"Please. I'm a tough old bird. It's Kula I'm thinking about."

". . ."

"I insist. Now, where is she?"

I quick stepped back across the room and pretended to be engrossed in a book chosen at random.

Miss Everts came in and walked straight to me. "Mr. Gable would like you to sit for him again." She fell down into the chair next to the fireplace, her skirts bunching up in a heap.

"All right."

She drew one hand across her eyes. "Well? What are you waiting for? Go." Her free hand waved at the door, and I caught in her expression something I had not seen before. Such sadness. It radiated in waves. A moment's pity ran through me. "Miss Everts—"

"Go!"

I went.

Mr. Gable's courtly manners were endearing and his studio pleasant. But this time he made a request of me.

"Now, not to offend you, my dear. I should like you to loosen your hair. And sit with this draped about you." He held up a large, heavy, coarse wool blanket.

His request didn't bother me, I was so preoccupied with other thoughts. I let my hair down; it fell into the long braid that I had made to pull it together. I threw the blanket around my shoulders. "Like this?"

He twisted the pencils in his hands. "Not quite. May I?" I nodded.

Mr. Gable took my hair and shook it completely loose, and pulled it about my face, catching it and lifting it until it made unsightly knots. "Now, if you don't mind, and please don't take this the wrong way, I should like you to bare your shoulders."

I knew he meant no harm, and there was trust between us. I went behind a screen and removed my shirtwaist and chemise and wrapped myself modestly in the blanket.

"Perfect." He beamed.

He sketched for almost an hour before he spoke again. "I'm making you one of the centerpieces of this panel. You brought my attention to something, Miss Baker. I've spent the last days in parts of this city that I'd ignored, even though I've lived here most of my life."

I wasn't supposed to move, but I couldn't help shifting my shoulders.

"Ah! Wait! A little to the left . . . your chin . . . there. That's perfect. There. I was saying . . . I find that terrible things have been happening here, right under our noses, and little has been done."

"Yes, I've seen it."

"I'm sorry for that. No young woman should have to see these things."

"You're wrong."

He stopped drawing. "Please?"

"Isn't that why you're drawing this now? Drawing me in this state? So that others will see what they've been blindly ignoring?"

Sebastian Gable placed his pencil on the table and rubbed his eyes.

"There are other girls who should be sitting here, not me. Not me, getting paid for this."

"It's respectable work, Miss Baker."

"That's not what I meant." I clenched my fist. "What you are doing is most wonderful. I meant something else. I came to

San Francisco looking for one thing. I wanted to save my family. Now . . ." My eyes welled. "There's such despicable behavior, all around us. So much sadness, so many others. I didn't expect . . ."

He lifted his eyes to me. "Kula, please don't move. Please." And he began to draw on a new sheet like a madman.

So I let my lip tremble and let those tears roll down my cheeks, and I didn't try to stop them or rub them away or think them sober or anything. I let the tears come until my bare shoulders were shaking up and down, and poor Mr. Gable had to stop and fetch me a cup of tea and a large white handkerchief. And even then I wept, for there were so many souls for whom I had to shed tears.

When it came time to leave, I didn't bother to pin up my hair, but only combed it and pulled it into a ribbon at my neck. And I kissed Sebastian Gable on both cheeks, and hugged him as if he were my uncle.

I arrived home only to see that a carriage sat at the curb before Miss Everts's house, a carriage bearing the crest of a dragon, tongue darting in flame.

Will waited in the drawing room. Waited for me.

"The auto is in repair. But would you like to take a drive? The sunset is worth the slow pace. And I can still manage a horse." He laughed, then paused. "What have you done with your hair? But"—and he reached for a long curl that had found its way over my shoulder—"it's most lovely. Like you."

I waved him away. "Will. Please." I was too drained to put up with his pretty words.

"Please what, Kula?" His voice sounded hard. It surprised me.

"I'm sorry. I'm awfully tired." And, I realized, probably without a bed to myself, since my unexpected guest was still hidden in my room.

"I can't imagine why. You don't want to see me? What have you been up to?" The playfulness had returned, but his charms were not working on me this evening.

"I didn't say that."

Will lifted his hand again, this time to tug at my belt. It was a familiar, possessive gesture, and it bothered me. "Now, Kula. I've come out of my way to entertain you."

I put my hand over his, met his eyes. "Please don't."

"Well. Fine then." My perfect easy Will turned stony. I could not let him go like this, not if I ever wanted to get him back. And he was all I had left.

"No. You don't understand."

For a moment, all things hung in balance. Will eyed me, lips pursed. I swung on the end of his finger, where he'd wrapped it through my belt loop. Then he burst into one of his incandescent smiles.

"Tomorrow, then."

I nodded, forcing a smile in return.

And before I could resist, Will pulled me close and kissed me firmly on the lips, one of his hands finding my waist, the other my loose hair, so intimate I was shocked, and further shocked that I let myself drift into his embrace and let him kiss me, all desire.

"Tomorrow." His voice was soft, and he left me standing in the middle of the room on wobbly legs.

I climbed the stairs to my room, trying to steady my heart, my mind.

Yue was awake, and Mei Lien was attempting to detangle the rat's nest of her hair. I sat on the floor with them.

"After this, she needs a bath." I wrinkled my nose as I plucked a louse from Yue's scalp and pinched it between my fingers. "And we have to get rid of these." I groomed Yue gently, swallowing my grief so I could see my task; and every nit I picked I crushed with a vengeance, thinking of Wilkie.

In the night, as I slept curled in my stuffed chair, my eyes found the painting on the wall, illuminated by moonlight. Yes. That was the key—that relationship between the families, between Baker and Henderson and Everts. Will knew more than he'd let on. Dragon symbols, and the brotherhood, and imports, and his father . . . the question of where to find the key to these interlocked secrets, I had to hope, could be answered by Will.

Chapter TWENTY-SEVEN

April 16, 1906

"Tradition and location unparalleled, beautiful surroundings, the splendid beaches of the Pacific Ocean, and the famous marine wonder of Seal Rocks, on which hundreds of sea lions have found a congenial roosting place, make the northwestern point of our peninsula . . . one of the most popular, attractive, and interesting points in the immediate vicinity of San Francisco."

—Charles Bundschu, *Merchants' Association Review,* April 1902

WHEN WILL ARRIVED THE NEXT MORNING, I WAS READY to leave with him right away. I didn't want either Miss Everts or Jameson hovering. I needed to be alone with him, for more than one reason.

"I have plans today to drive you all over the peninsula," he said. He leaned close to my ear as we walked out the door. "So much nicer without our chaperone, eh?"

Our chaperone: David. I turned my head away, bit my lip. David was gone. And I needed Will, and I also needed his answers to my questions.

Will's automobile was waiting for us, repaired, and so there was no possibility of conversation until we reached our destination. The weather had warmed considerably after the rainy cold spell, and Will had removed the bonnet from the top of the auto. He gave me a scarf to tie over my hat and handed me a long coat—a duster—to keep my clothes clean. We drove west to the ocean.

The ocean!

We stopped once for a bit of view, shaded by chaparral. Will spun me around to face him and smiled his melting smile. Everything in me said: Kula Baker, don't be a fool; but his angled features, perfect chin, soft eyes sucked me in, and common sense left me. I let him kiss me again, even though I knew I was being stupid. I didn't feel for him the way I felt for David. And there was something about Will, something not nice about how quickly that smile went from dazzling to mean, that bothered me. But his lips on mine felt so lovely that I let him kiss me on and on, his soft lips on mine.

The passing of other tourists and the fact that we were so obvious tugged me out of my reverie. I was grateful that we were out in public, if only to save me from myself. At last, Will helped me back into the automobile; heaven knows I needed the help.

Will drove all the way west to the Cliff House, to show me that magnificent structure and the rocky promontory on which it sat above the golden sands. Cliff House was all turrets and arches and balconies. We took lunch at a table by a window, and I had no eye for the food: I wanted to watch the waves and sea lions below. The sparkling sea with its foaming breakers. The gulls floating as if suspended.

Yet this brilliant day—with its rich salt smells and softly thundering waves, and with Will's constant attentions, his fingers playing with mine—was clouded by my worries. I had to open the last door between us, get everything out in the open. I had to uncover what he knew because I needed his help. Time was running out for my father. And I needed to be sure about Will and his feelings for me. It wasn't until we were strolling along the sand, after he'd kissed me yet again, as he tossed rocks out into the water, that I ventured my question to him.

"What do you know about the connection between your family and the Everts . . . and mine? Henderson and Everts and Baker, and the brotherhood?"

Will's rock sailed out over the waves, splashing far out. He shielded his eyes and looked at the blue Pacific. "What should I know about that?"

"In the past, our grandfathers, or great-grandfathers, were friends. And I think that seal, your seal, with the dragon had to do with it. We're all connected. Isn't that something?"

He bent for another rock, and hurled it even farther out. "That's something."

"Listen, Will. I need you to listen. The reason I came to San Francisco. My father . . . he owns a box with important things in it. He said it was here, and he asked me to come and find it. But it's been lost. I must find it. It's . . . it's life and death."

"You've told me this already." Will weighed a rock in his palm, turning it in his fingers. "You told me about the box at the party. Your father's an outlaw, and you need some box he had. Your father, Nat Baker, a most wanted man."

The wind was knocked clean out of me. I'd been so foolish at that party, how could I have been so careless as to have told him all of my secrets? I had told him about the box. I had told him my father was an outlaw.

But I was convinced I'd never told him my pa's name.

"How—how do you know about my pa?" My voice trembled. Had Will had been lying to me? He knew about Pa. What else did he know?

Will threw the rock, hitting an outcropping out in the surf.

"Kula, I know all about the box. I know all about you. About your little pretense. Artist's model? I don't think so." Will's smile vanished, replaced by a chiseled, cold expression. He did not look directly at me. "Why are you ruining our nice day with these questions? Why ruin everything?"

"I'm ruining everything?" I tried to keep my voice light.

"Leave it alone, Kula, and we can still be friends."

"Will, I can't leave this alone. This is why I'm here. My father's life is at stake."

He sighed, an exasperated sigh. "I know. Fine. You've already spoiled it. All right. Yes, I know all about the box, and I also know Josiah Wilkie. There, are you happy?"

My legs buckled, as if they would collapse under me. I reached out my hand to him, my hand grasping at the air between us. "You know Wilkie? He's . . . he's tried to hurt me, he's framed my father—"

"Really."

"Will." I was practically pleading now. "Will, you asked about my name. We talked about your family crest, the dragon symbol. You knew everything all along?" I prayed he would be honest with me. I prayed he wasn't deceiving me now. I prayed he hadn't been deceiving me about his feelings for me.

He glanced at me and away again. "I think it's time I took you back."

"Will, please?" I put my hand on his arm. He pulled away. He turned and looked at me, and the hard stare he gave me was like a hand shoving me away.

"Your foolish questions spoiled it all. I was trying to keep you from finding out, so we could still have a good time. What did you think, Kula? Did you think I was going to *marry* you?"

Of course I had. I'd thought he cared for me. I'd thought he'd save me, save Pa. A heavy weight pressed on me. "I . . . I thought you liked me."

"Liked you! Of course I liked you." His eyes were cold, steely. "I still like you. Very much. But I could never marry someone like you." He laughed, harsh. "It was fun. And you're very pretty, lots of fun. But look at who I am. Look at who you are. I could never be serious about you. It doesn't matter who your grandfather was. Your father's a thief and you're a maid! My father would never approve of you—you're not suitable. You, and your father. You're both—"

"Oh, Will. Stop." I put my hand over my mouth. Now I understood. That day in the rain, at his house. He didn't want his father to know he'd taken me in. His father wouldn't approve of me.

"And that box of yours? That box belongs to *my* family. And I've got it now. Did you think that I'd give it to you or something? That I'd help you find it? No. Your father can't have it. He's a criminal—he killed a man. And I won't let him ruin all my father's work, just so he can—what? After all he's done? What makes you think that I'd save your father from hanging?" He practically spit the words at me.

"You— You have the box." I barely breathed the words.

"Of course I do. For goodness' sake, Kula, you don't think Wilkie would do this on his own, do you? Who do you think Wilkie works for?" Will's voice shook as he spoke, and it was the only reason I didn't fly into a rage and attack him there and then.

"Just what do you think is going on, Will?" I asked. "Do you really know what Wilkie does? What he's done to others? How could you hire him, knowing all of that?"

"I know all I need to." He walked away from me. "That box is for my father. And he's proud of me for getting it for him." Will stood with his back to me; I could sense the uncertainty that radiated from him, even as his words flew like daggers. "It was a mistake, spending this much time with you. At first I only did so because my father wanted me to keep an eye on you. And then it was easy. You're so . . . entertaining. As long as you didn't know anything, we could have fun." His voice softened. "I didn't expect . . ."

"What?" That he'd grown to care for me? "Will?"

"I'm taking you home."

There was no hand-holding now. I hugged the passenger side, staring out the window, worrying that I would be sick, right there in Will's automobile, for all the awful feelings rising inside me. I'd believed Will, trusted him. I gripped the door handle tighter, fighting the urge to shout angry words at him. My head throbbed, and my heart pounded. I was betrayed, and all alone.

Will did not see me to the door. For that, I was glad.

I went up to my room, where I found that Mei Lien paced and fretted and Yue wept silently. I wasn't sure I could take anything more. I was near to broken.

I sighed. "What's happened?"

"Wilkie. He came here. To the house."

I began to tremble "He came here? Why?"

"He knows where we hide her. He knows she runs here."

A fierce protective feeling for Mei Lien and Yue rose up in me. I had nothing left to fight for except these girls. Pa was as good as dead; my heart was turned to stone. I had no power over Will and his father. I'd lost David; I'd lost Will. The box was in Will's hands, or by now his father's—it made no difference. My future was a bare ruin. I had nothing left except to take my revenge on Wilkie for what he did—for what he was still doing—to these girls. "What did he do?"

"Talks to Jameson." She wrung her hands. "I hide up here with Yue."

All my sorrow coalesced into anger at Wilkie. "He can't take her away. She's not his slave. He doesn't own her."

"He think so. She a slave to him."

"How could he know where she is, Mei Lien?"

"Someone tells."

I shook my head. "But, who . . ." Miss Everts—it must have been her. I stormed out of my room to confront Miss Everts at once, but she was not in her room. Jameson materialized in the door.

"Where is she?"

"She's gone out." His blank eyes regarded me.

"Jameson, I— I wish to do some shopping. Take me into town." If I couldn't find Miss Everts, I'd look for Wilkie. I'd look where I'd seen him before.

Everything was at an end for me. David was gone. Will had betrayed me. My pa . . . I had no more hope. I had nothing left to lose, except the fight over these girls.

It was time to make an end of this business.

Chapter TWENTY-EIGHT

April 16, 1906

> *"The Barbary Coast! . . . That sink of moral pollution, whose reefs are strewn with human wrecks . . . The coast on which no gentle breezes blow . . ."*
>
> —*San Francisco Call*, November 28, 1869

JAMESON TOOK ME DOWN TO MARKET STREET. I ASKED him to drop me near the department store where Miss Everts had purchased my gown.

"I'll walk home." Jameson looked skeptical. I didn't care. "I'll be back by four." By that time, I knew I would have found Wilkie, or I'd have given up.

I went into the store and made a few purchases with some of the money Mr. Gable had paid me for the sittings. Things for Yue, mostly: a shawl, a skirt and shirtwaist, and some underthings, all of which I arranged to be delivered to Mei Lien at Miss Everts's.

Then when I was sure Jameson had left, I slipped out the side door and headed straight for the alley where I'd last seen Wilkie.

It was silent and deserted. I walked all the way down to the end, but found nothing save for scraps of paper that eddied along the gutter. I turned and headed back toward Market. The sun didn't reach to the ground in this alley, and the place felt like the underworld.

I was glad to be on my way back toward safety, and stumped as to where to look next, when a door in a brick front opened ahead and Wilkie stepped out into the alley. Quick as a fox, I darted into the shadows along the wall.

He was the very devil. I felt like I'd called him up from the depths of hell. But now that I'd found him, what on earth was I going to do?

I'd follow him. Perhaps I'd discover something I could use against him. Something to put him behind bars for good.

Thankfully, he didn't look in my direction but stopped to pick his teeth, his other hand resting casual on his hip. He tossed the toothpick into the street, tilted his hat forward over his brow, and walked out of the alley and onto Market.

Stepping as quietly as I could, I followed him down the street. When he paused, I paused, staring into windows at my own reflection, or rifling through my things, my back turned to him. Wilkie had caught me unawares too many times before—I would not let it happen again. I'd honed some keen skills for stalking in the woods, to the misfortune of more than one rabbit.

Wilkie marched down Market toward the Embarcadero, the ferry landing and trolley station at the edge of the bay. He seemed fixed on a destination; I was fixed on him. Cable cars trundled past; autos honked and tooted; boys whistled. The air was choked with the acrid, raw smells of the city, masking the clean salt smell that wafted in only when the breeze picked up.

I was a block or so behind him when Wilkie suddenly turned

right, and I stopped, realizing where he was headed. The Barbary Coast.

I waited for what felt like several long minutes, but was most likely only a few seconds, staring across Market, dwarfed by the buildings that towered above my head and blocked out the late-day light. Fear pressed against me—I dared not go back to the Barbary Coast. And yet the thought of Yue hardened me.

I took a deep breath and pressed on. When I reached the intersection where Wilkie had turned, I stopped again.

Wilkie had disappeared. I'd waited too long, and lost him. I stared down the street. Within sight of the thriving businesses of Market, the Barbary was a seedy refuge, with saloons spilling music and raucous laughter. I took a few halting steps.

Men staggered and women leaned and loitered. At one tavern a man thrust his head out the door and hollered at me, using foul, coarse words. I kept my head up and continued walking, looking for Wilkie, determined to find him.

But instead I found Min.

She hovered in a doorframe just beyond the corner, slipping in and out of the shadows, but there was no mistaking. I stopped, then stepped backward, turning to put the corner between us. She'd saved me from Wilkie—perhaps this was my chance to help her at last. If she was finally alone, away from Wilkie, why then, maybe I could spirit her away. But I needed to be sure.

From the far end of the alley a man approached Min's doorway. I jerked back from the corner, plastering myself out of sight. I put my hands on the cold stone, pressed my back against the wall, mashed myself against it, closed my eyes. David. The man coming down the alley toward Min was David.

I heard their voices; I was only just around the corner. I couldn't make out words; in fact, they spoke in their own tongue. Their tone was enough. Familiar, hushed, affectionate. David, familiar and affectionate with Min. With Wilkie's Min.

David had let me go. He hated Wilkie. It must be that David was trying to rescue Min, just as I was. But for different reasons. Of course, David and Min—it made sense. They were the same.

I shut my eyes. I could hear them talking, so familiar. A tear rolled down my cheek, stopped at my trembling chin.

David's voice became animated; I opened my eyes and leaned around the corner, trying to see.

"Ah, missie. And here we are again." That familiar cadence, rasping and harsh, came from behind me like a slap right between my shoulder blades.

I'd forgotten how big Wilkie was. He stood so close, my stomach clenched from the stench of his breath.

A bubble of loathing and fear rose up quick at the sight of him. Fear that was compounded by the thought of Min and David standing just around the corner, unaware that this evil man was merely a few feet away. A prickle of sweat beaded on my forehead.

I sucked in my breath. "Wilkie, I was looking for you." I tried to edge down the wall away from the corner, to draw him with me and away from David and Min. But he only angled closer, so I couldn't move.

"Ah! Well, what d'you know. That makes two of us. Me looking for you, too, that is. And you know what? You thought I didn't know you were on my tail?" He gestured with his finger. "You weren't following me, girl, I was following you."

"Stay away from Yue." My knees shook, but my voice was sure.

His eyebrows shot up. "Now, Kula, that's no way to talk to your friend."

"I'm not your friend. You stay away from those girls. You don't own them."

"Ah, don't I now?"

"No, you don't! Stay away. And I'll make sure you suffer for every injustice done to them."

He smiled, that missing tooth a gaping black hole. "You can make sure of nothing, girl. I got to your father, and now I have you."

"No one has me."

"That so? You know, you'd fetch a fair price, you would. Now what if I was to tell you them girls is mixed up in the business about your pa's box?"

That stopped me, choked my words in my throat. From a distance I heard a steamer horn and the clang of a cable-car bell. "How is that possible? You don't even have the box anymore—Will told me."

"Oh, so you know that everybody's mixed up in it. Will, that Miss Everts, and that man of hers is, too."

A weak sickliness weighed on my limbs. Wilkie moved closer to me still, close enough I had to turn my face away. My back was pressed so hard against the bricks, I thought I might push right through the wall.

He whispered. "You ever hear tell of folks being shanghaied? It's when someone's knocked for a loop and wakes up to find hisself—or *herself*—on a ship. Bound for the Orient. Where there's good money for girls like you. Just a wink and you'd be gone, and no one would ever find you. This place around here, nobody cares what happens."

Even though people moved about and it was broad daylight, anything I did was useless. What had I been thinking coming after him? Coming here? Wilkie could throw me over his shoulder and march me away, and even if I screamed, it'd merit scarcely a look. No one knew where I was, and even if they did, no one in this town cared for me—not Will, not Miss Everts, not David . . .

David— David was right around the corner. David and Min. Wilkie had followed me, and I'd led him straight to a meeting between David and Min.

I didn't want Wilkie to see them together. I feared for them, too. I thought about the money I'd earned from Sebastian Gable. "What if I told you I could pay you?"

"You?" He threw back his head and roared with laughter. And then to my horror, he stepped to one side, and caught David and Min in his line of sight. Wilkie's laugh cut short, and I saw David and Min, their faces, and I knew. And so did they. We were all caught in Wilkie's web.

"Well," said Wilkie. David stepped in front of Min, putting himself between her and Wilkie. "Ain't that a pretty sight. And don't that beat all. And now I know who's been betraying me." Wilkie's face grew dark, and I saw in it the hurt, the anger, and all directed at Min.

I tried to reach Min before Wilkie did, but she was faster. She pushed past David and past me and went direct to Wilkie. He took her chin in his great fist as David tried to press on them, but Min thrust out her arm against David. She succumbed to Wilkie.

"Shall we have a talk, yes, my love?" said Wilkie.

Min's eyes closed, and she nodded as best she could.

"You leave her alone." David started forward.

"Or what?" Wilkie turned his narrowed eyes on David. He lowered his voice. "What are you going to do to me? Look around. You think you start a fight in here you can finish? I got more friends in this here byway than you have in the entire country. So back off. You think you can protect that one there, too?"

He meant me, and now I saw—David could not help Min and me both, not here.

"Back off," Wilkie repeated.

David stepped away.

Min reached her hands up and took Wilkie's in her own. "I love you."

"Yes, I'm sure you do. And I love you, too, my Jezebel. So off we go then, right? And you"—Wilkie looked back at me—"don't you worry none, I'll come find you again, girl. I'll find you." Wilkie took Min's arm in that vice grip, and David and I, helpless, watched them walk away, Min stumbling behind Wilkie.

"He'll kill her," David said. I heard the anguish in his voice.

"He loves her. I've seen it. He hurts her, but he'd never . . ."

David looked at me as if I were simple. "Do you think that matters anymore, Kula? Come on, Wilkie was right. We're fish in a barrel here in the Barbary."

"You were here for her."

He laughed as if I was an idiot. "She's a spy. She watches Wilkie's movements. That's what he meant—he knew there was a spy on him, and now he knows it's been her. She's been helping us so we can find out where the girls are, when to get them out.

She's been doing this for months. And if you hadn't interfered, it wouldn't have turned out like this." David grabbed me by the shoulders. "What are you doing here? You've been interfering right from the start. All that business about your father's box. You've been messing with things that we've set up, and so many lives in the balance. You've cost us so much. And Min's life, now, that's almost certain."

"I was trying to help!" His words stung—though I knew they were true. It was because of me that Min . . . I'd as good as led Wilkie right to her. I pressed my palm to my forehead, shut my eyes.

"No, Kula. You weren't helping anyone but yourself. Let's think. You said you were trying to find a way to get your father out of a jam, but really you wanted whatever treasures were in that box. When we first met, you pretended to be Miss Everts's guest, not her servant. You played all sincere when you just wanted to become a society girl. Between me and Will, you chose Will because he has the money, the power. You've been playing two sides of the fence for too long."

I pulled away from him and leaned back against the bricks. "You're right." I knew what my heart wanted now, but it was too late. Too late.

He waved his hand in the air, not looking at me. "That won't help Min."

"What can we do?" I'd lost him forever, but I couldn't lose Min.

"We need to see Miss Everts."

"Miss Everts—no! David, she's in league with Wilkie. I've seen it! We can't—"

"No." David shook his head, with a harsh laugh. "No, she's not.

Phillipa Everts has been walking a very tight rope for a very long time. You'll see."

"But I saw her giving him money. She's—"

"Come on. You'll understand." I followed him out of the alley, and out of the Barbary, but he wouldn't look my way.

David was right. I hadn't saved my father. I'd let myself believe that I stood a chance in Will's world, and threw away the one man who held my heart. And I hadn't saved Min, but doomed her. David was right. I'd had my mind fixed on myself.

Chapter TWENTY-NINE

April 16, 1906

"It was then I began to understand that
everything in the room had stopped,
like the watch and the clock, a long time ago."

—*Great Expectations*, Charles Dickens, 1861

MISS EVERTS WAITED IN HER DRAWING ROOM, ALMOST as if she knew we were coming. At first glance, she looked as she always did: done up in her silk and satin. But when David and I walked into the room, I noticed something new. The dress she wore today—expensive, surely, for the fabric was blue silk and the details finely made—was fraying a bit along the hem, and the lace had been mended more than once. And she wore no jewelry.

David spoke first. "Miss Everts, Wilkie discovered Min with me. He knows about her."

"That's unfortunate." She spoke softly and, I was surprised to hear, not without compassion.

"We have to get to Min—"

Miss Everts pursed her lips and didn't respond.

I clenched my fists. I could no longer play these games. "Miss Everts. I'm hiding a girl in my bedroom. I'd wager you know that already."

She nodded. "The clothes you bought her were delivered in your absence. And Jameson isn't blind." She smiled, a fleeting smile. "I'm proud of you for thinking to protect the poor thing."

I straightened my shoulders. "And I saw you with Wilkie. I saw you hand him money at the Hendersons'. You're working with him. You've been working with him all along." My voice rose with every word I spoke.

David, standing at my elbow, coughed.

She said, "Well, now. David, tell her, for pity's sake. She knows enough of it anyway and is only going to keep getting it wrong."

"Kula, Miss Everts is trying to save the girls. But to do that, she has to either buy them or steal them away. It all has to be done with great care and secrecy; that's why no one told you anything. No one in the law wants to get mixed up in Chinese business. No one in the government will back us up. Wilkie has powerful connections. We have to do what we can."

"I have a home across the bay, if you remember," Miss Everts said. "That's our way station. We smuggle them out, to safety."

"So," I said, "Yue and Mei Lien, you stole them?"

"Not Mei Lien," said Miss Everts. "Jameson bought her straight off the docks. We've let Josiah Wilkie think that Jameson has a . . . fetish. That's what you saw me doing that night—buying girls." Miss Everts sighed. "But it's expensive. I haven't enough money left for buying these poor girls outright. I've just about run through everything. Stealing them before Wilkie gets his hands on them is our only recourse now."

The candlesticks, the silver, the worn clothes, the missing jewelry. I knew where the money had come from. She was, indeed, trying to save souls. I'd misjudged her, and badly. In that instant, Miss Everts gained my undying devotion. I bit the inside of my cheek, took a breath. "But I don't understand. Mr. Henderson was there when you paid Wilkie . . . How are the Hendersons involved? And what about my father?"

David spoke up. "Wilkie's been in and out of the business for years, trafficking in human flesh. The Hendersons, well, William Henderson, and now Will, employ Wilkie to do various bits of their dirty work."

This was beyond imagining. "But how could they? How could the Hendersons let Wilkie do such a thing? Trafficking in girls . . ." I could hardly form the words.

"They don't know." Miss Everts was firm. "At least young Will does not. He thinks it's all import and export of art and other goods, not slaves. When you saw me in that room, Kula, William Henderson thought I was paying Wilkie for some stolen art."

I whispered, "Why didn't you tell me?" I thought about what I might have done differently, what might have changed . . .

David said, "We didn't want to involve you. This is dangerous business. We didn't want you to know."

"But whyever not?" My blood boiled up. "If I don't know about it, then I can't help to stop it, can I? I hate it! It's outrageous and ugly."

"Of course it is," said Miss Everts. "Dear girl, it's the way the world works. Unfortunately, there's much that is ugly about life."

I thought I knew. I thought I knew so much, about Miss Everts, about the girls . . . about everything. I'd seen ugliness and conniving and tricks and ways to manipulate, and I thought I'd understood. I thought my world was a harsh one, and if I just escaped my own life, it would all be so much better. Everything I believed was turned upside down and inside out, and ugly things were tumbling from its pockets.

"I want to help," I said.

David spoke. "We have to get Yue out of here and across the bay. Wilkie knows Yue's here, but I don't think he'll act, at least not yet. Still, we don't have much time. William Henderson is managing a shipment of art that leaves here early on the morning of the eighteenth, and that's our cover." He turned to me to explain, and I saw the emotion in his eyes. "Miss Everts takes the art, stores it, and when she disperses it to customers, that's when we smuggle the girls out of San Francisco with the art." He brushed his hair back from his forehead. "It's a tricky business. We use oversize crates to get them across the bay. Everything is done at the last possible moment. The last thing we want is for any of them to suffer further."

"And when they reach Sausalito? Where do the girls go then?"

"We have connections," said Miss Everts. "Thank the good Lord there are still decent people left in the world. They find employment elsewhere, where people will treat them right." She watched me for a minute. "Your father, Kula. He's recently become one of our connections."

I cried out. "Why didn't you tell me? Why didn't he tell me?" All of the lies, the betrayal . . . I could have helped them. I pressed my hand to my heart.

She waved her hand. "I didn't see how you could help. I'm concerned that your father's current situation is a result of his involvement."

David said, "We think he was set up. He and a Quaker family just outside of Yellowstone Park were tending to one large group of girls we had traveling through."

"The Blacks," Miss Evert said. "I imagine you could put the rest of the picture together."

I was right—Pa had been set up. And finally, I understood. Those girls were Pa's unfinished business; that was why he hadn't joined me at Mrs. Gale's. Mr. Black: murdered, but not by my father. And murdered because he was helping the girls. "Then we have to uncover their scheme. Expose them all. It's the only chance my father has. The only chance any of them have." My voice was firm.

David and Miss Everts exchanged a look.

"What?" I asked. "I will help with this—you're talking about my pa here."

David said, "We'll try. Let's get the girls out first. And Min."

Miss Everts reached for her fan. "Heavens, it's warm for April. David, please open some windows."

I gripped my arms tight, hugging myself as if to keep my heart from exploding from my chest. Everything I believed in was shaken from me, even my old suspicions. Saving my pa had been all about me; now saving my pa was about something larger. I watched David as he unlatched and shifted the windows open, letting in the warm, moist late afternoon air.

Miss Everts said, "Now, Kula. I do have something for you to do. Mr. Sebastian Gable has asked that you attend the opera with him tomorrow night."

"What? Me?" Opera? I was clueless.

"Caruso is singing. It will be quite the event."

"I don't know who that is. And really, I don't see how that will help anything. It won't help me find the box. And it certainly won't help Min or those girls."

"Ah, but it will. Wilkie often acts as bodyguard to the Hendersons. And both father and son will be attending. They will all be at the Opera House on Tuesday night."

"But what has that to do with me? I don't understand!"

"My dear girl, you want to help. By attending and drawing the attentions of Mr. Henderson and his son and Wilkie, not to mention keeping an eye on them, you will afford us a window to get the crates ready for the next morning. Thanks to Min, we've learned that a ship with girls is due in during the night Tuesday and the girls offloaded into a warehouse. David needs to bribe the guard and spirit the girls out of the warehouse and out of the city at dawn on Wednesday. I must assist him. I shall not be missed at the opera if the Henderson eyes are upon you." She raised her fan, beating it vigorously about her face. "I wonder if we shall have storms. This stillness and heat are unnatural."

I would hear Caruso, whoever he was, sing opera, whatever that was. I had twenty-four hours to learn what I could from Miss Everts about both so I would not appear foolish. I had no time to find another gown; I'd have to wear the scarlet-colored gown again. Perhaps it would remind Will of a time when he looked on me with favor. But after our argument at the beach, I wasn't sure I wanted him to look at me at all—not after what I'd learned today. Not after knowing that he had my father's box, that he might even be involved in the slavery of Chinese girls.

But still, perhaps I could help draw his eye. Maybe I could confront him and shame him into revealing the location of the box. More than anything, I wanted to help David. I knew now what I wanted, who I cared for. I had two deeply intertwined goals: to help David help the girls, and to save my pa before time ran out.

Chapter THIRTY

April 17, 1906

"I had sung in Carmen that night, and the opera had one with fine eclat. We were all pleased, and, as I said before, I went to bed that night feeling happy and contented."

—Interview with Enrico Caruso about
his experience of the Great 1906 Earthquake,
The Sketch, London, reprinted in *The Theatre*, July 1, 1906

THE HEAVY SCENT OF ORCHIDS WAS OVERWHELMING. As was everything else about the lobby of the Grand Opera House in San Francisco: the enormous cut-glass chandelier that descended in three tiers from the ceiling, the jewelry that adorned the necks and wrists of the society matrons in silks and satins who were escorted by their overstuffed husbands, the blood-red carpet covering the stairs in a velvet nap so thick my feet nearly disappeared.

Mr. Gable led me to his personal box, where a chilled bottle of champagne and several flutes waited next to the tufted chairs. On one seat cushion lay a set of gold spyglasses—opera glasses, as I'd been instructed, the better to see the singers from the refined heights of the expensive box seats. Mr. Gable was so solicitous and kind, I finally relaxed a bit. I no longer cared what the other patrons thought of me, of why I might be his companion. Their petty snobbery disgusted me.

I declined the champagne; I'd learned that lesson, thanks to Will. My interests lay in finding the Hendersons, not in dimming my wits. I picked up the opera glasses and scanned the boxes for the one that Mr. Gable said belonged to William Henderson. It was empty.

Rustle and chatter and soft laughter filled the hall. Every few minutes someone knocked on the door behind us, and Mr. Gable admitted yet another member of polite society who had come to converse with the artist and also ogle his companion—me. I felt like a piece of artwork myself, expected to smile and utter polite nonsense while strange men worked their gaze up and down my figure, and their wives bared teeth in forced smiles above their diamond-encrusted necks. This visiting and conversation continued even as the house lights dimmed and the orchestra struck the first stunning notes of *Carmen,* turning my body rigid with anticipation. I turned in my seat to find the Hendersons right across from me.

They'd entered the box and been seated, Mr. Henderson and Will, with Wilkie standing behind in the shadows, his eyes shining like two pinpoints. A thin-lipped, blue-eyed blond girl sat to Will's right, and Will was bent toward her, with his arm resting casually over her chair back.

One little part of me seethed with jealousy. But then I thought of Will's sharp words, and David's kind eyes, and I smiled to myself as Enrico Caruso stepped to the front of the stage and, pulling a flower from his breast pocket, serenaded his love.

Oh, my stars. What a voice. With his rich and wide-ranging tenor, Caruso commanded my full attention at once, and the emotion he packed into his plaintive love song brought goose bumps out all over me. When he finished the aria, I, together with the entire house, jumped to our feet in a spontaneous rush of cheering and applause.

And so it was for the entire performance. When Caruso was not singing, I turned my attentions to the Hendersons. They remained in their box, and Wilkie, too, thank goodness. At least I did not have to worry about David, who was making arrangements to spirit girls out of Chinatown at that very moment. Once, while I was watching Will, his eyes turned toward Sebastian Gable's box and met mine, and I quick lowered the glasses, but I'd caught his expression.

He was sad. He was not smiling, not jovial, not flashing his blond companion that dazzling smile that had made me melt.

I turned my eyes away and back to the stage, where Don Jose was becoming increasingly desperate for the unwilling Carmen.

When Don Jose finally plunged his knife into his defiant, willful lover, I choked with sympathy. Even though I couldn't understand the language, I was transported. The audience called again and again for Caruso to take the stage, and he was pelted with roses and wild cheers.

The opera was over, but the Hendersons remained in their box, clearly enjoying the attentions from the streams of society types who filed in and out under Wilkie's narrowed eyes. If Wilkie had seen me across the way, he didn't acknowledge it. Of course, he couldn't, not with so many respectable people around. Mr. Gable rose; it was time for us to leave. I turned one last time and found Will Henderson's eyes on me. He gave me a wan smile. I stared coldly back, knowing that I'd been unable to confront him about pa's box, vowing to do so the next day. At least I'd served Miss Everts's and David's diversionary purpose.

It was past midnight, and I yawned, openmouthed, as Sebastian Gable escorted me from the Opera House and into his waiting carriage.

"Only a few hours until dawn," Mr. Gable remarked.

"Yes." I thought about how, at dawn, at least a few of those desperate girls would find a new and better life, thanks to Miss Everts and David. I thanked Mr. Gable for a lovely evening and, on arriving back at the house, wearily climbed the stairs.

My room was now my own again, as Yue had joined Mei Lien in her room. I was exhausted, and yet I slept fitfully. It was warm and still, with no breeze coming through my open window. My miserable sleepless state and my open curtains had me up with the first dawn light.

It was an eerie morning, silent. I'd spent so much of my childhood in the woods that I knew how the first light of day was always accompanied by the racket of rising birds. On this day, there was no sound of birds. It felt all wrong. The ticking of the clock in my room sounded like a hammer, pounding. Five o'clock. There was no more sleep for me; I got up and dressed. The scarlet gown lay draped over the back of my stuffed chair.

I had just finished dressing, but with my hair still hanging loose in its single braid, when the world around me fell apart.

Chapter THIRTY-ONE

April 18, 1906

"I was within a stone's throw of that city hall when the hand of an avenging God fell upon San Francisco. The ground rose and fell like an ocean at ebb tide. Then came the crash. Tons upon tons of that mighty pile slid away from the steel framework and destructiveness of that effort was terrific."

—Fred J. Hewitt, *San Francisco Examiner*, April 20, 1906

I KNEW AN EARTHQUAKE, THE JOLT WHEN IT FIRST HIT and the roll that followed. I'd experienced the rumblings of the earth a time or two in Yellowstone. But those little knockabouts were nothing compared with this. The floor began to heave, and I was thrown to my hands and knees.

The house creaked and groaned, and the plaster crashed and framing wrenched and wood splintered to fragments. The portrait of my Blue Boy swayed against the wall like the pendulum of a clock. The clattering of bricks tumbling to pavement lifted through my open window and a rumbling noise like thunder that seemed to come from the belly of the earth itself.

After a minute that felt like an eternity all motion stopped, and an eerie silence settled over the house. Thunder rumbled in the distance as walls—whole buildings, from the sound of it—that were shaken loose fell to earth. I stood, all shaky, and had just dusted off my knees when the second shock hit.

This time I ran for my door and stood in the frame, clutching it tight with both hands, for this shock was far worse than the first. The house rose and fell like the ferry would on the roughest sea; porcelain crashed to the floor in the hall below. Outside, something close at hand—one side of the house?—fell with a violent rending and hammering. And the bells. Through my open window came a clamor of bells. Bells in all the steeples of all the churches in the city rang and rang, as if calling to heaven, pleading for help.

When this shock was finished, I stood for a minute, getting my bearings. Then I ran down the stairs toward Miss Everts's room. She clutched at her bedpost, her face drawn and tight. I pulled an evening coat from her wardrobe and threw it over her shoulders.

"Come on," I said to her. "We have to leave in case there are more."

She came with me, like a child, obedient and silent.

In the downstairs hall we were joined by Jameson, Mei Lien, and Yue. Together we stumbled out into the small front yard.

Up and down the street people in various states of undress were also outside, clutching odd belongings—a porcelain vase, a birdcage, a set of books—and everyone was silent in stunned confusion. The only noise came from animals. Dogs barked and horses screamed; birds flapped and squawked in every tree.

The houses on our street had mostly survived, even if their chimneys had not; one house farther down the steep hill shrugged to one side, its front porch on the verge of sliding off like a layer on a tilted cake.

Miss Everts's house had held up surprisingly well. It lost its chimney, which must have been the noise I'd heard, and the bricks were scattered in a fan at the foot of the outside wall. Several windows on the ground floor were broken. An image of Sebastian Gable's wall of windows came into my mind, and I was sure they could not have been spared. I wondered what had happened to all his paintings, and if he was all right.

"Well." Miss Everts seemed recovered. "What an alarming wake-up call."

Jameson stared down toward the city center. "Look." Smoke billowed skyward from several places around the southeastern end of the city.

There were no sounds now: no cable cars, no more church bells, no people; no one moaned or cried out; even the animals had gone quiet. We had all been struck with reverential silence at the awful power of nature.

Mei Lien touched my arm, and I looked at her. "Girls, in cellars."

I started, and turned to Miss Everts. Her lips were set in a thin line. "Yes. In the cellars. We were to move them in half an hour. David might already be there. They would all be trapped if the buildings fell."

"I'll bring round the automobile," Jameson said.

"I shall get dressed. Mei Lien, you and Yue stay here and help Kula—"

"No! I'm going with you." I would not be left behind, not knowing if David had been crushed in the midst of his rescue. I knew he thought I was silly and selfish, but I didn't care; I could only think of him. "Miss Everts, you should stay here."

"Absolutely not," she replied, turning on her heel and marching up the steps and inside.

Within a few minutes it became clear that there were other problems to consider. No water came out of the taps, nor was there gas from the stove. And the automobile could not be brought round until the rubble of the chimney was cleared from the drive.

Miss Everts, dressed now, put her hands to her hips. "There's a hand-pump well at Simpson's Grocery down at the bottom of the hill. Mei Lien, you and Yue will fetch water. We can't survive without water. Kula, you and I will stay here and keep the house safe."

"I'll go find them," said Jameson, meaning David and the girls.

"Please let me go with Jameson," I begged. "He can't manage alone, and I can move fast."

Miss Everts pursed her lips, and then nodded once.

Jameson had long strides, but at least we were headed downhill and I was able to keep up. Once we were out of the Nob Hill neighborhood and into the area of tightly packed tenements, the effects of the earthquake became clear. That's when we began to see real destruction.

Many of these poorly constructed buildings had collapsed entirely, falling in on top of people. We passed a man in nothing but a nightshirt sitting, stunned, upon a pile of rubble. Others were digging through the bricks in an attempt at rescue. Still others stared in the direction of Market Street, where several of the plumes of smoke had grown larger.

Jameson knew just where to go; the girls David had been seeking were warehoused in the Barbary Coast. We threaded our way through people who now carried belongings away from the ruins, in a migration to nowhere, in a state of calm. It was eerie, that calm, broken only by the crying of infants. The adults and older children—it seemed we were all a blank.

Shock, I thought. We're all in shock.

The Barbary, that refuge of all that was foul, was a ruin, her residents, in nightshirts or tuxedos or, most shockingly, nothing at all, drifting along the streets. I averted my eyes as Jameson gave his coat to one unfortunate man, who was naked as a jaybird and who only stared back blank-eyed and confused. Others sifted through the ruins calling after friends in this otherwise friendless place.

Jameson stopped suddenly in front of a pile of rubble, and I realized why. It was gone. The evil building where the girls were imprisoned was gone. The buildings to either side had collapsed as well. I sank to my knees in the rubble. There was no one else here; no one seemed to care about this place. No one searched for loved ones. Only Jameson and I had come looking.

And David. Where was David? I would not picture him buried in this. My mind could not comprehend it.

Jameson clambered over the piles of bricks and broken timbers. After a moment he called out, "Kula, here!" I gathered myself up and ran to him, to the girl he found.

She lay pocketed beneath a timber that had collapsed over her and sheltered her from the crush. Jameson and I had to work at the rubble to dig her out. She was conscious, with scrapes along her thin arms and legs that the scrap of clothing she wore barely covered. She was so small. Her hand fit fully in mine.

We found two more girls buried in this way; we helped them to the curb while we kept on searching. I thought of all who were lost beneath the weight of all those bricks and timbers. I set my teeth and hoped that Wilkie lay buried deep somewhere in this city's pile of death.

I'd seen dead people before. Once in Yellowstone a soldier'd been thrown from his unruly horse, right in the Mammoth parade ground, and he'd landed just so, and there he died. I was carrying a load of my clean washing between buildings. I dropped it all in the mud to run to the boy's side—for he wasn't but a boy—and I saw his blind eyes and his unnaturally kinked neck. I'd been sick, then, right there next to him.

I'd scrubbed that linen for hours after.

Here, a hand, a cold stiff hand, sticking up through the rubble. There, a girl, her hair covered in dust; when I turned her over, her eyelids were creased with black. There, alone, a shoe: tiny, black, like the shoe in Miss Everts's automobile. And there, a flower made of folded crimson tissue paper, someone's only treasure, still perfect, an unblemished paper poppy lying in the rubble.

I couldn't afford to be sick here. We had to save those we could.

We'd just pulled the third girl out when a policeman found us, told us we had to move out.

"But there are people here . . ." I couldn't finish; my throat closed. David. Where was David?

"Miss, we're moving everyone. They're going to blow up buildings to try and stop the fires."

"Blow up the buildings—you can't! There are people trapped here."

"It's the only way to stop the spread of the fires, getting rid of buildings that will burn. You have to leave." Then I understood; in the forests during a fire they cleared swathes of trees to create a firebreak so there would be no fuel for the fire to spread.

Jameson and I continued to search as the policeman moved on to round up others, but there were no more signs of life in this ruin.

We helped the three girls we'd found away from the ruin and

made our way toward Nob Hill. I picked up the smallest and carried her, as she clung to my braid as if to a rope. Jameson carried another and tucked his arm around the shoulders of the third. We made for home. My stomach heaved, but I swallowed it.

"Move along!" The militia was out, men on horseback with rifles. "Looters will be shot!" Fire trucks raced by, their bells clanging, heading for the area south of Market. "Make for Union Square," the police ordered. We tried to hurry, bucking up the hill, carried along in the tide of people who dragged their few belongings bumping behind them. The thud and scrape of trunks on the pavement filled the air, making up for the silence of conversation.

No one seemed able to carry on anything more than a polite, "Pardon me." Or, "May I help?" I made note of people's courtesy, so striking in the circumstances. Or perhaps they could say nothing else because so much of their lives had changed in an instant.

We reached the house with the girls as Miss Everts was setting up a small wood-burning cookstove on the front lawn.

"A policeman came by with orders not to cook inside," she said. "The gas lines are broken and leaking. Mei Lien and I wrestled this old thing out of the smokehouse." She looked us all over, noting that David was not with us. "Let's get these unfortunates inside."

Mei Lien and Yue and I took the girls up to the bedrooms, where we helped them clean up as best we could with so little water, and we gave them fresh clothes. By now, detonations rocked the air every few minutes or so, causing the girls to whimper. I went to my window.

Smoke rose over the city in ever-growing spires. Every minute some new thread rose up to join the cloud.

I went outside, plucked at Miss Everts's sleeve. "Miss Everts, have you heard from David?"

She shook her head. "It was early. He might not have been in the building . . ."

"The telephone—"

"Is not working."

I turned to Jameson, who brought wood round for Miss Everts. "Is there any way—"

An aftershock shook the ground. The girls all cried out, stricken and terrified, and ran out of the house. They huddled on the curb after that, draped in blankets and throws, refusing to go back inside.

Jameson had just cleared the rubble enough to bring out the horseless when a small troop of soldiers made their way to the house. "We need that automobile," their commander said to Miss Everts.

"We do, too," she countered.

"Sorry. We got orders and need automobiles. For the good of the city."

Jameson stood his ground at the door of the vehicle, and the soldier leveled his gun, pointing it at Jameson's chest.

"Roddy," said Miss Everts, laying a hand on Jameson's arm.

I watched them take away the automobile, my fists clenched at my sides. "Miss Everts, I've got to go back and find David."

"No, Kula. It's becoming too dangerous. These men roaming around . . ."

The stream of people escaping the burning lower city became a river. The fires were spread by the broken gas mains. The biggest fire was a black plume over the lower city, filling the sky, drifting up the hill to cover us.

I tugged at Miss Everts's sleeve. "Please."

She turned away.

As did I—I could not wait for her approval. I would find David, so help me. I started off.

"Kula!"

Miss Everts moved toward me. Jameson, bringing another load of wood, placed it on the ground and rested his hand on Miss Everts's shoulder, stopping her. "Let her go."

I went out into the street, moving against the stream of people, pushing against the current, through the faces all hollow and lost, people pulling trunks and pushing wheelbarrows, people with clocks and chairs and books and fine china. I thrust myself through the torrent that became a flood that yanked me back, but I would not be stopped.

Chapter THIRTY-TWO

April 18, 1906

> *"Downtown everything is ruin. Not a business house stands. Theaters are crumbled into heaps. Factories and commission houses lie smouldering on their former sites."*
>
> —Combined *San Francisco Call/Chronicle/Examiner,* published on the presses of *The Oakland Herald,* April 19, 1906

THE MILITIA HERDED THE SWARM OF HUMANITY AWAY from the city center. I couldn't follow the main streets; I had to keep ducking behind abandoned wagons and into side alleyways to keep from being herded away from the city myself.

I made my way down those infernal steep hills—even having grown up in the mountains as I did, these San Francisco hills wore me out—trying to make for Chinatown. It was the only place David would be, other than buried with the girls in the Barbary. Knowing him, he was trying to rescue the entire brotherhood of Chinese people.

I remembered the street along which he and I had walked in Chinatown when I arrived here, but when I reached the bottom of Nob Hill, I recognized nothing. So many buildings had been demolished by the quake, I could hardly get my bearings. Only remnants stood: single walls, one fluted cornice, piles of brick.

A fine white ash had begun to rain down, and the smoke from

the fires rose into the sky, dimming the sun. I slipped behind an overturned cart still attached to its dead horse, trying to avoid another troop of soldiers, who by the look and sound of them had been drinking as they patrolled the now nearly empty streets. They laughed and cursed as they passed my hiding place. I saw small valuables tucked into their belts or slung from their bayonets, and half-empty bottles hung from their hands. I barely breathed until they were away out of sight.

I followed the signs as they changed from English to Chinese to find my way into the ruins of Chinatown.

Here the streets were empty but for scurrying rats and the cats that skulked after them. Smoke from fires rose not far off now. I had no idea where I was. I stood in the middle of the street and called David's name.

My voice echoed among the buildings; from the near distance came the thunder of an explosion.

"David! David Wong!" I shouted again.

From an alley some hundred yards away a figure dressed all in black shouted something at me, gesturing.

"David Wong!" I shouted back.

He threw his hands in the air and turned away and disappeared.

I felt drained, as if all life had slipped out of me. I was lost. Without David, I realized, I was lost. I sank to the ground, careless of my once fine skirt, placing my palms on the earth that was now dust and rubble and ash.

My pa's death loomed ever closer; Will had betrayed me; David was gone, perhaps buried in the ruin that lay around me.

Another explosion rocked the ground under my fingers, closer still, and a tower of flame rose into the air, and I threw my arms over my head as bits of wreckage dropped around me. It was no use; it would do no good for me to die here. I stood and made my way back toward the north, back toward Nob.

The stream of people moving up the hills was reduced to a steady trickle, and the sky was gray and black with smoke. The sidewalk was riddled with cracks, like the glaze on an old pot, as I put one foot in front of the other, climbing that hill, my heart heavy, my legs trembling.

"Kula?"

He stood in the street. I'd reconciled myself to the notion he was dead, so at first I thought perhaps it was his ghost, his hair and face and clothes so gray with ash and dust. "David?"

And then he opened his arms, and I found myself wrapped in them, and I didn't care who saw us or what they'd think. I wept into his shoulder as he stroked my hair and whispered, "Shh, shh."

I pulled away so I could look into his eyes. "I was lost."

He put his hands on my cheeks. "And now you're not." He kissed me on the lips, soft, our first kiss, and sweet. He pulled back and used his thumbs to brush away my tears. We didn't speak for a long time. We were together. I was whole. Whole and forgiven.

Then David's face grew serious. "Kula, I found Min. She's dead."

"The earthquake?"

David's face grew dark. "Her throat was cut."

"Oh!" I covered my mouth, thinking I might be ill. "Wilkie . . . ?"

"Who else? He is a true demon."

"Hey!" A soldier came up, two others behind him. "Get along." He glared at David, and then at me. His rifle sat in the crook of his arm. "Clear the street. There's a curfew on, and looters will be shot. *Sabe*, Chinaboy?"

"Sabe," David said, his voice tight.

I didn't tell the soldier that the only looters I'd seen were wearing uniforms.

David pulled me against him as we climbed the hill to Miss Everts's house.

"I talked to some of the firefighters. There's no water," David said. "The mains are all broken and leaking. They can't stop the fires. We have to hope they can keep the fires contained. All the area south of Market is in flames. One of our people who worked with dynamite on the railroads said that those manning the dynamite don't know what they're doing. They're using far too much. And black powder, of all things! They can't control it. They're blowing up too much and hitting gas lines and throwing sparks everywhere and making things worse." His arm drew tighter around me. "This city will never recover."

Miss Everts saw us coming up the street and sent Jameson to greet us. It was a sweet reunion, even though few words were spoken.

We all turned to stare over the lower city, a city in flames.

"Perhaps they can stop the fires before they reach us." It was the most I'd ever heard from Jameson.

Miss Everts cooked everything left in the house, and we handed out what we could to those still passing us by on their migration up the hill—even water, as long as we could spare it. My shoulders ached; my shirtwaist was dirty and torn; my skirt hem was frayed. I rolled the waistband of my skirt to hike it up so I could work without tripping.

But each time I caught a glimpse of David, my heart pulsed with happiness.

The detonations continued through the night. The flames burned like glowing coals below us; the city buildings crumbled and fell, one after another. More families marched by, struggling with their few belongings. No one slept. Jameson and David alternately patrolled, but there was little need; the militia was everywhere, and order was maintained.

The occasional rifle shot in the distance attested to that; David felt sure they were shooting looters.

We all stayed outside in the night. In the cooler night air the fires ebbed somewhat; but I knew wildfires and how they could trick you that way, getting quiet at night only to explode with the sunrise.

The smallest of the girls lay with her head in my lap and her thin arms around my waist as I sat on the porch steps staring down the hill. I stroked the poor girl's face. She shifted and began to suck her thumb, clutching the tail of my braid in her other fist.

So young to be so ill used. I'd thought myself a slave to my life; I hadn't understood. I'd never suffered like that.

Thursday dawned red and gray and sunless, and ash continued to fall around us like delicate snow. Thursday. It had been only a week since the Henderson ball. How was it possible for the entire world to shift its moorings in only a week?

About noon, the militia came again. Their captain dismounted and approached Miss Everts. "Ma'am, you'll all have to leave. The fires will be here within hours."

Miss Everts clutched her skirts, then dropped them, several times in succession. "Girls," she said, "each of you take a piece of artwork, something you can carry. Jameson, you know what to do. David, come with me." She turned to the captain. "We will leave shortly."

He bowed and stepped to the side, but he did not leave until we did some hours later, our arms full. Miss Everts hauled one laden trunk on wheels and David a second. Jameson pushed an old two-wheeled cart stacked high.

For my part, I carried several things, but the largest was my Blue Boy. As we marched up the hill, herded by our soldiers, I turned and looked back. The conflagration had reached the lower part of the street. I could see now that Miss Everts's house would burn in the night.

It seemed that all San Francisco would burn, and it wasn't over yet.

Chapter THIRTY-THREE

April 19–22, 1906

"Light shocks all night and every half hour explosions from the city, where they are blowing up all the buildings. All San Francisco is gone now out to 20th Street on one side and Dayton and Union on the North Beach side . . . the Earthquake broke all the water mains . . ."

—Letter from Maria Cochrane Praetzel
to her cousin, April 18, 1906

FIRE PURIFIES, SO THEY SAY. ASHES TO ASHES.

I'd seen fires in Yellowstone, mostly in the late summer and fall, when things got dry. Flames would jump from treetop to treetop with the slightest spark, and burst like exploding candles. I'd seen the pillars of smoke that rose into the air, towered into the air like thunderclouds lit beneath by a hellish red. There's no stopping a wildfire when it gets going. Only nature can bring a change that will turn the tide.

My pa, he'd pack us up and out of the forest before a wildfire. "There's no safe place here until the snow falls, boys."

With the mains broken, there was no water to fight the fires here in San Francisco. The weather was hot and dry and unseasonable, and the fires made their own grim weather.

There'd be no stopping these fires, not without a miracle.

We left Miss Everts's and kept walking, until, footsore and

exhausted, we arrived at the marina at the north end of Van Ness. There we set down a makeshift camp in the park adjacent. Miss Everts had brought blankets and quilts, and by scrounging for rope, the men were able to rig a tent of sorts. Every one of the refugees there with us was kind, no matter their station. It seemed that ahead of the conflagration swept an epidemic of kindness.

We all waited and watched as San Francisco lifted in flames, like a brilliant phoenix, into the night sky.

The fires crawled up Nob Hill and consumed the home of Phillipa Everts. They consumed the home and all the artwork and papers and sketches of Sebastian Gable; I didn't know where he was, but I hoped he was somewhere safe. The fires consumed mansions and tenements, brothels and castles. They consumed the palatial homes on Russian Hill and the side-by-sides of Telegraph Hill. We watched them all burn.

When the fire reached Miss Everts's house, or thereabouts, as we could gather, I went and held her hand. We stood together staring out over the hellish scene.

She didn't cry or fuss.

"Well," she said, when it seemed the whole of her neighborhood was in flames. "Well, that's that."

All day and into the night Thursday, the east side of San Francisco burned. It burned hot through the vile, mean streets of the Barbary Coast, sending hundreds of miserable alleys to the heavens as a pillar of smoke.

The fires burned through Market and destroyed the Grand Opera House, where I had seen Caruso sing just two nights ago, and the Palace Hotel, where he slept; though Miss Everts heard from one of the police in the camp that he escaped with his life, all his costumes were lost. Not even the rich and famous were immune to the flames.

I stood next to David, our fingers entwined.

We watched the billowing smoke in the afternoon as it approached Van Ness Avenue, that broad street that lay like a river between us refugees and the flames. Soldiers came through to tell us to be ready to move again, to the west, ahead of the flames.

We stayed ready, waiting.

We all huddled together—orphan slave girls from China, Jameson, Miss Everts, David, and me—through the night Thursday while firefighters fought with blankets and shovels and single buckets drawn from the sea to keep the flames from crossing Van Ness.

On Friday morning, we were warned again. Buildings along the east side of the avenue were dynamited. The fire crested Russian Hill, taking the largest of mansions in its ceaseless hunger. It drove for us with a vengeance.

Midday Friday they came calling for volunteers. David and Jameson leaped up. We'd all readied for another evacuation and were waiting for directions.

I would not leave David's side. "Miss Everts . . ."

"Go." She shooed me away. "And please, Kula. My name is Phillipa."

David, Jameson, and I ran together toward the avenue, me with my skirts hoisted right up. The firefighters needed men to haul hoses up from tugboats moored at the docks, to pump seawater. Jameson took off with a crowd to grab a section of hose.

David and I found ourselves with a pile of rugs and linens—Oriental carpets, finely woven; silk quilts—taken from some mansion, I was sure—and now we used them to beat out the embers that flew at us from the climbing columns of smoke and ash. For several hours we worked side by side, along with so many others. I smacked my small carpet of red-and-blue geometrics against the ground over and over until my shoulders screamed and the carpet was fraying and singed black and my lungs stung from the searing smoke.

It was sometime just past noon when the wind shifted. I could smell it. I stopped beating and stood, my eyes closed, and I turned my face west amid the beating and the shouting and I lifted up my face and smelled the sea, the cool sea breeze, pushing against us from the west. My spirits lifted as the temperature dropped.

"Look!" David grabbed my arm.

I turned. The fire was backdrafting—roaring back over itself, over the areas already scorched. A cheer went up from those around us. The fire was stopped at Van Ness by our sheer will and the gift of the shifting wind.

Great sections of the city were gone. All of the area south of Market: the entire evil Barbary Coast, Chinatown, Nob Hill, Russian Hill. The stinking alleyways of abuse and desperation were gone. The business district was gone. The palatial homes built by the nabobs of the 1849 Gold Rush were gone.

Miss Everts's house was gone, too, and everything left in it.

Many, many thousands were gone, though we didn't know it then. And we never knew how many, exactly, buried alive, burned to ash, souls who had no voice. Slave girls and lost sailors, desperate men and sorry women. Gone, forgotten, ash and smoke.

We stood in line for water and food, side by side with rich and poor, all patient, all kindly, all those who had lost everything. The woman in line in front of me was dressed in fine linen. Yesterday she'd owned a towering mansion on Russian Hill; today she was stripped clean of everything save the clothes on her back. Yet she shrugged, laughed. The cheerful moods of each and every one were infectious.

Inside our little tent enclosure I was able to sponge off some of the grime and soot coating my hands and face and neck. Mei Lien plaited my hair again into my one long braid, and I stepped outside for air.

I sat on an upturned bucket in front of our little lean-to tent enclosure and listened to the whispers of the girls with us who spoke in their native tongue, realizing that I was hearing some of their voices for the first time. David came and sat next to me.

"It's not over," I said. "Not for me. I still have to find a way to help my father. He's going to hang in a few days. If that box survived, it's my only chance." A heaviness drifted over me, an exhaustion more of the spirit than of the body, though my body was worn out. "Wilkie said Will had it. What if it's gone? What will I do?"

"We need to find Will Henderson."

My blood boiled. "Will Henderson." I spat; I didn't care how unbecoming it was. I was already a filthy, tattered mess. "He stole it. He stole the one thing that could save my father's life, when he knew what it meant to me. When he knew it was killing my pa."

David rested a hand on my arm. "Kula, I don't think Will's evil; he's just rich and ignorant. We don't know his side yet. There may be more to it."

"How can you—" I bit my tongue. David was right. How often had I assumed one thing and been shown that there was another side? My father's life still hung in the balance, but I knew Will was no Wilkie, no cold-blooded devil. "Fine. I'll pretend he took it for some good purpose."

David smiled, and I leaned my weary head on his shoulder. "Kula." I heard him whisper my name, felt his breath as it stirred my hair, felt his arm lift over my shoulders and wrap me up.

I turned to him and kissed him then. It was a full kiss, given with my full heart.

He said, "We'll have to wait for the morning. They've told us there's a strict curfew. They'll shoot to kill. The police chief has deputized new men all over the city, and some of them shouldn't be carrying guns, much less making life-and-death decisions, so it won't be safe at all now."

I chafed, but there was no help for it. In point of fact, we were all so exhausted by the emotion and labor and the day's doings that after a short supper of the potatoes and meats and stewed vegetables that had been given to us in the food line, we all fell to a dead sleep. Sometime in the night I awoke in our makeshift tent. After the hot days of the fires this night was chilly, and I was grateful for the warm blanket, but something had woken me.

Mei Lien, Yue, the three rescued girls, Phillipa, and I shared the tent; David and Jameson slept just outside the door, wrapped in blankets. The tent gaped, and I could see out into the night. Jameson sat up awake beside a small fire he'd set in the brazier over which we warmed our food.

He stared away from me, toward the smoldering, smoking city. Every so often he glanced toward the tent, then away again. Then he lifted his hand and opened a small portrait box, stared at it, shut it again.

Jameson looked at someone's portrait, a portrait he treasured enough to save from the flames. A realization dawned. One that should have been obvious to me long before this.

The thoughts that flitted through my mind made me sad. I thought about my pa and what he'd lost when they took my mother away from him. About what it meant to love someone when the world thought that love improper.

The next day dawned bright, and although the fires to our east still smoldered, men were already busy clearing the streets. It seemed there was no hesitation about what must be done to bring the city back; there was no question of it. It was all anyone talked about in the camp: bring the city back. The other refugees around us were not weeping and moaning. In fact, sharing our misfortune brought us to sharing all our goods. We gave out our bread; we were given coffee. Even our girls and David were given their due.

But we still couldn't venture into the city. Only a week remained before my father was due to hang. I needed to find Will—to find that box, if it still existed. I tried to keep busy, but my mind was never far from Pa, whose days were truly numbered.

Finally, on Sunday morning David and I were allowed to make our way back into the heart of the disaster, to see if we could find Will.

I fingered the key still hanging around my neck. So much had been destroyed in the quake, I was hoping beyond hope that the box had survived. The earthquake had opened a great gaping crevasse between my pa and me, and I had to make a leap over it now or lose him forever.

Chapter THIRTY-FOUR

April 22, 1906

"They [Californians] seem to be people without any remembered Past save as it may sometimes come to them in a confused sense of having been born in some other place at some vaguely remote period."

—Ada Clare, in one of her essays for *The Golden Era, San Francisco,* mid-1800s

DAVID AND I WALKED DOWN VAN NESS IN THE DIRECTION of Market to the Henderson mansion. It was odd how open and visible the streets were now that we could see across the landscape bereft of trees and buildings. The sad naked exposure tugged at my heart.

It had rained in the night—too late to save much of the city—and what fires remained were now largely quenched.

The Henderson mansion itself, so recently the site of my awkward debut into society, was nothing but a set of four stone walls, all of it burned out from within, its windows now like gaping eyes framing shifting, ghosting gray ash.

We stared at the ruin in silence. I thought about the artworks that had perished, the three stories of furnishings collected from all over the world, the personal treasures, the mementoes. The Hendersons had lost so much, like everyone else. I thought about Will, and that smile.

I touched David's hand, as if to remind myself that not every man would betray me.

As if thinking brought him to life, Will came from over the hill. He walked quickly toward us, with purpose, already lifting his hand as if to surrender or explain.

It should have been me who flew at him, but it was David. David lashed out at Will with both fists raised, facing him down with barely contained anger. "Why?"

Will spread his hands. His face was pale, his clothes tattered. Dark circles rimmed his eyes, and his hands shook. His eyes met mine, and all I saw there was grief. Nothing remained of the cocky, self-sure, rich young man I'd known.

I didn't care how much he'd suffered. "You stole my father's only hope!"

Will gestured, a fluttering movement. "Kula, I already told you. My father had been looking for that box for years. He said he needed it. He told me it was life or death. I had to."

"*My* father's life depends on that box, not yours! Did you even open it? Did you see what it was that was worth Pa's life?" If the box had been in this house, it was gone, and my father was doomed. I kicked at a rock, sending it skittering into the remains.

"I didn't open it. And it might have survived," Will said softly.

Somehow I managed to speak past the lump in my throat. "How? How could it have survived this?"

"I took it to the bank. Before the fire. It's at the bank." Will lowered his head, raised his hands to grip his head as if to contain everything inside.

"But didn't the bank . . ." David began.

"It burned," Will said. He lifted his head. "But I put the box in our family's private vault. The vault's made of steel—it was supposed to be able to survive anything. It could have survived the fire."

"Then let's go," David said through gritted teeth. He shook Will's shoulder roughly. "Let's see if you're right."

We walked down to where the bank had been on Market. Rubble littered the streets although already men gathered to clear the way. If I hadn't been with Will and David, they would have been commandeered into brick-heaving duty more than once, but as my escorts they could pass. The farther we went into the city, the more terrible the devastation appeared, with entire blocks of buildings gone, reduced to smoldering ash. So many buildings had been gutted with fire or reduced to rubble, and yet every so often we came upon a structure that for no obvious reason remained nearly intact.

As we drew close to where the bank stood we could see that the stone framework remained but the interior had been burned out.

David approached the outer wall. The bank had been one of the lower buildings on Market, no more than two stories high. "It appears solid, but Kula, you should stay here."

"No."

David shook his head but didn't argue with me. "Will, where was the vault?"

"In my father's office at the back." Will led us down the alleyway between two remaining outer brick walls. We picked our way through the ruin of fallen bricks and charred lumber, some still smoldering. I lifted my skirts nearly to my knees to avoid catching an ember.

"There, the vault's still there. See, it's still there!" Will pointed to the interior, where a vault stood half buried but sound in the shadows of the ruined bank.

David helped me over a mound of rubble and through a window and then lifted me into what remained of the interior.

It was sad, standing in the middle of this ruin. On the walls were the charred remnants of ornate carved-oak moldings. Here was a rolltop desk, incongruously spared; a window with no glass framed the ruined city. Above us the sky, a soft blue with pale clouds, formed the ceiling.

Will and David made their way through the ruin to the vault; they heaved off the ceiling timbers that rested against it. Will knelt and twisted the dial on the lock.

"Will?" Mr. Henderson stood with one hand on the window frame.

Only days ago William Henderson had seemed to me a titan. He'd been reduced to a slump-shouldered wreck whose eyes were glassy and unfocused. His three-piece suit was torn and filthy, his hair uncombed, his beard untended. "Will?" Henderson's voice quavered.

"Father! It survived. Our vault survived the fire."

"What are you doing?"

"I have to return Kula's box to her." Will straightened and faced his father, the door to the vault still shut. "Kula says her father will die without it."

Henderson slid down the ramp of rubble onto the floor, his feet faltering, his arms flailing. He came to a stop and breathed hard.

"Why do you want it?" I asked. "Why are you keeping it from me? It's not yours."

"There's no money in it, you know." He moved past me, toward Will. "There's no money here at all."

"No money?" Will sounded puzzled. "But I thought that's what it was. If it's not money, then . . . what is it?"

"That box is all I have," Henderson said to the floor. He looked almost like a child, slumped down.

"Mr. Henderson," I said. "What is in my pa's box that you don't want me to see?"

He placed his hand on the vault to steady himself. "It's nothing. It's only important to me. Just a bit of ancient history."

"I don't believe you." I stepped forward. "My father sent me here to get it—it's the only thing that can save him. Will, open the vault."

Will shifted his glance from his father to me and back. "I'm sorry, Father. She's right. I can't keep on like before. Everything's different now. What could possibly be in this box that's so important to you that it's worth a man's life?" He shook his head. "I have to give it back."

Henderson didn't argue. He backed away until he could rest against the wall. "Your father and I were friends, Miss Baker," Henderson said. "There were three of us. We were as close as our own fathers had been, and our grandfathers before them. Baker and Henderson and Everts."

Will's eyes followed his father. He twisted his hands, knotting his fingers together. Watching him, all at once I understood the lies, the betrayal. Will had been doing the same thing I was—trying to save his father. Trying to win his father's love. His actions were clumsy and foolish and hurtful, but I understood. His desires were not unlike my own.

Will bowed his head again, and then bent to the task, and the vault door popped open. Will straightened, my father's box in his hands. But now we all—Will and David and I—waited on William Henderson's words.

"Three boys, each an orphan, on a ship from England bound for America in 1840. Three boys whose lives were linked by fortune, or misfortune. They pledged to remain friends forever, pledged for themselves and their unborn sons."

William Henderson studied his hands, spread his palms open. "They found their way west together and set up a business. They bought land. In a few short years Baker and Henderson and Everts had settled in California territory. Then one of them struck north. Why? Curiosity, hunger for the unknown, or just the desires of a young man." Henderson shrugged. "It doesn't matter why. What matters is Henry Baker went to Alaska and returned two years later to the port town of San Francisco with a native bride, Kula. I have a fondness for names, you know. I rarely forget a name."

Kula. My great-grandmother. I steadied myself.

"She was beautiful, so they say. Proud and dignified. Gave birth to her only child the same year that gold was discovered on the land owned by Baker and Henderson and Everts." Henderson gave a little nod. "Gold. Men lust after many things, but none so much as gold."

Will stared at the box in his hands; it seemed to grow suddenly heavy, or hot; he put it down on the bed of ashes at his feet.

His father pointed at it. "It's all in there, what I'm telling you. All those secrets. I tried to keep them from you, Kula."

"What happened?" I said it soft.

"John, Theo, and James—they were the three boys of the next

generation, born into gold wealth. Kula, she died giving birth to John. Henry died not long after. So young John went to live with Charles Henderson, raised up with Charles's son James as if they were twins. John Baker and James Henderson were nearly inseparable from their friend Theo Everts. That is until Theo met Hannah Porter. Then Theo wanted his share, out from their partnership. He and Hannah had plans.

"Now, John and James, they'd married, too. John Baker had a son, Nathaniel. James Henderson had a son, William—me," Henderson said, and he pointed at himself. "Nat and I were best friends."

My pa: Nat Baker. Best friends with William Henderson, one of the richest men in San Francisco. The man who'd stolen Pa's only chance at freedom.

Henderson spoke again. "Hannah and Theo had no children. They moved across the bay to Sausalito, while Theo pressed his case to split the partnership and take his share of the fortune. There was a heated argument, the threat of lawyers. In the middle of all of this, round about when Nat and I were ten years old, Nat Baker's parents died in an accident on the bay. They were on a ferry that rammed into another ferry in the fog."

My grandparents. Mr. Henderson was talking about my grandparents, my pa's parents. Why had I never heard any of this from Pa?

"Then Theo was killed. He was taking a shortcut through the meaner parts of San Francisco one night. He was murdered in cold blood. Knifed in the back. A Chinese man was blamed. Hanged for it. No trial, just a hanging. In the street, from a lamppost."

David, next to me, moved a little.

"They died, and Theo died, and everything changed. Just like that."

Henderson went on. "After Theo's death Hannah Everts was shut out of the inheritance by my father. Theo's sister, Phillipa, became the third partner."

"Miss Everts!" I blurted.

"Yes, your Miss Everts. Her fiancé took pity upon poor Hannah and eloped with her. For which Phillipa suffered a keen loss. Hannah Porter Everts eloped with Edward Gale to the Montana territory. This left all the property and the gold in the hands of my father, along with Phillipa Everts, and the young, newly orphaned Nat Baker."

Henderson shook his head. "Nat. My parents adopted him; they treated him like their own son. We were like brothers. And, well, I was happy to stay right here, but he persuaded me that we had to see the world. Guess he was more like his grandfather than he knew. We were sixteen when we left San Francisco; I came back two years later. Nat stayed behind in the greater Yellowstone.

"See the world, he'd said. But we never got farther than Montana. We fell in with some rough types. Nat's a bit of a devil. I expect he still is, isn't he, Kula? He liked the whole outlaw business. He thought it was exciting." William Henderson met my eye. "Until he met your mother. That changed him."

My mother. Henderson examined the ash at his feet, as if he could divine something important in it.

"What's in my pa's box, Mr. Henderson?" My hand rested on

my throat, on the key that still hung by the chain round my neck. "What's in there that will save his life?"

He laughed, a short, harsh laugh. "Nat. He lured me out into his wild world."

I pressed the key against my breastbone. Above it, above my fingers, I still wore my mother's cameo.

"I left Montana, I came home. Well, there's the irony." Here, he let his head drop. "I came home to find everything had changed." Henderson pointed at Pa's box sitting at Will's feet. "I never knew it existed. That's because it was in the hands of Ty Wong. Ty was one of the brotherhood. He'd gone east with Nat and me. Nat trusted him and gave him the box to bring back here, to keep it safe here. If I had known then that your father had what was in this box . . ."

Will dropped his head into his hands. David bit his lip.

"What?" I asked, softly, half not wanting to hear the answer.

Henderson's eyes grew bright. "I would've destroyed it! My parents blamed me for running away. *Me!* I came home, and, out of spite, to punish their natural-born son, they had given Nat everything—he owned it all. After we'd left, they'd disowned me and sent the deeds to Nat in Montana. I was right there with him, and he never said a word. He never told me. Oh, he told Ty Wong, sure, but he never told me, me who was like a brother to him. Nat Baker owned everything that was rightfully mine."

"But . . . your house, the business . . . How did you . . ." I trailed off. My father was a struggling outlaw; Mr. Henderson was a scion of San Francisco society.

"When my parents told me what they'd done, I was furious. How could they disown their own son? But then my father died of sudden heart failure. After that my mother was not in her right mind. So I took control of things. I paid to change the deeds and even cut Nat out of his share and left him penniless. I made it all look legal, even if it wasn't. I didn't know about the box then. Ty was clever, and he hid it from me. Because the papers in it? They make what I did null and void. They're originals of my parents' deeds. If he wants it, your father will have everything, and I'll have nothing. So I had Wilkie get that box," said Henderson. "And Will took the box from Wilkie and kept it safe, didn't you, Will?"

Henderson looked at his son with something like pride; Will stared at the ash-covered floor.

"I thought it was money," I whispered, half to myself. David's fists were balled up tight, his jaw worked hard.

"There's no money in that box, Kula. There's an entire fortune," Henderson said.

"But . . ." Desperation swallowed me. "I don't understand how these papers can save my father. He's going to hang, and soon. These papers, how can they change anything . . . ?"

"They can't."

"What?" I choked, steadied myself. "What?"

"There's nothing in there that can save your father, Kula. And surely he knew that. When he told you to find it, he meant for it to save you."

Chapter THIRTY-FIVE

April 22, 1906

"The Federal Troops, the members of the Regular Police Force and all Special Police Officers have been authorized by me to KILL any and all persons found engaged in Looting or in the Commission of Any Other Crime."

—Proclamation by E.E. Schmitz,
Mayor of San Francisco, April 18, 1906

"NO." I WOULD NOT BELIEVE THAT I'D COME ALL THIS WAY and spent all this time and still could not save my pa. "No!"

"I didn't think he'd hang. How could I lose it all? How could I give it all up? Will . . ." Henderson turned to his son. "I couldn't give it all up, now, could I? We'd have been broke. You would have lived like a pauper."

Will stiffened. "This isn't right, Father. You know it isn't. You should have told me what you were doing . . ."

The clatter of loose brick caused us to turn.

Josiah Wilkie.

"Well, Mr. H, I think you've about said enough. And I've been here long enough to catch the best of it." Wilkie carried a Winchester, and it was pointed at us. He lifted his lapel. On it he wore his silver star. "See, I got myself deputized here, in San Francisco. I been a marshal before and now a proper California deputy. We don't want looters roaming through the streets, now, do we?"

David snorted. "Who in his right mind would deputize you? You're a cold-blooded killer. You killed Min."

Wilkie's face worked with fury. "Min! You killed her, that's what. She was all I had, and you as good as killed her, with your scheming and spying, you filthy Chinaboy." Wilkie spat, and the Winchester shook; his eyes were like brass buttons fixed hard on David.

David braced, and I placed a hand on his arm.

Wilkie went on, his voice a rasp. "There's a lawlessness all about. It's a mess out there. I am the law."

"We'll see about that," David muttered.

"It don't matter what you think, son. I have the gun. And here I happen upon this happy little scene. Do I see an open vault? Looters to be shot on sight, that's what I was told."

"It's my bank, Wilkie," Henderson said.

He moved away from the wall, went to stand before Wilkie. Will still stood by the vault; David and I were a few feet away. It was the three of us facing the two of them, Wilkie and Henderson.

"Oh, is that right, now, Mr. H.?" Wilkie said. "That's not what I heard. In fact, just now I think I overheard something different. I think the rightful owner of this bank would be somewhere in Montana."

"I didn't want him to hang," Henderson said. "I never wanted him dead, Kula. Never wanted anyone dead." Henderson's eyes never left Wilkie. "Mr. Wilkie, here, framed your father. He murdered that rancher, Black. I told him to get Nat out of the way. I didn't ask him to kill."

Wilkie was a killer. I'd known it all along; this just confirmed it. I said to Wilkie, "You murdered that poor man."

He laughed. "Oh, girl, it's all in a day's work."

"Just to set up my pa."

"Well, I did get me a couple good horses. Oh, and that Black was hiding those Chinese girls of mine. Got them back, too."

I bit my tongue, tried to settle, to control my boiling anger as best I could. "And you"—I turned to Henderson—"you put him up to it?"

Henderson said, with a touch of surprise, "Can I help it if Wilkie killed Black? Killed his woman? And Ty? Killing them was his choice. I'm sure he did it for the sport. I only asked him to take care of things."

"Now why'd you have to go telling them every little thing?" Wilkie asked. "Mr. H., you've just gone and made my job so much more difficult." Wilkie gestured around the room at David, Will, and me. "Now, you're all a problem for me."

Every muscle in my body tensed. Wilkie was going to kill us all.

Henderson's mouth worked. He glanced at Will; his eyes betrayed a shift in his thinking. He smiled at Wilkie, a tight smile.

"Now, just hold on." Henderson stepped closer to Wilkie, slipping his hand into his jacket pocket. "Let's see if there's anything in that box that might smooth this all over. Will, open the box."

"No." Will shook his head. David put himself between me and Henderson and Wilkie.

"Will," I said, with a note of warning, "I don't care about the box anymore. It won't save my pa. Give it to your father." I pulled out the chain, pulled it over my head, took the key, and bent and unlocked the box. "There. Give it to him."

Henderson took another step closer to Wilkie. "Will, why don't you hand the box to Mr. Wilkie?"

Wilkie smiled. "See, that's what I like about you, Mr. H. You know how to worm your way out of a tight spot. Always have. Why, does your son know we've been working together for years, buying these girls over in China?" Wilkie turned to Will. "Your father provides the money, and I take care of the girls. Together, we make a tidy sum of money, don't we now?"

Will said in a hushed voice, "Father, what's he saying? You import art."

"And you." Wilkie waved his rifle at David, his lips curling. "You kept interfering with that enterprise. With your spies and such." He lowered his voice. "You took Min from me, and I ain't never gonna forget it."

David moved toward Henderson. He seethed with anger, directed at Henderson. "All this time, all those children. You're to blame. You're the cause of all this. You were behind this—this pig—all the time. You and your greed."

Henderson raised his hand toward David. "The girls were already slaves back in your country. Already bought and paid for. Wilkie was the middleman, and I just handled the money. And I never touched a one . . ."

David moved so fast it startled us all. He had his hands wrapped around Henderson's throat, shoved him back against the wall.

"David!" I yelled.

Will swayed, uncertain.

Wilkie took a step back, his rifle still pointed at David.

"You disgusting . . ." David yelled as he throttled Henderson, who flailed back, unable to get purchase, unable to pry David's hands off his throat.

"David!" I ran to him and grabbed his wrist. "No! It won't do any good." Even though I hated Henderson myself, I had to stop David. He loosened his grip, left Henderson sputtering.

Behind me, Wilkie raised his rifle again, cocked the mechanism. "I'm done. Time to end this little party." We turned; Wilkie aimed his rifle straight at Will. Straight at Will's heart.

Will lifted his hands and dropped his eyes.

"No!" Two voices spoke as one, mine and Henderson's.

But it was my shout that drew Wilkie. He turned and leveled the gun at me. "You first, then, missy. I've had enough trouble from you."

I heard the report at the same moment that I saw David lunge at me and felt David's hands wrap my waist. He spun me away, and as I turned I saw his face, saw his expression change from determination to shock as the bullet struck him—the bullet meant for me that struck him in the middle of his back. That went right through his back into his heart.

His heart. Oh, my heart.

I must have screamed, but the rifle report echoed in my brain and damped all other noise. What happened next came back to me much later in pieces, like torn photographs, bits and pieces of image and noise. At that moment I didn't hear Will shout or his father shout; I didn't hear the second shot.

I fell to the floor with David. Our eyes locked, and I watched his go dull and then close, but I didn't hear what he said. I didn't hear it, but I read his lips as we dropped in a slow dance, his hands on my waist, his hands spinning me away, onto the floor together. I read his lips as he said it.

Kula.

David's body cushioned my fall. He was beneath me, his right hand still on my waist, so that I landed on top of him. He was dead before he hit the floor.

I put my fingers to his lips, put my head to his chest, ripped open his jacket to his shirt; no breath, no beat. A great pool of blood spread underneath him, soaking into the dust and ash and debris that littered the floor. His shirtfront grew wet; it was my tears that soaked his shirt. I closed my eyes and laid my head on his chest, still feeling his hand on my waist, and I sobbed.

"Kula?" It was Will's voice; I ignored it.

Henderson's voice, next. "Is he dead?"

"They're both dead," Will replied. "Wilkie, too."

Wilkie was dead, too.

It didn't matter that Wilkie was dead. I'd never forgive him for taking David from me. I'd never forgive myself for not telling David how I truly felt.

I believed I'd never forgive this miserable city for laying my heart wide open to love and then taking all love from my life.

Chapter THIRTY-SIX

April 22, 1906

"It is at present impossible to estimate the amount of damage to property in this city . . . Many of the structures which from the outside show little apparent damage, on closer examination prove to have been so badly twisted and racked by the shock that it is feared they will have to be torn down."

—*The Call/Chronicle/Examiner,* April 19, 1906

IT WAS WILL WHO GOT ME TO MY FEET, PULLED ME away from David. Will, whose face was ashen with grief.

Will's father stood, his head hanging, his arms limp by his sides. In one hand he held a small pistol. The Derringer that he'd pulled from his pocket and used on Wilkie.

There were papers everywhere, like feathers, drifting in lazy swirls around this shattered wreck of a room. The box lay open, upside down, papers scattered. Wilkie lay facedown in the dust.

Will left me standing above David and made to collect the papers, picking up one after another. I watched as if from a distance. I gazed on David as if from a high heaven. His was the sweetest face I'd ever seen. I fell to my knees again, beside him, stroking his cheek.

It was some time before Will went to find help. More time passed before that help came, in the form of soldiers. I stayed with David, kneeling by his side, until someone pulled a blanket over his body and someone else lifted me up and helped me through the rubble to the street.

A wagon took David and Wilkie away together. I tried to stop them from putting Wilkie's body next to David's.

"He's just a Chinaman. A dead Chinaman. He don't care who's in the hearse next to him."

I didn't have the strength to slap the face of the soldier who'd said it.

Henderson confessed what had happened inside the bank right there, to the captain.

The captain lifted his hat and scratched his head. "All the earthquake and fire and death and misery going on in San Francisco right now, and we can't get away from greed and revenge and cold-blooded murder." He shook his head. "Sad."

Will put his hand on my arm, and I leaned into it. "My pa . . ." I whispered.

"Father, tell them. They have to get word to Montana. Free Kula's father. Tell them." There was something in Will's voice; there would be no arguing with him.

"My pa'll hang," I said. "He's only got days. You've got to get word there now."

The officer scratched his head again and nodded. "All right, then. You all come with me." He looked at Henderson. "I'm afraid you're under arrest. The law'll straighten this out one way or the other."

Henderson's face was cast down.

We all went to the makeshift police station, one of the remaining mansions commandeered for that purpose. They had telegraph service. I listened as the captain made his report to his senior officer, and that officer took it to the telegraph.

These troops were volunteers who'd just arrived from Montana to help in the city. The officer in charge had been garrisoned in Great Falls. He knew exactly where to send the message. Luck was with me. As much as it mattered now. Within a short time, I knew that my pa was safe, that they would not hang him, but that he'd remain in prison until the new information could be brought to the court. But in the meantime Nat Baker wouldn't hang for the murder of Mr. Black.

Will came and told me. My pa was safe, and I wouldn't lose him.

That was when I collapsed, my legs giving way there in the crowded room filled with milling soldiers. It was Will who caught me and carried me to a bunk. There, I turned my face to the wall and wept.

Will didn't leave me. He sat in a chair next to me and didn't leave me, even when his own father was taken away in handcuffs.

Hours later, a carriage took Will and me back to the tent where Phillipa Everts, Jameson, and the girls waited. I crawled onto my makeshift bed as Will explained everything to them. I had saved my father. I had lost David. Miss Everts cried out once; Mei Lien sobbed. Will's voice droned as I drifted into exhausted sleep.

I woke in the night. I thought it had all been a dream. I peered through the tent flap, and someone slept right where David had slept the night before, and my heart lifted for a moment. Then I realized it was Will, lying on David's blankets. He was homeless, just as we all were.

And Jameson still sat as he had before. Staring out over the park, holding a portrait box open in one hand, the firelight glinting off the glass.

I hadn't spoken to Miss Everts, and I didn't until the next morning. We sat side by side, the sun rising behind us and the shimmering sea in the distance.

"I know why you put me in the room with the portrait." The portrait still leaned, wrapped in its canvas covering, against the wall of the tent where I'd propped it. "You wanted me to discover it."

She looked away down the hill toward her old neighborhood. "That's your grandfather, in the painting."

I pondered that. My grandfather, in a fine painting. Kula Baker, daughter of an outlaw, a girl who grew up longing after fine things, found herself newly rich and in possession of a portrait of her high-society grandfather. "How the world turns," I said. I shook my head. "What about the ring he wears in the painting? That dragon ring?"

"They each had one, the three partners. Everts, Baker, and Henderson. That ring was their crest, the imperial dragon was their symbol. They were tied to one another and to the Wongs. Your grandfather's ring was lost when he died in the ferry accident. I don't know what became of Henderson's."

"And so then the one I saw on Mrs. Gale belonged to Theo." And now I understood something else: Mrs. Gale had known who I was and how we were connected, knew it from the moment Pa had returned her rings to her.

Miss Everts nodded. Then she dropped her eyes. "I didn't shut William Henderson out. That was his parents' doing. We were partners, as much as I hated it. Once he finagled his way back to his share of the fortune, I had to humor him. Especially once I suspected that he was involved in that other wretched business."

"So he financed the slavery . . ."

"And I bought the girls. He didn't know that, of course, any more than I was certain he was the money behind Wilkie."

"You were pretending. With me, with Henderson. Pretending about being angry with Hannah Gale, pretending not to know my pa . . . it was all so you could save those girls."

She did not meet my eyes.

"How many did you save?"

She shrugged. "I don't know. As many as I could. Until I ran out of money. My well ran dry not very long ago."

"Where are all the others?"

"They've moved across the country. I always try to find them a place to go where they'd be well looked after. That shoe you found—that thread was gold. They wore the little wealth I could give them in their clothing. It wasn't much. But at least it was something to start with." She leaned toward me. "Now, Kula. Our work isn't done. I need someone like you here, to help me. These girls . . . they need you. You can teach them a good skill. One they can use. Embroidery, sewing. Something useful."

"I don't want to stay here." I bit my lip.

"Why not?"

"There's nothing here for me. There's no one here for me, not anymore. I need to get home to my pa. I can work for Mrs. Gale." I rubbed my palms against my skirt. My pa would be fine. I wouldn't have to work for Mrs. Gale; I had my own fortune now, my pa's fortune. "I miss Yellowstone." That much was true. But it wasn't the real reason I didn't want to stay. I looked at my hands, grimy and calloused. "I just don't know that I can stay here in San Francisco with him gone."

"Yes, I'm sorry about David," she said. "I truly cared for him."

I swallowed and shut my eyes. David. The ache wormed its way through me. I'd never lose it. After a few minutes I found words again. "You were in love with Ty, his grandfather."

She was silent.

"And I wager he was the love of your life. That's why you never married. That's why Hannah married Edward Gale, and you didn't."

"It was convenient for me to pretend that Edward had abandoned me. It removed the prying eyes." Her hands fluttered to her hair, tried to pat the loose strands back into place. "It was convenient to pretend to be angry with Hannah."

Another pretense. She was a surprise, Miss Phillipa Everts. Well, I had a surprise for her. "You do know, of course, that Jameson is in love with you."

She started. "Nonsense."

"He is. He's probably been in love with you for years."

"Roddy? Nonsense." She turned her head, looking out the tent to where Jameson, silent but steady on, was busy adjusting ropes, fixing supplies, seeing to the comfort of us all. "That's impossible."

"No more impossible than you loving Ty Wong." No more impossible than me loving David—or David loving me.

She stood. "I've heard that we can get across the bay now. We can get to my house in Sausalito. I think that's the next order of business."

She went outside to Jameson. I watched her. She spoke to him, clearly telling him that it was time for us to pack up and move, that we would go to Sausalito. Just as she turned away, she placed her hand on his arm. And left it there. And he leaned toward her, just ever so little.

Through all my own sorrows, I could still feel glad.

Will looked up at me as I left the tent.

"I'm going to go to the beach. I'll be back."

"I'll take you," he said.

"No. Just point me in the right direction. I want to walk. By myself." I did not look at Will.

"We'll leave on the evening ferry," Miss Everts said. "You could walk to the Golden Gate, but be back here by three."

I'd walked many a mile in my life; this walk would not be difficult.

All around me the city was shoring up. Cleaning up. The soup lines were long but amicable. Children laughed and played while their parents gossiped. This part of the city had seen earthquake damage but not the fires. Still, bricks littered the streets; buildings were collapsed, tilted, gaping. Great cracks crisscrossed the streets. In places the paving was lifted right up to a cliff. I had to take care as I walked.

But the walking cleared my head, even if it could not mend my heart.

After about an hour or so, I reached the Golden Gate, where the bay meets the ocean; I tripped down the rocky slope into the grass-covered dunes, right down to the narrow strip of beach where the ocean rolled and roared against the sand and the rocks. Sea lions with their great, slinky bodies lounged and barked on the rocks, and I knelt and pushed my hands into the damp sand. The sun was in my eyes so that I could hardly look at the water, sparkling as it was like a million jewels.

I wished I'd come here with David. I let myself cry again. I let it go. I let him go. David.

I rocked gently on the sand, let my love of David sink with my damaged heart into the waves that sparked so, the cut-glass edges of the waves slicing me up until I was all pieces, floating, washed, strewn on the sand, David forever with me, forever gone.

At least my pa was safe now. And it really began to dawn on me, I had inherited some kind of fortune. I didn't need to marry for money now; I no longer needed to work, whether as a lady's maid or an artist's model. I had my own means. I'd never dreamed that I'd have my own means. I could support as many girls as I could free from slavery or, better yet, use it to fight the import of them altogether.

There was much work to be done here, so much could change. The city at my back had to be made new, and I could be a part of that.

I just had to accept what I was and what I had to give.

I understood now. I understood that forgiveness was the path to happiness. That I had to learn to forgive in order to be happy.

Wilkie had been lost in his desire for money and power, unable to forgive Min, the woman he loved.

My pa had been unable to forgive himself for losing his beloved Anna, my ma.

William Henderson had been unable to forgive my pa for taking what William thought was his.

I'd been unable to forgive almost everyone. Not Maggie or my ma, not my pa, not Will or his father. Certainly not Wilkie.

I'd been unable to forgive this city for stealing my heart.

I'd been unable to forgive myself for being what I was: a simple girl with a hard past and an uncertain future.

Until now.

I stood up and brushed the sand from my hands and skirt. I looked out over the ocean toward the west. I had some decisions to make.

Chapter THIRTY-SEVEN

April–May 1906

"I thought of all the solitary places under the night sky where I had slept, and how I prayed that I never might be houseless any more, and never might forget the houseless . . . I seemed to float, then, down the melancholy glory of that track upon the sea, away into the world of dreams."

—*David Copperfield*, Charles Dickens, 1850

MISS EVERTS'S HOUSE IN SAUSALITO HAD LOST ITS chimney and a part of its porch. Jameson and Will made a full exploration of it before allowing us all inside.

We had no running water, but there was an old well out back, so we could hand pump water until things were repaired. And the house was comfortably furnished. It was a large and rambling structure that held all of us with ease.

Will had become a part of this odd family we'd formed. He had nothing left. He went back and forth across the bay to look after his father, who would stand trial for his crimes.

Now William Henderson, as well as my pa, was in jail.

Word came down from Montana and Mrs. Gale that my pa still had to serve time for his part in certain robberies. As for the murder of that rancher, Black, he was deemed innocent.

The girls we'd rescued became like sisters to me, and I started them on learning to embroider. After all, I had to bide my time while sorting out what to do next.

Will's handsome eyes followed me when we were together. I didn't love him in the way I'd loved David, but I liked him well enough. Liked him, but didn't need him. Funny, that. How I'd always thought I'd needed a man to raise me above my station, how I'd needed to marry rich. Now I could do what my heart told me was right, and my station was of no importance.

Every day now, in the evening, I made my way to a point of land from which I could watch the sun skimming across the water. Something about looking over the water soothed the ache in my heart. Once, Will went back up Mount Tam with me, and we walked in silence over the hills at the top, to that same point where we'd once stood with David. Now we stood and stared in silence toward the far western horizon.

One morning about a month after the earthquake, the fog came in. The fog rolled in around the city from down the hills above us, rolled across the bay, wrapped the house we were in like a shroud. I sat at the window and saw only the gray wall of fog. San Francisco had disappeared.

From the small parlor came the sound of soft laughter. One of the girls. It was the first time I'd heard one of them laugh, and it struck me then, hard. Not just what they had been through, but what lay ahead for them. Phillipa had places for them to go, paths she'd laid out before, trails blazed by the other girls who had been spirited out of their terrible quarters and given a new chance at life. They would find new homes in safe havens in the West, the Midwest, the East. I was teaching them skills they could use, ways to control what happened to them in the future. Yet their nightmare past would linger, and they would meet with other trials, and their road would not be an easy one.

And me?

The fog had weight. It rolled around the house and moistened the windows so that they ran with soft drops. I put my fingers on the glass, and it felt cool to my touch.

I went back into the room where Mei Lien and Yue and the other girls waited. They were so patient. I picked up the stitching we'd started and began again with the simple stitches. They were learning quickly, I could see that, and then they could make their way out of here. They could choose a new life. They'd be free, and I'd have helped them. Just like I could help make San Francisco new.

One day, I would return to my high and snowy peaks, to my bubbling springs and endless skies. I'd return to my pa and we'd make a life together. But for now I would stay in this broken place to heal my broken heart.

It was a new century, and all things could be made clean and shiny, even a city destroyed by earthquake and fire. Even the soul of a girl who thought she knew what she wanted.

The soul of a girl who had lost all hope, lost love, and needed to be made new as well.

We worked all day, and the fog lifted just before sunset.

I left the girls to their work and went out to the porch and looked across the bay. It looked as if it was on fire, sparking and flashing. Across the bay, San Francisco was already coming back from the ashes. I wanted to help bring that city back to life. I wanted to help others find a new life. I'd discovered how to find my own life, how to open my heart.

Kula Baker was ready to live.

AUTHOR'S NOTE

The truth, however, is—judging by an analogy and all the light that science has placed within our reach—San Francisco is in very little more danger of a disastrous earthquake than the Eastern States of being flooded by an overflow of the Atlantic ocean..."

—*San Francisco Real Estate Circular*, April 1872

When I began writing *Forgiven* it was with the intent of following Kula, a secondary character in *Faithful*, for whom I'd developed a strong attachment. Kula is feisty, strong-willed, and action-oriented; I wanted to see what would happen to her if I put her in difficult circumstances. I decided to let her mature a year and a half "offscreen," and this was partly because I was attracted to the idea of sending her to San Francisco so that she might experience the great earthquake and fire of April 18, 1906 (*Faithful* is set in the summer of 1904). What I did not know until I began my research was the extent to which San Francisco of that time was a city divided.

The wealth of the Gold Rush of 1849 coupled with the westward migration of many of the tycoons of nineteenth-century industry gave rise to a population of immense wealth. Nob Hill and Russian Hill were crowned with extravagant mansions. At the same time, San Francisco was a seaport and gateway to the Orient. As a result, the extreme poverty and dissolution that often follow the hardworking homeless sailor lay side by side with enormous wealth.

Furthermore, the government in the city of San Francisco at the turn of the nineteenth century was acknowledged to be corrupt. In the notorious Barbary Coast, a young man who let himself become too inebriated was subject to being "shanghaied," a condition in which he would wake up to find himself an unwilling seaman in the middle of the Pacific Ocean. The Chinese population, so important to the economy of San Francisco, suffered constant harassment. And I discovered the horrors of child slavery, wherein young girls were sold in China and brought to San Francisco and housed in terrible circumstances. This last fact became an important part of Kula's story.

Several books were important to my research, including Herbert Asbury's *The Barbary Coast,* first published in 1933, James Smith's *San Francisco's Lost Landmarks,* and Bill Yenne's pictorial, *San Francisco Then and Now.* The Virtual Museum of the City of San Francisco (http://www.sfmuseum.org/hist1/index0.html) is a treasure house of photographs, movies, period newspaper accounts, and scholarly articles. Two fictional accounts also made an impact on my understanding of the various cultures of San Francisco: Isabel Allende's *Daughter of Fortune,* and Laurence Yep's *Dragonwings: Golden Mountain Chronicles 1903.*

The earthquake and fires of 1906 did have something of a cleansing effect on that great city. But the exploitation of children—degradation, humiliation, the worst forms of abuse—continues in all parts of the world even today. A portion of the author's proceeds from the sale of *Forgiven* will be donated to the National Center for Missing and Exploited Children. It is my hope that my readers will become aware of this continuing problem and choose to act on behalf of children everywhere.

ACKNOWLEDGMENTS

The first draft of *Forgiven* became my creative thesis for my MFA in Writing for Children and Young Adults at Vermont College of Fine Arts. I could not have written the novel without the guidance of my thesis advisor, Leda Schubert. Her patience, vast knowledge, encouragement, and editorial skills sustained me when I needed them most. Leda, I'm grateful and proud to call myself your former student and forever friend.

My critique partners, Kathy Whitehead and Shirley Hoskins, read bits and pieces of the novel as I struggled to bring it together, and as always, their wise words guided me through thick and thin.

My friends in SCBWI, in the classes of 2k9 and 2k10, and at the Vermont College of Fine Arts—you are my heroes. You have come through for me time and time again, when I felt I couldn't go on, or when I needed guidance, or when I needed to know that the struggle was all worth it. My ThunderBadgers—especially my friends and confidants Kari Baumbach, Anne Bustard, and Lindsey Lane—I love you all.

The faculty of Vermont College of Fine Arts is without peer. My advisors, Sarah Ellis, Jane Kurtz, Uma Krishnaswami, and Leda Schubert, provided me with craft tools I will use forever. And Kathi Appelt and Cynthia Leitich Smith—you are my special Texas connection, boosters, and sweet friends.

Wayne and Martha Sellers, and Tim and Randi Jacobsen—thanks for being there, and for supporting my craft, again and again.

Alyssa Eisner Henkin—you are my agent; but you are also my rock. I can always count on you, and I love you for it.

Jen Bonnell, my talented editor—you are amazing. You cut right through to the heart of my story, every time. I am in awe and forever grateful.

The other fabulous folks at Speak/Penguin—Kristin Gilson, Eileen Kreit, and Caroline Sun, and all the wonderful folks in School and Library Marketing—thank you for believing in me and in my stories. And thank you, Jeanine Henderson, for giving me two of the most beautiful covers an author could desire.

And last, but oh so not least, thank you to my husband, Jeff, and my son, Kevin. You tolerate my moods, my late nights, my roundabout discussions of character, motivation, plot, and you both have the wisdom to advise me when I desire it, support me when I need it, and leave me in peace when all else fails. I love you.

Turn the page for a preview of

FAITHFUL

PROLOGUE

I KNOW A PLACE ON THIS EARTH THAT CONTAINS wonders enough to stop the breath. A place where the very rocks whisper and whine, where the rivers boil and the snow-studded peaks thrust into a bowl of blue; where great shaggy beasts press the earth with cloven hooves or threaten with claw and fang; where new life and lurking death coexist in the shallows of varicolored pools.

I went to this place to search for what I had lost, but instead found a life unexpected.

Chapter ONE

May 31, 1904

To lose ones' faith surpasses
The loss of an estate,
Because estates can be
Replenished,—faith cannot.

—"Lost Faith"; *Poems*, Emily Dickinson, 1890

THE TRAIL WAS TOO CROWDED FOR A HARD RIDE. Too groomed, too manicured. I wished I could fly, could gallop away from my raging confusion, but I couldn't give Ghost my crop and set him off at a canter. I urged him into a fast trot instead and even then I saw it in the faces we passed: the raised eyebrows, the surprise, the disapproval. Disapproval draped over me like a funeral crepe.

I pressed my lips together. I imagined the glares I'd receive if I rode astride instead of sidesaddle. Mama had worn a split skirt when we rode. When I was little I'd thought it fun—they all watched her, my mama! But when I reached my teens I saw the attention for what it was. The eyes had skimmed from Mama to me. I was guilty by association.

I sighed as I slowed Ghost to a walk, then bent forward and caressed his silky neck with my gloved fingers and stuffed my warring thoughts all the way down.

Ghost twisted his ear toward me. "You're always ready to listen, aren't you? I wish you could come with me. That would be such a comfort. But I have to go, and you have to stay. It's not forever, old friend. Only a little trip. I promise I'll be back." Promise. Like Mama had promised me. I squelched that thought, the misery of broken promises. My lips drew tight. "I promise."

Ghost tossed his head; he understood. I sat up in the saddle and thought it all through again.

Papa's plans, having come from out of the blue two days ago, had thrown me into conflict. First, I'd felt excitement.

"There is some suggestion—only a possibility, mind you," Papa had said. I tensed, waiting. "Your mother was there before. We took a trip out west, right after you were born. You stayed in Newport with your grandparents, but we went west. Did I ever mention it? No? Well. Your mother and I were there, years ago."

Papa's eyes had grown bright; he leaned toward me with a smile. "Your uncle John's been investigating. He's made some discoveries. There may be a chance, only a chance . . ."

"What?" A chance she was alive? My breath quickened. I reached out my hand, tugged his shirtsleeve. This was the thing I'd prayed for these many months. "Papa, are you saying she's alive and we can find her?"

But Papa looked away; he didn't answer. He bent and picked up the train schedule, flipped it open, and pointed. "If we leave within the week, we'd be there by the middle of June."

"Wait. So soon?" My mind twisted in another direction, my feelings in conflict. Elation turned to shock.

Leave within the week. This week. Be somewhere out west in the middle of June. And back—when? To find Mama was my greatest hope. But to leave Newport at this very moment, even to find her, was . . . I pressed the heel of my palm against my forehead to quell the ache. We'd be gone well into the start of Newport's season.

"Papa, wait. How long will we be away? You know I have so much to do! Kitty and I have so many plans!" It was my season, and it should have been Mama planning with me. The conflict in me began to boil and my voice rose with it. "There are the clothes, and the orchestra, and the flowers, and the invitations . . . all the little details to manage."

It was my sixteenth spring, the eve of my debut. This was the summer I'd dreamed about for as long as I could remember, the summer in which my future would finally be sealed. A debut required hundreds of preparations. The ball alone would take weeks to plan. Most girls planned theirs with their mothers, but my mama was gone. I was on my own, with only Kitty to help me. Yet now, here suddenly was the possibility of Mama . . .

Mama. I wanted to know what my uncle John had learned, out there in the wilds of Wyoming. For the past year I'd stubbornly insisted that Mama was alive; now Papa had given me fresh hope.

I felt dizzy. My hand clutched at Papa's shirt, twisting the cotton. My stomach twisted, too.

It was unfair that this was happening now. That Uncle John and Papa would make this unnamed discovery now—it was unfair! I didn't expect Papa to understand how much my debut meant to me. If Mama had been here she would have understood. I like to think she would have understood.

Ghost whinnied and brought me back to the moment. I caught the eye of Mrs. Wolcott as we passed on the trail. I smiled; her return was faint, not quite a sneer yet not a smile. I stiffened. A glittering debut with all the right trappings was one of the few things that might make the Mrs. Wolcotts look at me new. Since Mama had left, I'd tossed and turned at night, alone with my wretched thoughts. And now, when I'd finally begun to make some peace with my life, to let go of my desperate insistence that she'd be back, now everything was about to change.

I'd asked Papa two days ago (two days! A lifetime!), "Can we be back in time? If we're back by July, that would be all right. Maybe Kitty can manage till then. But Papa, we have to be back by then." I remembered tightening my hold on his sleeve.

"Yes, yes," Papa said, waving his hand, the train schedule flapping, brushing off my questions. He paused and looked at the floor, tugging his mustache with two fingers. "There's something else, Mags. Listen. You must promise not to tell anyone that this is anything but a pleasure trip. You must promise especially not to tell your grandparents." He looked up at me with a piercing gaze.

I was taken aback. "Not tell? But . . ."

"It's important, Margaret." Papa took my free hand. "You must promise. I don't want to give them false hope." He searched my face, his eyes unusually bright. "Lord knows your grandfather is angry enough with me."

His grip tightened around my hand, so I put my other hand on his and lied. "I understand." Why wouldn't he want my grandparents to know that he may have found their daughter?

"Good girl. Now, I have some things to do, eh?"

"But, Papa. I want to hear what Uncle John . . ."

"Margaret, please." And he ushered me out of his studio and shut the door. I stood in the dark hall, alone, my lips pursed in frustration.

Ghost snorted and I stroked his neck again. He knew me better than anyone, my Ghost. "I have to go." I sighed. "I'll miss you, my friend." I would miss the pleasure I took in our daily rides. I'd miss our unspoken connection.

There were many things I'd miss. Like Kitty. And the first round of parties that Mama should have been here to help me prepare for. Sad, gray, boring winter had yielded at last to spring—my spring. In only a few weeks the wealthy from all over the East Coast would descend on Newport to hunt, sail, mingle, and play the complicated social game.

Which seemed simple in comparison with the tangle of feelings weaving through me now.

I adjusted my seat, restless, and fidgeted, the wool riding habit chafing my thigh even through the silk of my petticoats. Most people said Mama was dead. Now I'd be proved right. When we found her, out in that terrible Wyoming wilderness, we'd bring her home. We'd make her well. Then the matrons of Newport would forget her eccentricities. I'd have everything—Mama, my season, my future, everything.

But there was the other possibility. We might go west and not find Mama. Mama might return to Newport and find us gone. I picked unhappily at a loose thread on my velvet cuff. I wanted to find Mama and have her back home with me. But even if we did find her and bring her back, there was still the chance that she could drag me down with her unsocial behavior . . . or with her madness . . .

That unspeakable thing. I reached my hand to Ghost's neck and smoothed the stiff braids lacing his mane. I ticked the riding crop against my knee, *tick-tick, tick-tick,* tapped the pace of Ghost's footfalls. The breeze, carrying the faint scent of salt water, lifted the veil on my hat. Ghost's ears twitched.

I wanted a normal life. But I also wanted Mama.

Normal had not defined Mama; *bohemian* had. Other mothers served tea, my mother painted landscapes. Other mothers wore hats, while mine wore ostrich feathers. My mother laughed, openmouthed with joy; thin-lipped sedate smiles were all the others could muster. Even as a child, I'd watched Papa gaze at her, awestruck; I'd seen how other men stared at her, too. She was compelling, magnetic. Her silky black hair always ended up falling loose, the buttons open at her throat, her cameo pinned low.

Bohemian was a likable word once—a flamboyant word, like ripe grapes on the tongue, conjuring something naughty but fun—but now it fell harsh on my ears. I now understood the flinty looks of Newport matrons and felt the slights from their daughters for myself. Her cameo hadn't only been pinned low; it had been eye-gathering low.

And the whispers—I'd heard them, too, about her lonely walks on the Cliff Walk. Whispers that she was mad.

But I pretended not to hear for as long as I could.

Last June, they grew so loud I couldn't ignore them any longer. And on a morning when I stood in the doorway to her room and witnessed a dreadful thing, I feared they were right.

"Mama?"

It was a glorious summer day and I wanted a new shirtwaist, something cool for the coming heat. I went to Mama's room to persuade her to take me to town, where we could shop and have tea and sweet cakes. My mood was so gay, I was unprepared for what I saw.

Perched on Mama's splay-foot easel was not her usual dreamy landscape, but something ugly. A nightmare vision of hideous vapors and smokes. It was unfinished, a painting of frightening landforms—spires and terraces in the reds, ochres, and oranges of hell. Other new paintings like it leaned against the walls, against her dressing table. Fire . . . bubbling, steaming pits . . . it was grotesque, the product of a sick mind. While I knew Mama had been distracted of late, here I saw that she had drifted into something dark and horrific. And I hadn't noticed until that moment.

She'd left her oils to pace before the brilliant window, her form a dark silhouette framed against unearthly light. Her watered-silk dressing gown gaped open. I froze, staring from the hall at her and at those hellish landscapes, misery flooding my body. She did not see me. I suspected that she could not see me.

"Mama?" I repeated, louder.

She stopped pacing, her face tilted away, her hair cascading in unkempt waves loose to her waist. "I don't know where she is. I can't find her." She resumed pacing, never looking my way.

She was talking nonsense. I bit my lip. I balled my hands into fists in frustration. I whispered, "I wish, I wish . . ." I wished Mama would turn and look at me.

"Mama?" Nothing. I turned away into the empty hall.

My chest formed tight knot. She wasn't normal. If she loved me, she wouldn't act this way. Whispers snarled in my brain: "she's mad," "she's shocking." I leaned against the wall and swallowed the hot tears that rose into my throat. I wanted a mother who played by Newport's rules, not a mama who was peculiar.

Not a mama who frightened me with her odd behavior. With the thought that I was too like her.

I pulled up on the reins. Lost in memories, I didn't realize that Ghost and I had reached the far end of the trail. I was surprised to feel the fresh sting in my throat, as if I'd stood in Mama's doorway only moments ago. Across the rolling granite outcrops I spied the gray ocean, the ocean that I hated, the thieving sea. Light danced on the water, scattering sparks that made me blink. A gull keened; how lonely a sound that was, and how deeply I felt it, sadness like a weight pulling me down. My hands tightened on the reins.

I turned back to my season and the preparations. Kitty would have to do it all.

Kitty. Dear Kit. We both lived in Newport year-round. We went to the same schools, moved in the same circles. But I knew what a closer look revealed. Kitty's parlor never wanted for callers. Her tray was filled with calling cards by the end of each Sunday afternoon. Our parlor had been empty for a long time, long before Mama's accident.

Or disappearance. Or departure. Or . . . I'd heard so many euphemisms for it this past year.

I squeezed my eyes shut and opened them again, as if that might bring Mama back. I missed her even though I was tarred by her behavior. Even though I feared we were alike.

I clicked my tongue at Ghost and we set off for home.

Uncle John had made some "discoveries." Papa's words: "only a chance, mind you." But it was a chance to find her. A chance was all we needed.

My shoulders grew stiff despite Ghost's easy gait. Newport society was unforgiving. By going west with Papa I could miss my chance to make Newport see me differently, to see me for me, and not as my mother's daughter. I'd miss friends who hadn't seen me since Mama disappeared and who thought I was tainted by her scandal.

Friends like Edward, who I hoped was more than a friend. He

wasn't due back from New York before mid-June. Edward's dark hair and soft eyes floated in my daydreams. Last summer, at one of the first cotillions of the season, he asked me to dance. After that short waltz, I was smitten. My cheeks burned now, and my heart beat faster as I remembered Edward choosing me over all the other girls.

He could be a perfect beau. But we made no lasting promises. No promises could have been made before now, anyway, before my season and my introduction into proper society. And now . . . Now everything was uncertain.

I inhaled deeply, pulling the faintly briny air into my lungs.

Maybe I'd driven Mama away. I was ashamed of Mama, and so angry at her. Those paintings frightened me. After that day, I'd hardened against her. Maybe it was my fault that she'd gone; here was my chance to make it all right.

Ghost, sensing my emotions again, picked up his pace to a trot. Finding Mama, bringing her home, and making her well could solve everything. I would be absolved. We could plan the season together, and I could have my debut. And Edward. Society would forgive her, and I could forgive myself. Going west with Papa and bringing Mama home could make everything right.

The sun was low in the west as Ghost and I approached the end of our ride. I turned him in at the gate that led back to the stable. As he trotted through the narrow file and I leaned to avoid an overhanging branch, a sudden kick of sea breeze flicked the branch at Ghost and he bolted.

I hung on, caught unprepared, my chest tight with fear.